Puleo, Alessio
Night and fog / Alessio Puleo
328 pages ; 24,4 x 17 cm

This book is a work of fiction. References to real people, events, establishments, organisations or places are intended only to give the impression of verisimilitude. Any resemblance to reality is purely coincidental.

© 2019 Alessio Puleo

All rights reserved
Reproduction in whole or in part is prohibited
The cover art has been designed using images from Freepik.
No part of this book shall be reproduced in any identical form, in whole or in part, by any means or process, mechanical, computer, recording or photocopying, without permission of the publishers.

Layout by Salvatore Pecoraro

INDEX

PROLOGUE	9
1	13
2	17
3	23
4	35
5	47
6	53
7	67
8	73
9	77
10	95
11	103
12	105
13	123
14	129
15	133
16	137
17	145
18	155
19	159
20	165
21	171
22	175
23	179
24	181
25	187
26	193
27	203
28	209
29	211
30	215

31	217
32	221
33	225
34	231
35	237
36	241
37	243
38	247
39	251
40	255
41	261
42	267
43	275
44	279
45	283
46	287
47	289
48	297
49	299
50	303
51	309
52	313
53	315
54	319
EPILOGUE	325

ALESSIO PULEO

NIGHT & FOG

PROLOGUE

Love and hate.

These are the words that remain echoing in my head after reading *Night and fog*.

The possibility of writing a prologue for this book was a proposal that took me by surprise, since I had never done it before. However, when I found about the subject matter and the author, I said yes with my eyes closed.

I had somewhat high expectations when I received the text, which was more than covered.

Much has been written about the period during which the Nazi regime was in force; there are also a number of voices being raised in what might be called "LGBTIQ+ literature". However, a novel that gives visibility to both in the same story mobilised me to read it, both for its novelty and its necessity.

A story that calls everything by its name, not without care for prose and style. But with big slaps in its narrative, of which the reader is already warned by its subject matter.

I am interested in the importance of this book being published at this moment, at this time, when testimonies and opinions are democratised, but also when strong hate movements are reaffirmed, when non-tolerance is imposed, when language is the object of great transgressions and writers are called upon to take a stand.

The fundamentalism present in the historical ideologies in which our protagonist narrates his life is embodied in figures of hatred, being a different way of loving the response with which Alessio Puleo surprises us.

It is no longer just a matter of living, but of trying to live better, of counteracting suffering and giving firmness to the decisions of subjects trapped under ideas of pathologisation, criminalisation or punishment.

The character of Ben, in my opinion, represents the reader's eagerness to know more about what happened before and the surprise that, to this day, some things have not changed.

The importance of these voices, like Puleo's, taking their place today on the shelves of bookshops and in the libraries of their readers is a great reason to consider love as that engine that allows roots and motions to be set, that allows life to be made a little more bearable, whatever the era.

I hope that readers will enjoy the book as much as I did and that they will have opportunity to think, to be moved and, why not, to propose a change in the face of hatred.

I paraphrase Stephen King when he points out in his book As I Write what is the great secret of his success: a stable marriage and love for his work.

May that determined desire move us to make our days and those of others more livable. Because the laws of destiny have their surprises in store, so it is better that we are not alone, but contained and with many stories to tell... as happens with the protagonist that Puleo proposes to us.

Welcome to *Night and fog*.

Luis Ávila

"Even homosexuals are forgotten victims of the Nazi regime. It is unknown how many have been condemned and interned in concentration camps, due to the destruction of part of the archives, and because many of them, like other categories persecuted by the Nazis, were captured and made to disappear under the edict Nacht und Nebel (Night and Fog), issued by Hitler on 7 December 1941, with the aim of eliminating 'subjects dangerous to the Reich', without leaving a trace".

Vittime Dimenticate
(Forgotten victims)
Giorgio Giannini, 2011

1

I look at my reflection in the mirror, I hardly recognise myself. Square chin, hard features, crooked nose and dull eyes. I dig deep into my soul, beyond the opaque iris, and detect no trace of the joyful child I once was, nothing. Nothing. I see nothing but nothingness, no innocence, no dreams, no longing for freedom. My hair is intertwined with silver threads and my face is furrowed by the streets I have travelled. The jacket, which covers my body deteriorated by time and the pains that life has bestowed on me, makes me look even older and more tired than I am.

I look at the numbers tattooed on my wrist and wonder where I could begin to tell this story; if it has a real beginning, if it all makes sense. And, above all, how to explain the horror and terror of what it was to someone who didn't experience it first hand.

With great difficulty I try to sort out the ideas in my head. My memory is not what it used to be, and Ben is only seventeen.

"Grandpa, then, are you telling me that story or not?" he grumbles, unable to wait.

I smile at him and calmly settle into the couch with the help of my faithful cane.

"It's a long, long story... Will you be patient enough to listen to it all?" I ask, smiling sweetly. He is a curious boy, and every day he looks more and more like his father.

"Of course, I will. I'm not a child anymore!" he nods his

head vigorously, trying to reinforce his affirmation."

"All right! But first of all, you must make one thing clear to me. Are you sure you want to know everything? There are things that you might not like or that might disturb you."

"Yes, Grandpa, everything. I'm a man now and, as my history teacher says: 'We must know our past if we want to build a better future!'"

"Even if some things seem strange to you?"

"YES!"

"Then we can start, but don't say I didn't warn you."

"Grandpa, wait, wait! I have to turn on the video camera. I also want to warn you that from time to time I will interrupt you to make a historical picture. I want my work to be well done and as interesting as possible. But don't worry! When I've finished, I'll be able to erase the parts you don't like."

He gets up from the couch where he had curled up on and very professionally places the video camera on the tripod.

My dear Anna comes up to me and brings me a cup of steaming coffee. I look into her eyes, silently thanking her. Despite the ravages of time, she is still a beautiful woman.

"Are you sure you really want to do this?" she asks me with sincere concern.

I look sideways at her.

"Anna, it's 2005!"

"Yes, but he's only seventeen!"

"He has to know. Back then, you were only fourteen."

"Do you think he'll believe the stories of a lunatic and lovable ninety-year-old?"

"Of course he'll believe me!"

A sound of hurried footsteps in the corridor interrupts

our conversation.

I rest the cup on the table next to the couch, and little David joins us.

"What's going on?" he asks intrigued.

"Grandpa is going to tell me a story, it's for a school project," Ben is quick to emphasise.

"Can I listen to it too?"

"You have to finish your homework!" Anna interjects, gently taking him by the hand and encouraging him to leave the room with her.

"Phew, how boring!" protests the little boy as they make their way to the kitchen.

Once we are alone, Ben looks me in the eye and gives me a nod of approval. A red light comes on and the video camera focuses on my face. I take a deep breath, but before I can begin to tell the story, Ben takes the floor to introduce his *DocuFilm*.

2

27 February 1933

The night in Berlin is cold, silent and strangely calm. The sky is clear and full of stars. The frosty air of the harsh German winter caresses the faces of passers-by and makes them shiver with cold. The temperature outside is about two degrees below zero, and yet one man, standing still in front of the gates of President Hermann Göring's residence, is sweating. His face firm and determined, his square jaw, his expressionless eyes fixed on the map in his hand. He has studied it so carefully that he knows it by heart; he could describe any particularity without any mistake.

He tilts his head first to one side and then to the other, crunching the neck bones. With his right hand, massages his sore biceps, then he presses the chest of his dark shirt with his hands, before putting his plan into action. Everything has been meticulously arranged, prepared and studied down to the smallest detail, so that there is no risk of running into any snags or surprises.

Göring's residence is the only access to the Reichstag building when the parliament is closed. Thus Karl Ernst, leader of the Berlin SA, together with a very small number of loyal storm troopers, enters the central heating ducts of the president's residence at night in order to reach the building unobserved.

They are highly trained men, capable of anything to complete the task entrusted to them.

They trudge through the narrow ducts. Once they reach the far end of the tunnel, surrounded by a funeral silence, they spray petrol and other flammable chemicals all around them.

Once they have completed their assigned task, they walk along the duct again, but in the opposite direction, then leave the residence and quickly disperse through the streets of the city, proud of having accomplished their goal, faithful subjects of that black swastika sewn on their arms and souls.

At 9:14 p.m., not a minute earlier and not a minute later, a Berlin fire station receives the alarm: the German parliament building is on fire. A fire brigade frantically makes its way to the scene of the disaster, while the flames rise, almost touching the stars, the only silent, shy and silent witnesses to what has really happened that night.

Some distance away, a young Dutchman watches mesmerised by the spectral dances that the long blue and red tongues paint in the sky, tearing through the darkness.

As soon as law enforcement arrive, a huge explosion engulfs the deputies' room in flames. The fire brigade immediately begins to extinguish the blaze, trying to save as much as possible.

Karl Ernst, in the distance, enjoys the distant sounds of sirens and the chatter of people crowding the street and wondering what is happening. On their faces, the terror and panic are more than evident.

That mission has been brilliantly executed: the real objective was to cause disarray and chaos in the city in order to enable Adolf Hitler and his henchmen to gain freehold.

It is no accident that, on New Year's Eve last year, Hitler swore to one of his greatest supporters, Ernst Hanfstaengl, that 1933 would be the year of change. He is aware that he must act with caution because the party is going through a difficult phase, but Hitler is a skilful orator and a great leader of the masses, and it was not difficult for him to win the office of Chancellor on 30 January. This is how nationalism has begun to seize power.

While the fire brigade juggles to control the fire, the police immediately mobilise in search of clues. Shortly afterwards, they find Marinus van der Lubbe hiding behind the building, half naked and dirty with smoke. At exactly that moment, Adolf Hitler and Hermann Göring arrive. The gendarmes drag the young man in front of them, claiming to have found the person responsible for the fire.

Taking advantage of this advantageous situation - and Van der Lubbe being a known communist - Göring claims that the fire can only be the work of communists and has the party leaders arrested, while Hitler declares a state of emergency and incites the old president Paul von Hidenburg to sign the Reichstag Fire Decree, which abrogates most of the civil rights provided by the 1919 constitution of the Weimar Republic.

According to the police, Van der Lubbe claims to have set the fire in protest against the expansion of Nazi power. Under torture, he confesses again, and is brought to trial along with the opposition communist party leaders.

With their own leaders in prison and without access to the press, the communists are heavily defeated in successive elections. Those Communist deputies, and some Social Democrats, who are elected to the Reichstag, are not allowed by the SA to take a position in Parliament.

Hitler is propelled to power with 44% of the vote and demands that the minor parties give him a two-thirds majority for his decree of full power, which gives him the right to rule by decree and to liquidate many civil liberties.

At the Lipsia trial, held eight months later, Van der Lubbe is found guilty and sentenced to death. He is beheaded on 10 January 1934, three days before his 25th birthday.

The night of 27 February 1933 marks the beginning of Nazi power in Germany. Adolf Hitler, after winning a parliamentary majority with the German National People's Party, begins to reveal himself as the man destined to create a new Germany.

Thirteen years after the Nazi party publicly admits the desire to separate the Jewish stripe from the Aryan stripe, on 23 May, the law gives Hitler de facto right to rule and legislate without the need for the Reichstag's consent. Thus, the nightmare of the racial laws is given the green light.

"Ben, it's very nice how you tell it and it's the historical reality, but I assure you that everything is much more complicated than how it is narrated in your book. The facts are correct, the names are correct, the dates are correct... all very detailed! But the pain, the fear, the desperation are missing... I can't tell you anything more, historically speaking, about the events narrated in your book; but I can tell you about the people, Jewish and German, about hetero and homosexual love, about emotions, about the lives of young people a little older than you who had the misfortune to be born in the wrong place and in the wrong year. If this is what you want to know, then sit down and listen!"

3

"Of course, I do, Grandpa, that's exactly what I want. The documentary, in fact, will be made with my off-camera voice, describing the purely historical facts, and with your real, concrete and emotionally charged testimony."

"All right, Ben, but I warn you: it's a long story that might upset you a lot."

I take a deep breath, squint my eyes and prepare myself for a trip back in time. Suddenly, I'm young again...

Dawn doesn't seem to want to break. I move slowly, enjoying the silence of a city still asleep. My only company is the crackling of the fire that makes the seemingly endless night less dark. Yawns come one after the other. My eyes water for a few seconds. My head throbs.

I need a coffee. I pick up the coffee pot and pour some into the cup as it releases its aroma. I love the smell of coffee: it tastes of home, of love, of intimacy...

"I can see it, Grandpa, I can see it!" Ben exclaims, interrupting my narration.

"I understand your excitement, but let me go on."

After drinking the hot coffee, I grab the slice and, with an automatic gesture, acquired over time, I throw the uncooked bread into the oven without even looking at it. I've been doing this job for so long that I could do it with my eyes closed!

I still wonder how long I will be able to continue the activity that once belonged to my father. Since 19 March, Jews in Berlin have been banned from practising law, and since April, teachers and civil servants have also been banned from practising their activity. It is true that these are prestigious positions, but why would Hitler prevent us from working as bakers?

I defy any German to envy my life: eighteen years old and the weight of a business on my shoulders, Dad depressed by Mum's death, poverty and misery to spare. And yet it is my life and I love it as it is, with the daily sacrifices and small joys, the affection, the friendships and the first disappointments in love, while I am still not quite sure who I really am.

Suddenly, a dizzy spell hits me and I almost fall over. I close my eyes and lean against the counter behind me. I may have overdone it the night before. As usual, it's Matt's fault!

I struggle to get back on my feet, although it's difficult, considering that I slept for an hour and a half at most! But it was worth it. I remember a few moments and shivers run down my spine.

"Grandpa, even now you don't sleep much, and it doesn't seem to affect you."

"Ben, now it's sleep that's gone away from me."

"Isn't it the same?"

"Sometimes, when I sleep, I wake up startled by terrible nightmares and find myself in a state of panic. That's why insomnia is such a blessing today. At that time, no;

back then, I was young, full of life, always starving; the sleep of a bear in torpor and with energy to give away. And that day I was dying of sleep..."

The smell of freshly baked bread pervades the room and, for a moment, I forget my adolescent revelry, my desires, even my most intimate ones.
I grab the slice and pull out the buns: they look great, golden brown and crispy, just right! I place them in the basket, and bake some more, quickly. In the meantime, my mind travels again.
It's strange to savour this new feeling. Still, I'm happy, I finally feel at peace with myself, I finally know what I really want. My life is anything but easy, but I have so many dreams, so many ideas and so much desire to spread my wings and fly. I think about how I was two years ago and I find it hard to recognise myself. I admit, the credit for this big change goes to Giona.

"Grandpa, who was Giona?"
"Giona was my first love, my great love. I think you've lost your mind for someone already, or am I wrong?"
"Oh, yes!" he sighs, biting his lip. "Let's leave it there, Grandpa. It was just a disappointment!"
"It's okay, but sometimes you learn more from pain than from joy. In a few years you'll understand, you'll realise it when you manage to distance yourself from this feeling and when you're be able to look at it as a stranger would. Then you'll understand many things and you'll thank God for having given you the possibility to have met someone and to have loved."
"I understand that, Grandpa, but... Isn't Giona a man's name?"

"Yes, Ben. Giona was a very attractive boy. Our feeling was true, deep, intense, turbulent, consummated in miles and miles of letters. I loved him, I'm sure of that. He was the first man I ever loved in my life."

"A man... Grandpa, are you gay?"

"Yes, Ben, I'm gay and I've struggled a lot. First, to know my true identity, then to recognise it as such and, finally, to get others to accept or at least respect it.

In those days, I tried hard to go out with girls, I even tried to sleep with them, to love them physically, but it was a tragedy! I couldn't get aroused in front of a naked woman. Just the thought of it made me feel a reluctant sensation, almost a slight nausea... I was sure, women were not my thing!

I wouldn't want you to be ashamed of me with this confession or, even worse, for the teacher to send us a visit from the social services. Talking about homosexuality, even though they say we live in a modern, uncensored age, is a great transgression. I wouldn't want you to get in trouble because of me."

"Are you serious? It's a bomb, Grandpa! My friends will be proud of me."

"Never use other people's pain and problems for your own benefit. You can't even imagine what kind of consequences these behaviours can lead to and what hidden bombs they can set off."

You want me to tell you, and I will, but not so that they can say you are the best, rather so that my story can make you and others reflect on many often-undervalued aspects.

Back to that day, Ben, where had I been... Ah, yes!"

I'm in the bakery, looking at my profile in the

reflection of the steel slice. I know I'm not attractive. My features, typically Jewish, are surely no help considering what is going on.

I sigh. I wish I was a little taller, a little more muscular and a little blonder. Maybe I'm asking too much?

I think of Giona again. He's really someone to admire. All he has to do is flick his hair to provoke childish giggles from young, wild girls. His perfectly defined muscles, his gleaming white smile. His perfect jawline and those dimples that are marked every time he smiles.

Those dimples... I could have kissed them for a lifetime.

With him I experienced my first time.

He helped me discover who I really was, my true nature; he helped me to let go and live my life like everyone else. He taught me how to love, in bed and out of bed. I owe him everything.

Too bad he disappeared without a trace, from one day to the next, without reason or motive. Even today, every time I think of him, I feel a strange emotion run through my body: a mixture of affection, desire and rage.

I take a slow breath and, for a moment, I seem to feel his body on top of mine, skin against skin.... God, how I miss him! His hugs, his cuddles, his lips. My mind takes me back to the days we lived together, when everything was tinged with the bright colours of the rainbow, when the world disappeared over the horizon and the only protagonists, the only real actors that filled everything, absolutely everything, were the two of us.

God, what melancholy! Even today, when I think of him, I inevitably lose myself in a parallel dimension.

The sound of the doorbell startles me. I stop abruptly, snapping back to reality. My mind had already catapulted me between those purple silk sheets. I try to compose myself and turn around. My breath hitches and my face flushes. I squint to see who is entering. I sigh in relief. It's Matt.

"Hey, mate!" he greets me.

This couldn't be a worse time!

"Hi" I reply, a little embarrassed, unable to shake off that nagging feeling of having been caught red-handed.

"Can I have a piece of bread? I'm starving!"

"Take as much as you want!" I reply in a slightly squeaky voice.

He smiles at me, and I let myself be carried away by our sincere and fraternal friendship.

It means a lot to me his affection, his love and knowing that he is happy. He is the friend we have all dreamed of. A perfect friend, an example to follow, the only one capable of accepting my confessions and my secrets without staining them with the dark colour of evil tongues; the only one who can understand me. A sincere and loyal accomplice.

"What are you doing here? Don't you think it's time to go home?"

His breath reeks of alcohol, but he doesn't look drunk.

"I needed to see you..." he continues.

He approaches me, as if he was a nomad begging for a glass of water.

In general, he is the strongest, the most self-confident, the cool one; the one who gives advice and invents strategies. I am the shy, sometimes a bit clumsy friend. But now, at this exact moment, the roles seem to be reversed and this situation, if on the one hand flatters me, on the other scares me. I laugh in embarrassment.

"Say it now! What could have happened to you so terribly? You're the mythical one, you always have the solution ready for everything. I'm the one who always needs your approval for everything, even to be free to dream without feeling dirty. And now you tell me... 'I needed to see you'?"

My voice sounds frightened and disarmed by the simple fact that I don't feel up to the situation, I have a terrible fear of letting him down.

It seems he didn't hear a word I said. For a second, a doubt takes hold of me: did I speak or did I just imagine it?

Matt continues right where he left off.

"I have to tell you something." His brow furrowed.

I throw him a piercing glance, wishing my eyes could free my heart from my stupid fears, inhibitions, and the anxiety that haunts me. But no matter how hard I try to get his attention, his eyes are drawn to the oven.

"You're burning the bread!" he shouts.

"What?"

I leap forward and push the charred loaves of bread to the floor with the slice, cursing. The bread is completely ruined!

Matt feels sorry.

"Sorry, it's my fault... I distracted you! Maybe I

should come by another time!"

I watch him take a few steps back and decide that the situation can't get out of hand, at least not this time. The only time my best friend, my only point of support, seems to need my help. What do I do? Tell him to go away as if he were anyone else? Just for some burnt bread?

No! Although that's what I really wish. Not for the bread, which I don't care about, but rather for my stupid fears. No! I can't let my stupidity slam the door in his face.

"No!" My imperative tone surprises us both. I blurt it out as if nothing has happened, and indifferently continue: "What have you got to do with it? It's my fault, don't worry. Nothing serious happened. Tell me, what did you want to talk about?"

I go back to the bar and sprinkle flour on the counter. Without eye contact I think it will be easier for me to pretend to be self-confident and translate that into the advice I'll have to give... But what advice? Blessed is anyone who helps me!

Matt takes a deep sigh, clears his throat and earnestly confesses to me:

"I've found the perfect man for you!"

"What?" I ask in surprise.

I can't understand what he's trying to tell me.

Damn it, couldn't it be that for once, just once since we've known each other, he was the one who needed me? All those thoughts, for what? For nothing!

He's here for me.

But... But, damn it all! Now he gives himself the right to find me a man... A man, a new love... God knows...!

Suddenly, anger and indignation are transformed

into a dream wrapped in tenderness and mystery.

"I set you up on a date with a fantastic guy. Tonight."

"What?" I ask. "Have you lost your mind?"

"Yes, don't worry, I'm sure you'll like him. And it might be just the right time for you to get Giona out of your head."

There were only two shots in the chamber, and he fired them straight into my heart.

"Explain yourself better." I try hard to participate, although I wish I could be buried alive.

"I can't say more, it's a surprise! See you tonight at the Kleist at eleven o'clock."

I know the name of the club, but it doesn't tell me anything in particular, it's a place like all the others.

"Are you joking? I understand that you want to spend a different night, but do you really want to go to the Kleist? It's a normal casino!" I exclaim intrigued.

Matt starts rubbing his hands together, he has a mischievous look on his face, eager to reveal what's going to happen. He looks at me with a smirk on his face and adds:

"Dear friend, that's the most interesting thing. Every day it's an ordinary casino, but tonight it won't be at all." And, like the good actor he thinks he is, before going on, he creates an atmosphere of suspense: "I want to take you there because tonight they're organising a gay night! Come on, my friend, we'll have a lot of fun. I beg you, let's go together."

My eyes widen in amazement, and everything I've heard from my customers these days comes to mind. Of course, I need to get out of the house a bit, but... At what price?

"I... How do I do? Race laws! Matt, are you crazy? I'm

a Jew!"

I look up with a serious expression. Matt has it easier, he's a German, but I...

Since Hitler came to power, things aren't as easy as they used to be, if I think of how they were before the Nazis came to power.

Germany was one of the best countries for homosexuals. Berlin offered a thousand opportunities to find one's soul mate in freedom and without shame. But now... now paragraph 175 has been proclaimed!

If it is already difficult for German homosexuals in itself, one need not imagine how difficult it is for Jews.

"Grandpa, are you telling me that when you were young, homosexuality was conceived and accepted?"

"It was! If you read history properly, you would realise that homosexuality is not a modern phenomenon, quite the contrary. It is as old as the world, only now it is more talked about, it makes more noise, because homosexuals have decided to come out of the closet and assert their rights; like the right to marry, for example.

Germany before Nazism was one of the most avant-garde places when it came to sexual diversity: there were at least thirty gay magazines where it was possible to publish personal ads; there were tailors who made tailor-made clothes for transsexuals; and same-sex love was neither a disease nor a perversion, but rather a natural trait. Ah, if I had been born a decade earlier, then I could have been myself with peace of mind. Now everything has changed, everything is more difficult and sometimes impossible. But well! We are going off the rails, where were we?"

"In paragraph 175, Grandpa, an argument that we have studied in depth at school. I know it was a section of the German criminal code, in force from 15 May 1871 to 10 March 1994, in which homosexual relations were considered a crime."

"I'm glad your teacher told you about it. Now I feel more at ease to continue with my story uncensored.... in a manner of speaking!

Just so you understand, Matt had involved me in that night using the hook of new love. I think it happens among you too, I mean, when you discover your sexuality. Just dreaming about a girl, her image constructed in your mind, even though in reality it is completely non-existent, opens up a world for you: new hopes, dreams, repressed desires and endless emotions. Sometimes you fall in love with love even before you fall in love with a person.

Then all it takes is a smile, a look, a word to fill you with hope and to know that she is there and that she has captured your heart."

"It's true, Grandpa... It's so true!"

"Let's go on, then."

>   Anyway, Matt reassures me.
>   "Don't be afraid, Thomas! At first glance it's a normal bar. There are very few of us who know what will happen inside. It's an exclusive night, with selected people. You know I would never put you in danger."
>   He hugs me with a strength that takes my breath away. Matt and I grew up together, we've known each other all our lives, we're each half of each other. I'm sure I'm his best friend, a brother, and he's a brother to me too.
>   I squeeze his muscular chest and hug him back, smearing flour across my apron. He smells so nice. In his arms, the fears and insecurities swirling around me

disappear.

I'm Jewish, I'm gay, and it's 1933.

I can't help but wonder what the future holds for me.

4

I'm quite nervous, I walk quickly down the street, without looking around too much. I try to stay in the shade, the rain is a great ally. It's very cold.

I pull up the collar of my mackintosh and pull my hood over my head a little tighter. I keep my eyes down so I can avoid eye contact with people. I feel like a thief, a criminal, a delinquent, and yet I'm not doing anything wrong.

I turn the corner and finally see it, the bright and imposing Kleist sign.

My heart is in my throat. I glance around for Matt. No sign of him.

Fuck! He's late. It's eleven o'clock, if he doesn't show up in five minutes, I'm leaving fast.

I shouldn't have come; I'm risking too much. The verses of paragraph 175 come to my mind, and I feel shivers:

"Unnatural fornication, whether between persons of the male sex or between persons and animals, is punishable by imprisonment, in addition to temporary suspension of civil rights".

Unnatural fornication...! Bah! What the fuck do they know what is unnatural? Love, genuine and sincere love, is never unnatural. And it is never bad when it makes us happy.

The roar of thunder startles me - what crazy weather!

I feel a blow on my back and, uneasy, I turn around and take a few steps backwards.

"We're nervous, eh!" Matt looks at me with a mocking expression. He's laughing his head off. I'd like to kill him!

"Fuck you, Matt. I almost had a heart attack, you're late," I complain.

"It's no big deal! It was only three minutes, who cares?"

The sound of our voices is muffled by the sound of the rain.

He obviously carries an umbrella. He is so careful, and has the gift of preventing problems before they arise or simply not worrying at all. After all, he is a magician: he always finds the solution to everything... or almost everything.

"At that time, I thought so."

In this case, I am the fragile friend, the one who must be protected and sheltered. He grabs me by the arm and pulls me towards him to shelter me from the rain. He is always so attentive! I don't know what I would do without him.

"So, shall we go in?"

I nod, swallowing saliva.

I'm shivering, and not just from the cold: fear of the unknown and anxiety leave me breathless.

We approach the front door; he, confident and proud of himself, and me a little less so.

I can barely control the urge to run out of the place.

Fuck, Matt, what kind of trouble are you getting me into?

A tall, blond, elegant, muscular man, standing in front of the door, gives us a dirty look. My friend obviously doesn't fret, but I almost piss myself.

Matt gives him one of his best smiles, the kind that makes men and women swoon. It seems to have no effect on that gorilla, as he continues to stare at us in disgust.

I turn to Matt, worried, and suddenly I see him take a pink card out of his pocket and show it to our silent interlocutor. He takes it in his hands, examines it for a few seconds and hands it back to him. Immediately, the bouncer glares at me.

"He's coming with me."

Matt wraps his imposing arm around my slender waist. I wonder if he can hear my frantic heartbeat. Fear washes over me like a giant wave, my instincts is to turn around and get out of there immediately, but Matt keeps holding me tightly.

The big man nods and moves, allowing us to enter the premises.

The warm air of the place comes all at once and welcomes us like a mother's loving embrace.

For a few moments I enjoy that pleasant sensation and even feel a little relieved. At least we are inside. The first step has been taken.

We find ourselves in a small, dimly lit lobby. My shoes are soaked with water, and they stick to the red carpet, giving me an uncomfortable sensation when I walk. I feel clumsy and out of place.

"Are you ready?"

Matt's hand is resting on an opaque glass door and

he looks at me with a dreamy air, as if he is opening the entrance to paradise.

He looks radiant, and I'm envious.

"Not exactly!" I cry out, but he's already opened it. A bright light shines down on us, forcing me to close my eyes for a moment.

We step forward and enter. The huge door closes behind us without a sound. I open my eyes, disbelieving, in front of me I see a huge, luxurious room, glittering, but half empty: gaming tables, slot machines, and more fill the room with sounds and flashing lights. Gorgeous croupiers cast seductive glances at me as they expertly shuffle packs of cards.

Not exactly what I expected. A young man in a suit approaches us as I take off my mackintosh and look at my friend, puzzled. On his chest is the casino crest. Is he coming to kick us out?

"Wait for me here," Matt says, stepping back a little. The boy whispers something in his ear, and walks over to me.

"Let me..."

He smiles distractedly at me, pointing to my dripping mackintosh.

Matt also sheds his coat and gestures for me to follow him. We walk down a side corridor, through a door and move to the back of the casino. We enter the powder room and go down some stairs. Loud music blares from outside; the volume gets louder and louder as we walk down the stairs; restlessness comes over me and I finally feel like I'm in the right place.

With difficulty we push through the last heavy iron door. What I see leaves me open-mouthed: in the basement of the casino there is a real nightclub, with

DJs, go-go dancers, bar, music, psychedelic lights and, above all, a mind-boggling number of people.

Matt smiles at me, though it's hard to see him, dazzled by the spotlights projecting multicoloured light effects. All around us, a whirlwind of bodies moves to the music. He takes me by the hand and drags me through the tumult. I'm thrilled and stunned by what I see: it's even better than I expected!

We head straight for the bar. I'm glad: a drink is exactly what I need to immerse myself in this wonderful atmosphere.

The air smells of freedom, of delight, of nonchalance. I dive in headlong.

"What do you think?" Matt gesticulates. His eyes show euphoria, like a child on Christmas Day.

I flash my most sincere smile and respond with a big "wow".

I order two Danziger Goldwasser, which are served in less than a second.

Matt and I toast with a cheers, looking each other straight in the eye, and empty our glasses in one gulp.

I feel incredibly relaxed, free. Free to be who I am. Like everyone else here tonight. I feel the effect of the alcohol starting to invade my exhausted brain with speed. I want to have fun and think of nothing else.

"Another round! Double!" I shout, shooting a glance at the bartender. Meanwhile, with the back of my hand I wipe my chin, soaked with the liquor that has escaped from my mouth. Next to me, women are kissing passionately.

Two stools away, a man offers a drink to a blond man who, by the way, doesn't look bad at all. For an instant, I remember Giona and my face is troubled, but the arrival of the drinks manages to erase the memory.

"Here's to us!" Matt exclaims happily, raising his arm and slamming his glass against mine, and... in one gulp!

The vodka makes my throat sting and my right eye water.

The music seems louder now, pounding in my head, but it doesn't bother me. Everything is spinning around me, slowly, and I wonder if it's because of the alcohol, the music, or the earthquake of emotions that is stirring my soul at the moment.

Matt comes up to me and says something I can't make out; I try to read his lips, but my vision is blurry. Skipping dinner wasn't such a great idea.

Before I know it, I find myself with another glass in my hand: it has a pungent colour and smell. Without a second thought, I gulp it down in one gulp and feel a burning sensation in my throat.

I clear my throat, the temperature rises. It's hot, very hot. I see Matt utter something that sounds like "Ratzeputz". With gestures, he tries to tell me to take it easy, but I don't listen. Not tonight.

I order another glass of Danziger Goldwasser as the world spins around me.

I'm sweating, take off my jumper and lean it against the bar, letting the T-shirt show off my more or less manly chest. Sure, I'm not on Matt's level, but it's not bad either. I look him straight in the eye, the alcohol transforms me into someone more brazen, brave and bold.

Matt comes up to me, touches my hair. He's so sensual in every move he makes... The alcohol confuses my thoughts!

His image transforms: for a second, I see in him my first great love. It's my subconscious that claims him, it's my heart that seeks him, helped by the enormous amount of alcohol I've drunk.

I swallow and caress his biceps with my eyes. His face comes close to mine, everything around us disappears in an instant that seems eternal. If he kisses me, I'll die, I swear!

He rests both hands on my back and pulls me to him. His mouth comes closer and closer, brushing my cheek and resting on my ear.

I close my eyes as I listen to his words:

"Come on! I have to introduce you to someone."

"What?" I stay hard.

Fuck, it's Matt! It's Matt, I repeat to myself, trying to remember him as the alcohol clouds my sight, my memory and my senses.

He walks away and gives me a look to follow him, but I can't manage to take a single step: my legs refuse to cooperate.

I just want to sink into the abyss. My cheeks are burning and I can't hide anywhere the obvious disappointment I'm carrying.

For an instant I had the illusion of having the love of my life by my side again, I thought he hadn't left. I saw him here, with me, when in reality it was the drunkenness playing with my feelings.

I think Matt has noticed. I'm an open book to him, no one knows me better.

So as not to humiliate or hurt me, he continues as if nothing has happened and, with a brotherly gesture, ruffles my hair.

"Come on," he begs.

I walk a couple of steps when a gag suddenly stops me in my tracks. I close my eyes, take a deep breath, put my hands to my mouth and try desperately to block the vomit. I can't go on; if I move, I'll vomit, I'm sure of it.

My head is pounding and spinning like a crazy merry-go-round, I can't stop it. I wobble, I lean on someone. I don't know who.

I open my eyes with difficulty, my eyes are blurry. I still haven't gotten rid of the after-effects of last night and I've got too much alcohol in my body again. Fuck! I need some air…

"I can see that nothing has changed… You had fun just like we have fun now. You did the same stupid things you tell us not to do now."

"Ben, do you want me to continue?" I ask him. "I was young too, as you see, and I did the same things that all young people do, but thanks to the experiences I've had and the maturity I've acquired, today I can advise you on what to do and what not to do. Now, let me go on, for, if I return to reality, all those images will disappear from my eyes."

I look for Matt, but it's impossible to find him in the crowd.

I make a superhuman effort not to vomit on my shoes.

I take another deep breath, massage my temples and stagger again. I'm about to crash to the ground, but two strong arms prevent the embarrassing fall.

I open my eyes and see someone under my armpit. My feet lift, my body sways. I have the feeling that we're moving, but I can't figure out in which direction.

My diaphragm contracts with every step, the alcohol backs up into my oesophagus. I concentrate on not expelling it.

Finally, the volume of the music decreases and the cold air slaps my cheeks. Not far away I hear the sound of a shower.

I feel the water hitting my skull, running down my back and all over my body.

My clothes stick to me. Instinctively I shake my head and thousands of tiny drops form a wreath around me.

The smell of wet earth enters strongly through my nose. I take a deep breath, discovering with satisfaction that it is a great help against nausea.

Suddenly, I realise that I am out in the open, at the back of the premises. We exit through a secondary door. The street lamps in the square in front of us radiate an orange light that reminds me of a motorway.

I feel a hand on my chin, a thumb slowly running along my profile. I shudder.

Fuck! It's really cold, the water is freezing on me. My mystery man takes off his coat, patiently wraps it around me to warm me up and rubs me vigorously. I open my eyes and miraculously regain my lucidity. I stare at the stranger in front of me.

"Are you feeling better?" he asks. He looks worried.

I open my mouth, try to speak, but I'm short of breath. I barely have time to turn around when suddenly a week's worth of lunches and dinners crash to the pavement; a yellowish, foul-smelling stream pours out of my body. Whew! I'm a mess.

When I think I'm done, I try to get up but, unfortunately, I discover that my digestive system doesn't agree with me.

For the first time in my life, I am glad to live in a rainy city like Berlin. At least the heavy rain helps me to clean myself. More or less.

The stranger holds my head and encourages me to go on and get rid of everything. What a shitty situation.

Once I've puked my guts out, he helps me up, hands me some tissues, and I wipe my face with them. I blow my nose and throw the paper on the floor.

He hands me a bottle of water, I grab it, unscrew the cap and drink it in one go, as if I had been in the Sahara Desert for weeks.

Unfortunately, it's not enough to calm the fire inside me. I finally manage to see and think, more or less, clearly. Magically, my brain reactivates and I realise what has just happened.

I take a better look at the stranger and discover that he is the most beautiful man I have ever seen. His face looks sculpted: he's perfect! Slim, impetuous biceps, tall, light-toned… A perfect Aryan. An angel.

I blink, wondering for a moment if that heavenly image isn't just the residue of the rivers of alcohol. But no matter how much I open and close my eyes, the image remains there, motionless, staring at me curiously. I suppose my expression takes on a funny look as I assume that I am standing before a Greek god in the flesh, and that I have just made the worst fool of my life. He's laughing his head off. I'm not surprised to find that it sounds melodious. His teeth are white and perfectly aligned.

He puts one hand on the back of his neck and the

other on his abs.

Somebody tell me this isn't true! Tell me this isn't really happening. I pinch my arm, hoping it's a terrible nightmare. I just wish I could wake up in my bed and pretend none of this has happened, but... Fuck, it's all real! Not a bad start, to tell you the truth.

I continue to stare at him motionless, unable to utter a word. I wish I had a black bag handy so I could hide inside it for the rest of my life. My body shivers from the cold, my teeth chatter. It's raining, it must be about two degrees and I'm wearing only a ridiculous t-shirt, a jacket a couple of sizes too big and I'm all soaked. I huddle down. I try in vain to get warm. I approach hypothermia, which at this point seems like the best option.

Finally, my beau stops laughing and starts rubbing me again, wrapping me in a warm embrace.

"Let's go, or you'll get sick."

He takes my hand and I discover that his skin is soft and delicate. We take a few quick steps and reach his car.

He opens the passenger door and tucks me into the seat.

"My jumper..." I stammer.

"What?" he asks as he closes the door.

"In the premises," I continue without him being able to hear me. I watch him get into the car on my left and buckle up.

"Matt!" I exclaim, remembering my friend.

"No, David," he laughs, holding out his right hand. I take it and shake it with little determination. "My name is David."

"Thomas," I add.

I feel the roar of the engine; then everything goes dark.

5

As his Kübelwagen flies over the asphalt, I try to articulate the words as best I can. I recite my address from memory, but I can't keep my eyes open. I'm too sleepy and my head is still spinning.

In the distance, I hear David's voice, it has a warm, comforting intonation.

I can't follow the thread of the conversation; my mind is still very confused and all I want to do is sleep. I fall into a coma-like state within seconds.

Suddenly, David asks me again for my address, my "home" address; he specifies, "where you live".

It seems to me a misplaced clarification, I'm drunk, but I'm not stupid.

After a while, the car stops. David's hand gently caresses my left cheek.

"We've arrived, Thomas," he whispers.

I wake up. I look up into his face and lose myself in those fantastic blue eyes.

"Where?" I ask, yawning cheekily.

"To your house!"

I turn around, wipe my hand on the fogged window and look out; I hardly recognise the doorway of my home.

"Thanks," I murmur, struggling to get up.

I take off his coat and offer it to him, but he refuses with his hand.

"Keep it, it's too cold!"

I nod absently, too dejected to grasp the significance of the gesture.

With my right hand, I pull the handle and open the door: the icy air rushes into the car, making us shiver.

"Good night!" I exclaim, stretching across the seat towards him.

His soft lips rest on my cheek, and in no time at all, I'm aroused.

I see him rest his hand on his groin and I sense, to my astonishment, that the feeling is reciprocated.

I pause a moment longer to admire him, to memorise every detail of that wonderful face in my mind, while he starts up his military green Volkswagen again. His hands are shaking, he looks nervous.

"Good night!" he says without looking at me.

I close the door and, in the blink of an eye, he's gone. I'm all wet, freezing cold.

With an almost automatic gesture I move a huge potted plant, grab the keys that were hidden behind it, and go inside. I might have a fever...

I strip and quickly get under the shower, this time, hot. The water caresses my muscles, the steam envelops me and I start to feel better.

I remember everything that happened during the night, I wonder what Matt is thinking, or what he is doing. I hope he's not worried about me and that he's not looking for me. He'll certainly come to the bakery tomorrow, in fact, to be exact, in a few hours.

I think again of David and his surprising kindness. Suddenly I regret not having asked him any questions, not having done more research about this pleasant encounter. I know nothing about him: his address, his surname, his job.

I am sure of only one thing: he is not a Jew!

Although he didn't tell me explicitly, his physiognomy doesn't lie: tall and blond, handsome as a god. If he is not Aryan, then who is?

I wonder if he realised my origins. I suppose so, since only Jews live in my neighbourhood, and most Germans are aware of that. Could that be the reason why he was so nervous before he left? At least this is the feeling I got.

I lift my head, the water lapping at my forehead, then slowly trickling down through the folds of my tired body. I open my lips and for an instant I imagine them resting on David's soft, warm lips.

I miss him already. I long to see him again, but how is that possible?

I hardly know him, in fact, I don't know him at all. He's just a stranger who helped me throw up and drived me home.

Something like a supersexy hero. I think of the moment we said goodbye; the memory of that innocent gesture compels me to touch myself.

I surprise myself by imagining that sculpted body naked and available, and the pleasure grows until it takes me to goals I have never explored before.

I compose myself and catch my breath, but I find it impossible to get David out of my head. I wash myself, turn off the water and step out of the shower. I wrap the towel around my waist and start drying my still frozen body.

My balance is still not perfect, the alcohol is still coursing through my veins, and that cocktail of emotions is the coup de grace that doesn't make things any easier.

I'm amazed at the effect this young man has on me. I regret not having kissed him, but the situation and my breath prevented me from doing so, what a pity!

It would have been wonderful... Damn it!

I grab a pair of boxer shorts from the drawer and put them on with my pyjamas to go to sleep.

I slip under the covers, happy to be nice and warm. I lay my head on the pillow, fantasising about David and his physique.

I have to see him again.

Suddenly, I realise that it is almost impossible to find him in a city like ours. I don't even know if he lives in Berlin. I don't know anything.

Maybe he's engaged... or worse: maybe he's straight. But if so, what was he doing alone at the Kleist tonight? These thoughts obsessively torment my head, relentlessly.

I sigh, and continue tossing and turning in bed, unable to sleep. I want to see him, I want to touch him, to feel him. I want him to be mine.

The memory of Giona comes back to me. He was my first love, no doubt about it.

Meeting him changed me profoundly. Thanks to him I was able to free myself from my oppressions; with him, love was not gay or straight, man or woman: it was simply love. He gave me that intoxicating feeling of knowing that the most exceptional boy on earth, for some inexplicable reason, decided to fall madly in love with me. He was mine until he disappeared.

After him, I decided not to settle; I vowed to go all out.

And now I delete his image with the profile of another man: David.

In two hours, I have to be at work. There's no point in me lying in bed torturing myself...

And suddenly... an illumination.

I jump out of bed and run to find his coat, the one I left lying on the floor, looking for clues. Maybe I can find something that will somehow lead me to him, that will allow me to find him again, even if it's just to return his coat.

I hurry back to my room, turn on the light, sit on the bed, hold the precious booty to my nose..., inhale deeply..., smell his perfume: David.

A rush of adrenaline, excitement and disbelief moves my arms as I rummage through the pockets for anything useful. A pen, a notebook and a pocket watch. That's all I find. On the watch I see two initials, D and K, engraved. I open it and find a faded photo of a very beautiful woman, probably blonde and with the same eyes.

For a moment I lose my breath, but I calm down quickly: she must be his mother when she was young, or his sister. Too similar to be his girlfriend. I breathe a sigh of relief.

With a heavy heart I place everything on the bedside table and crawl under the covers.

I absent-mindedly leaf through the notebook and, once I get past the first few white pages, I find notes written in marvellous calligraphy: To believe is not to trust, to love is not to endure, to conform is not to live. And yet another: That which is permitted has little taste, that which is forbidden gives more pleasure.

I continue browsing. Near the end he writes about some events in Berlin in recent months and something about the fire a few months ago.

Without giving it much thought, I reread the beautifully written sentences scattered around the notebook.

I am impressed by the beauty of these sentences, brief but rich and full of meaning; by the depth of the words, the wonderful calligraphy, but what moves me most is the similarity with my innermost feelings.

That man is a lethal mix of glamour and intelligence. Suddenly, the solution to the riddle seems clear and simple: David must be a writer or a journalist!

He has it all: distinguished, cultured, good speech, perfect penmanship. It is not questionable. On the other hand, Berlin is the capital of the press and printing. Germany has a highly developed information system, more newspapers are published every year than in any other nation, although, if I remember correctly, on 4 February Paul von Hindernburg issued a decree limiting the freedom of the press and ordered the closure of all communist newspapers. This is why I deduce that David is not a communist, since he still writes.

In practice he is a columnist, single, attractive, sensitive and available. Or at least that's what I like to think. I switch off the light, dreaming of our next meeting.

I barely close my eyes and the damn alarm clock reminds me that it's time to go to work. Cursing, I unplug it and turn the other way.

6

Getting out of bed is very difficult considering that it is freezing cold outside and still dark. There is only a faint light that announces the new day.

For a change, I've hardly slept and I'm carrying all the after-effects of the hangover. But I'm already late, so I can't complain any more.

I crawl on the floor, get dressed with difficulty and leave the house without even having breakfast. I'm still nauseous.

The polar morning air wakes me up and activates me. In the meantime, I'm running late.

I'm opening the bakery late today. If my father knew about it, he would surely call my attention to me.

Halfway there I realise that it's starting to drizzle and, for a change, I'm not wearing a hat, umbrella or mackintosh, which stayed in the Kleist next to my jumper. Luckily, I'm wearing David's coat, which keeps me warm. I tuck myself in tightly, it's a bit big, probably one or two sizes too big. I feel incredibly safe in his perfume and clothes.

God, how wonderful!

I'm about to arrive, I reach into the pocket and reality reveals itself to me like a bomb, cruelly. Fuck! I have the keys to the bakery in my mackintosh, and the mackintosh is in the Kleist.

I slap my forehead, reproaching myself for my lack of responsibility. Luckily, my father always leaves an emergency key under a plant near the door. That's how I got into my house a few hours ago, but as far as the bakery is concerned, he doesn't come here anymore... There is no solution! I have to run to the casino in the hope of finding my things. I sigh, getting ready to run. I'm very late, soon it won't make sense to open the shop. Just as I'm getting ready to go back to that place, which scares me, a voice in the distance stops me.

"Thomas!" I hear my name shouted.

A silhouette slowly approaches me, it looks like a tall, muscular man with a good bearing.

My heart is pounding, that voice sounds familiar, it's warm and pleasant, like David's. Could it be...?

"David?" I call out to him.

He approaches, and the silhouette suddenly takes shape as my castle crumbles into a thousand pieces and falls to the ground.

"Who the fuck is David?" Matt asks.

What a disappointment! It's "just" Matt.

"Nobody!" I reply as I walk over to greet him and give him a kiss on the cheek.

"Where have you been?" he scolds me in an angry tone.

"I'm sorry. It's a long, long, long story." I try to justify myself. Actually, I wouldn't know what to tell him: I'm ashamed. "And, anyway, I don't have time," I add. "I left my keys in my mackintosh; I can't open the bakery and I'm already incredibly late. And I left my mackintosh at the Kleist, I must go and get it back."

I say it all in one breath, visibly agitated and exhausted. I can't control myself, I'm in a state of panic. What a crazy night!

"Where are you going? Calm down, I've got your stuff back, you fool!"

My eyes light up with happiness when I see my mackintosh hanging on his arm. Instinctively, I run to hug him.

"Thank you, Matt. What would I do without you?"

Matt laughs slightly embarrassed, but doesn't hug me.

I think back to that scene, a few hours ago, in the bar, when I thought he was going to kiss me. I blush, for fuck's sake! All that too much alcohol hasn't made me forget that slip-up.

I pull myself together, retrieve my mackintosh and find my precious keys in my pocket. I breathe a sigh of relief and put the key in the lock, then lift the heavy blind with Matt's help.

Once inside, we warm up in front of the newly lit oven.

"Let's see... Where have you been? And who is the famous David?" Matt jumps up.

He intends to find out every detail, and I know him well enough to know he won't give in easily, so I resign myself and blurt it all out.

When I finish my "report", Matt laughs and scoffs:

"I can't believe it! What a mess! What bad luck, only to you these things can happen, man."

I sigh, and then I add:

"And you, Matt, where have you been?"

"You have no idea, Tom. You won't believe it." He makes a gesture that resembles a smile. "This morning, I was awakened by the sweet rustle of the grass caressed by the cool breeze and, above all, by those icy droplets on my skin. Cool, then... icy.

I opened my eyes and a sense of disorientation came over me. I didn't know where I was or why. Inexplicably I was lying in a huge field, surrounded by magnificent plants. After a few minutes, with my eyes closed, with the first rays of sunlight, still lying in the wet field, with goose bumps from the night's humidity and the rain infiltrating my bones, I felt the touch of a leg.

Startled, I stood up with a quick, single gesture. I looked to my side and saw a thin, dark, hairy leg. With my gaze I ran my eyes up and down the leg until I reached the sex. I stared at it in wonder and awe, almost as if it was the first time I had ever seen a naked man. I imagined what might have happened during the night and regretted not remembering anything. The man slept peacefully, obviously enjoyed himself, and was surely completely satisfied." He smiles with pleasure. "I would have liked to touch him, to feel that young, brown skin under my fingers; I would have liked to lose myself in his folds, to entwine them in that unruly black hair, but I stopped, that was not the moment. I tried to wake him up by touching him with one finger, so that I could reconstruct at least a part of last night. It was hard for him to wake up, but when he noticed the first rays of sunlight, he immediately understood that the night was over."

Matt is delighted and, although he has no memory of what happened, he is very proud of the results obtained; on the other hand, it doesn't take much to understand what really happened, as the lawn mate was very nice.

"He ran off in a second. It was impossible to ask his name, the only answer I got was 'if it's our destiny, we'll surely meet again'. So, the mysterious boy, still half-naked, ran away, leaving me with my heart pounding: a little from the excitement, a little from the bitterness of not even knowing his name. What's wrong with you, Tom? You look weird!"

I sigh.

"I really like him, Matt! I'd give anything to see him again," I confess.

He becomes serious. He scratches his jaw with his right hand. He always does that when he thinks of something, but the ideas he comes up with aren't always brilliant; in fact, they almost never are.

"You said you have his coat, didn't you?" I nod. He sniffs in his pockets.

"I've already done it!"

"Are you sure you looked properly? You might have missed something."

"No." I shake my head. "I'm absolutely sure. I looked everywhere, believe me. Nothing useful!"

He goes on for a few minutes in silence, interrupted only by the crackling of the fire inside the oven.

"Maybe I should resign myself to the idea that I'll never see him again. Besides, he's German, and I'm Jewish: it could never work!"

"Man, don't talk nonsense."

Matt scolds me. He hates it when I start this kind of argument.

"I'm German too, so what? That has never stopped me from being your friend!"

"Yes, but you know how things are now… If you had seen the look on his face when he realised he was in a Jewish-majority neighbourhood."

"But weren't you drunk?"

"That didn't stop me from noticing his discomfort."
"But what are you saying?"
"I'm telling you it's like that."
"You're paranoid!"
"And you're too shallow!"

In an outburst, he grabs a handful of flour from the counter and throws it at me, smearing it in my face.

"Now you're pale and Aryan too, happy?"

I stare at him in amazement for a few seconds, then we start laughing, and, when he least expects it, I smash my hand full of flour in his face.

"What the fuck are you doing?" he asks.

"What is given, is received!"

I turn around laughing, and, in a second, he's on top of me. His imposing body holds me down, dominates me and crushes me on the counter. My back is to him, I can't move. It's an incredibly erotic situation, too bad it's only Matt, my best friend. If only David were in his place...

"Do you want war?" he asks, pretending to threaten me.

I swallow saliva. I feel his breath on my neck.

I move, trying to free myself, but he's stronger than me. In less than a second my face is full of flour again, as well as my hair, ears and neck; I'm all over. Matt, meanwhile, is having fun and laughing out loud.

The sound of the doorbell makes us jump. He takes a step back, and I try to clean myself as best I can. I look at the front door and my eyes can't believe what they see.

An angelic voice clears its throat.
"Everything OK?"
"David?" I ask. I feel like I'm experiencing déjà vu.

But this time the answer is different.

"Hey, yeah, it's me. Hello, Thomas." A halo of awkwardness lights up his face. "Uh... I hope I didn't interrupt anything... I just wanted to... you know, the coat," he stammers, crestfallen, from the doorway.

"Of course not! No, no... Absolutely not! Come in! You have interrupted absolutely nothing."

I approach him hoping to convince him. David takes half a step forward and enters my premises.

I can't believe it! The streets are deserted and I'm inside a bakery with the two most beautiful men on this earth.

"If the mountain won't come to Mohammed..." Matt mumbles through his teeth with a big nod of approval towards David. With a look, I glare at him, and introduce them.

"David, this is my best friend, Matt," I say, emphasising the word "friend". I want to make it clear that there's nothing between us, that I'm single and available.

"Hi, Matt."

David takes two steps forward and squeezes my friend's hand. Then he says to me:

"I was coming to get the coat. You know, I really... I really need it."

"Yeah, yeah, sure," I nod a little disappointed. "There you go." I point to the hanger by the door.

David takes it in a hurry.

"Okay, well... then... I'll leave you!"

"Wait!" I exclaim, almost shouting, and that feeling of déjà vu returns. I blush.

"How did you find me?"

"What do you mean?"

"How do you know I work here?" I ask. He looks at

me in confusion. I feel like an idiot, for the umpteenth time.

"You told me."

"I did?"

I understand this story less and less.

"Yes. When I asked you for your address to accompany you, at first you gave me this address. Once here, I thought it was strange, so I tried to get an explanation from you and you told me that this was your bakery and that you started your shift at about 4:30 in the morning. As it was still very early, I asked for your home address so I could give you a lift."

"Really?" I asked dumbfounded.

"Of course!"

He seems to be uncomfortable again.

I challenge Matt with my eyes, as he keeps "eating him up", and I'm making a real ass of myself. What will he think of me?

"I don't remember anything!" I admit, stunned and a little disappointed. I was expecting another kind of explanation, not so banal, and perhaps a little more romantic, from the guy who had moved heaven and earth to find me because he had realised I was the love of his life. But these things, unfortunately, happen only in the movies. Reality is much more difficult and boring.

"You weren't feeling well last night," he tries to justify me. And there is silence. I wish I could find something interesting to talk about, but nothing comes to mind.

Even Matt isn't much help this morning.

"I'd better go."

David says goodbye, already has his coat on and

opens the door, and I... can't find a valid excuse to stop him.

"Ok, see you soon," are the only words that come out of my mouth. I'd like to give myself a few blows...

Matt looks at me in disbelief, I can read his lips: he keeps nagging me.

The door closes gently and, in no time at all, David is out of my bakery and, it seems, out of my life.

I feel like I'm choking, my legs are shaking. I have butterflies in my stomach.

Without a second thought, I run into the street.

I call out to him, he stops, turns around; I rush towards him. We look into each other's eyes, and it is at that exact moment that I realise what it is between the two of us: a bond that cannot be described in words because it is too deep. It is in our gazes, in our skin, in our gestures, in the words not yet spoken. Before long we find ourselves against a wall. I catch him in my arms.

My lips on top of his, my tongue in his mouth and, after a second, I discover that my daring kiss is reciprocated.

Passion envelops us, I close my eyes and let that wonderful sensation of seductive gallant invade me in that whirlwind of tongues intertwining, caressing, searching each other; of lips biting each other and hands exploring unknown territories.

His essence penetrates me, I feel a flame burning inside me. I want nothing more than him. He drives me crazy. I hug him tightly; I still can't believe what I'm doing.

We're in the middle of the street, kissing brazenly.

Suddenly a car passes by, the window is rolled

down and three young men insult us without mincing their words, without mercy or modesty. The insults are followed by threats.

I step back for a second to catch my breath, and he regains his lucidity and composure. He looks around, terrified, and turns away from me. He continues to stare in bewilderment at everything around him. I look into his eyes, and I see terror in them.

"David... What...?" I utter excitedly, unable to speak. My breath catches. "They were just assholes."

He shakes his head and steps back. His gaze is lost and his eyes are watery.

"I can't, I'm sorry, I can't!" he stammers.

"Wait, I beg you. Explain! Why? What's wrong?"

I try uselessly to grab his sleeve. He runs away and rushes off like the wind. I stand there alone, staring at the edge of the pavement, my apron full of flour, my heart broken, and a terrible burning sensation on my skin.

"Wow, Grandpa! What a story! And then they talk about today's young people... But in Germany, what was happening in the area of raids and riots? How did they experience it? Were you aware of it?"

"Berlin, May 1933. The night of the 10th is a night I will always remember."

"Grandpa, is it the night of the 'Book Burning'?"

"I'm glad to hear that your teacher has told you about it..."

"Yes, Grandpa, while emphasising how lucky we are to be able to read whatever we want; then, sighing and looking up at the sky, she repeats, almost in a trance, a phrase from Heinrich Heine, the German poet of 1797:

'Wherever they burn books, they will also, in the end, burn human beings.'"

"How right your teacher is. On 10 May, the flames rose into the sky at Berlin's Opernplatz, piercing the darkness of the night."

The crackling of the burning books was interrupted only by the shouts of the Nazi students who applauded and glorified the *Bücherverbrennungen*; what you have rightly called 'The Book Burning'.

That night, hundreds of precious works turned to ashes: all the pages of authors, contrary to German ideology, mercilessly thrown into that open-hearth furnace.

Joseph Goebbels, Minister of Propaganda of the Third Reich, watched with satisfaction as the young men of the *Deutsche Studentenschaft*[1] fed that great bonfire with vehemence and conviction. A few days earlier, on 6 May, they had carried out an organised attack against the *Institut für Sexualwissenschaft*[2], instituted in 1919 by Hirscheld. They seized more than twenty thousand texts, including books and magazines, and more than five thousand pictures. On the other hand, they took possession of long lists with names and addresses of real or supposed homosexuals, which were kept inside.

Everything flowed like water. Goebbels, satisfied, stood in front of the microphone, stroked the huge black swastika that covered his glorious lectern in its entirety, and, addressing an audience of some forty thousand people, prepared to deliver his all-important speech.

Indifferent to the sweltering heat emanating from the impressive bonfire, he fixed his cuffs and straightened his shirt collar. After clearing his throat, he proudly addressed

---

1 *German Student's Association.*
2 *Institute for Sexual Knowledge.*

his audience. His voice was intensified by the loudspeakers:

> Comrades, men and women of Germany, the era of Jewish intellectualism is coming to an end and the consecration of the German revolution has also given way to the German way. The future German will not only be a well-read man, but a man of character. To this end, we want to educate them, so that they will have the courage to look at the merciless glare of death from a young age, to overcome their fear of it and to respect it.

He paused for a moment to enjoy the pleased gazes that surrounded him. It was one of his moments of glory, and he wanted to enjoy every moment. He continued:

> That is the task of the young generation. They are doing their duty by consigning the devilish spirit of the past to the flames at this time of night. It is a great, strong, symbolic act, a boundary that will testify to the whole world that the spiritual foundations of the Republic of November are gone. From these ashes will rise the phoenix of a new spirit.

At the same time, in thirty-four other German cities, on the same night, other students, in a single anti-Semitic dream, marched, raising their torches to the sky, while German teachers and officials delivered a ready-made speech, a faithful copy of the previous one: full of malignant energy, elegant, subtle, captivating, histrionic like its monstrous creator.

At two hundred and thirty-two degrees Celsius, the temperature at which paper is incinerated, the writings of

Einstein, Freud, Jack London, Theodore Dreiser, John Dos Passos and the marvellous golden, human geometries of Gustav Klimt were consumed in the fire and the ashes volatized. As your teacher correctly reminds you, in a kind of eerie premonition: wherever they burn books, they will also, in the end, burn human beings."

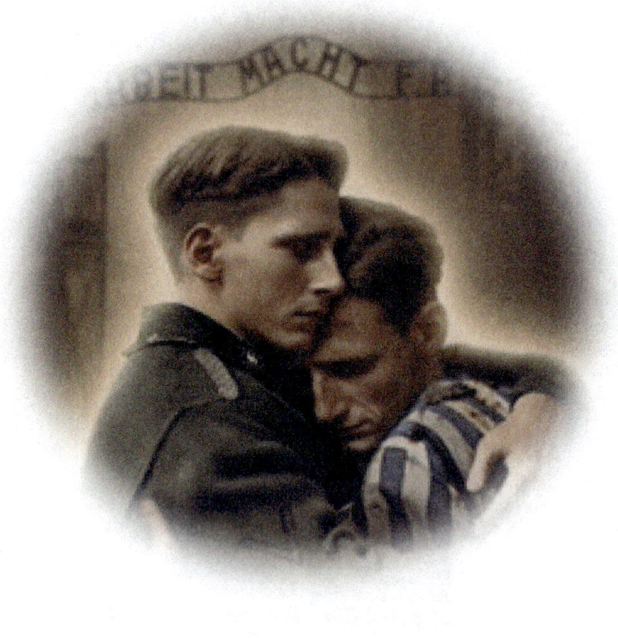
BEIT MACHT F

7

"And you, Grandpa, how did you experience that night of burning? Were you there? Were you able to see it?"

"I'm Jewish, Ben... I'm Jewish. I knew what was going on from Matt's stories and the customers at the bakery. At night I mostly stayed at home with my father, especially after the incident... The atmosphere didn't bode well. But do you want to hear more of my story, or do you think you already have enough material?"

"I'm sorry, Grandpa, go on, but... I beg you! Don't do like my teacher. You too, when you tell your story, look up and lose yourself in infinity."

"I relive, Ben, I relive everything that happened... I lose myself in the past, Ben."

I stand up suddenly, looking for some peace. My back is killing me, but it's not what's keeping me awake. In the last few weeks, I've immersed myself in work, neglecting everything else, including my physical health. I sigh. If only I could cancel that feeling.

The monsters that tormented me as a child, preventing me from resting peacefully, have once again become the protagonists of my sleepless nights, this time in the form of tremendous sensations: despair, regret, loneliness.

And that's how the darkness scares me again. Every time I close my eyes, the features of his face invade my head, making me drunk on him. It is a memory as sweet as lethal. A drop of love in a glass of poison you can't avoid.

I want him. I want him madly and I can't stop. It's constantly running through my head. I remember the wonderful feeling of his arms around my body, the taste of his lips, the smell of him, the passion that immediately erupted between us.

I get up and walk back and forth across the room, then sit on the edge of the bed.

I clutch my head in my hands, like a madman. I can't go on like this, I must find a solution!

I look at the time, shattered. I have to go to work soon, so I get dressed as quickly as possible and leave my room. I walk in the cold of the night, wondering if I'll ever see him again.

I dream every day that I meet him by chance on the city's roads, as often happens in romance novels.

I fantasise about our hypothetical meeting, imagining it romantic and moving. A string quartet plays in my head celebrating that perfect moment.

I can't smile, my life is going to hell. It's become an obsession. Sometimes I wish I'd never met him.

I look up at the sky, silently asking the moon to help me light the way to him.

As I'm thinking about the beauty of his face, suddenly the headlights of a car point straight at me, shining a light that forces me to squint.

I swallow bitterly. This situation doesn't seem normal to me. A halo of worry comes over me, but I try to ignore it.

The Germans' hatred of Jews is growing every day, the city is no longer a safe place. Still, I feel I should stay.

The car approaches slowly over the asphalt, without switching off the engine. A window is rolled down.

My heart stops for a few seconds - it's the same car as David's!

I take a step back, lowering my head a little to see the face of my interlocutor. I wish with all my might that it's him, but my lips reveal a bitter expression when I discover that the stranger has nothing to do with my beloved, in fact, he is not alone in the car.

"Excuse me, do you know where the zoo is?" he asks.

I think for a few seconds, then turn around and extend my arm to the right, pointing to the way.

"Go straight on and, at the second street, turn left. Go on for about five hundred metres and turn left again… No, sorry, to the right. Then go straight on and..."

I'm concentrating, thinking about the shortest way, which is why I don't pay any attention to the fact that one of them has got out of the car and approached me.

The words fade away and the blood freezes in my veins when I see his hand pull a knife from his pocket and hold it to my throat.

"Give me everything you're carrying, you filthy Jew," he threatens.

Instinctively, I take a step backwards and, in no time at all, I'm on the ground, blocked by three bodies that prevent me from moving, while legs repeatedly kick me in the face and head.

In vain I try to defend and cover myself, not really

understanding what is going on.

One of them goes through my pockets while another continues to kick me in the stomach.

I try to scream, but all that comes out of my throat is a desperate rattle.

I'm afraid to die, I only have a few coins in my pockets, and I know very well that they won't be satisfied.

I hear them cursing and insulting me, while the kicks and blows continue to fill my body. They insult me, not just because I am a Jew.

The metallic taste of blood invades my mouth and airways, forcing me to spit. I try to settle into the foetal position, aware that my time has come.

I can't see anything; my eyes are swollen shut and my ears are screeching so loudly I'm sure they're about to explode.

I'm given a minute's respite; something catches their attention. Matt's voice comes to my rescue.

"Tom, Tom... Fucking Nazi bastards!"

I try to crawl away, but I don't have the strength to move. I hear noises, and Matt's voice disappears amidst piercing screams. The sounds are garbled and distant, the pain stops me from breathing, I feel extremely tired and out of breath.

I spit out blood so as not to choke, my head is pounding terribly. Suddenly, the blows and kicks come again. I can't make out how many, I think it's three or four, maybe more.

They constantly utter words like "Jew" and "fag" with inhuman contempt. One of them tries to open my trousers, they try to pull them down, and terror seizes me because I understand their true intentions.

An unexpected rush of adrenaline invades my body and allows me to regain a modicum of strength, I move, I scream in desperation, I pray silently: I want to get out alive.

Numb with pain, I spot a glass bottle on the asphalt, grab it and try to hit one of them. I think I succeed because eventually the blows to my aching body subside and the shards of glass hurt my face and chest.

One of them ducks, while the rest run away. A confused voice speaks to me.

"Tom, Tom, don't leave me..."

Thank goodness Matt is safe.

I hear the sound of footsteps, the chatter of confused people. In the distance I hear a siren: someone has called the police or the ambulance.

Shattered, I stop fighting and let the pain invade me. Lucidity leaves me and suddenly everything becomes distant and unreal.

I wish I could just sleep and turn off this throbbing suffering that kills me. I wish I could scream, cry, react, but I am unable to do so.

I guess I have broken bones, because I can't move and I can't feel some parts of my body.

I feel cold, I can't breathe, I'm suffocating. I just want to die.

"Grandpa, this was the incident you were referring to, wasn't it?"

"Yes, Ben."

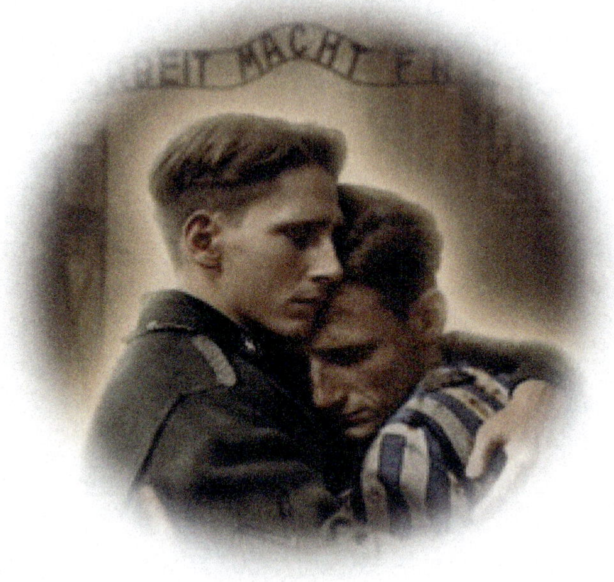

8

My father cannot sleep, not only because the wooden chair he sits in is uncomfortable, but also because he relives, as if it were a film, the events of the last year. For him and for the Jews, these have not been easy days.

Less than a month after the incident, while he was fighting by my side in a seemingly losing battle, Nazi policy had serious repercussions around the world.

"It's true, Grandpa, on 26 January Hitler, in order to stop Polish expansion which threatened Berlin's interests, signed a German-Polish non-aggression pact with Warsaw, and on 14 June he met Mussolini for the first time in Venice. Meanwhile, in Germany, Himmler, President of the Monaco City Police, declared that on Wednesday, 22 March 1933, in the vicinity of Dachau, the first concentration camp would be opened. This decision was taken in order to give the people peace of mind and to satisfy their wishes. And while all this was going on, you, Grandpa, were lying unconscious in the hospital."

"That's right, although it sounds almost like an excuse. In any case, even if I had been in full physical and mental capacity, there was nothing I could have done.

My father was convinced that I was attacked because I was a Jew, and I could not forgive him for it, but what is there to forgive? Should I have denied, or worse, cursed my own roots for the sadistic folly of a group of men? No!

But the reality was that his son was in a coma after a beating, and the cause of the beating was in his DNA.

Images of humiliated human beings, of men forced to be ashamed, to fear and to hide their own roots and their own lineage mingled and haunted in my father's confused and exhausted mind with my still image in that hospital bed.

He watched the spiteful faces of the Germans, their defiant, evil looks, and he didn't understand. He wanted... He wanted an explanation of everything that was happening. He saw it as a prelude to something even bigger, even more devastating, even more terrifying, but he didn't understand it... But deep down, who could?

He saw disconcerting images as he sat in the chair waiting for a change, for better or worse, that would put an end to this absurd agony. They were the flames and bonfires of terrible psychological violence.

Books continued to burn in a kind of symbolic extermination of man, his knowledge and his ideas.

He had no more tears to cry. Poor father! He was alone, tired and extremely affected. He did not know, or perhaps did not care, that Hitler hated not only the Jews, but anyone who opposed him.

And it happened at night, between 29 and 30 June: Germany ordered the purge carried out by the SS."

"It was the Night of the Long Knives, wasn't it, Grandpa?"

"Yes, Ben, a terrible night. Hitler assembled numerous members of the SS and police, and went to the Hanselbauer Hotel in Bad Wiessee, a small town in Bavaria. The SA were opponents of the regime, former enemies or former political comrades of Hitler, other strangers to German political or military life. It was a massacre!

The Reich Chancellor declared that seventy-one people were killed but, in reality, the total number of victims was estimated at between one hundred and fifty and two hundred. Only eighty-five of them are known by name. In reality, it did not matter how many or by what name, how or when, what mattered was to purge Germany of the enemies and of all the peculiarities of the individual, because from each subject the people, conceived as a single mass, had to be reached."

"Well, Grandpa, I know this part of the story, but... tell me about yourself. You were in the hospital with your father by your side, and then?"

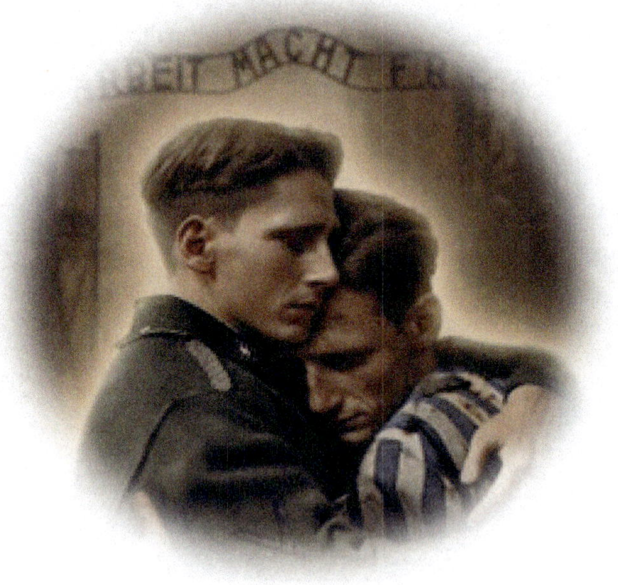
MACHT

9

I open my eyes, or rather, I try to open them, but a tremendous pain invades my temples, immediately forcing me to close them again. I groan in pain, still struggling to breathe. I don't know where I am, I can't remember what has happened to me. I can't tell if it's day or night, there's only darkness around me.

I'm scared, I feel panic coming over me. I try to move, but something stops me, I don't know what.

I feel a continuous and constant buzzing next to me, it pierces my eardrums. My head explodes, I want to vomit.

"He's awake, we need another dose of morphine, quick!"

I feel confused voices, I try to speak, but there's something in my throat, I don't know, maybe a tube, and I can't get a word out.

In an instant I fall back into a deep sleep.

For thirteen months my body has been trapped in the white sheets of the hospital, and my father has never moved from my side.

At my side, he has prayed silently, and now, what is happening looks like a miracle. It seems impossible.

I blink a few times; I feel like I'm dreaming. The images aren't quite clear, I mostly see shadows, but at least I don't feel pain.

The light bothers me, I try to put a hand to my face, but I can't move my arm.

There is someone around me, I can't recognise their features. I don't hear any noise, just a continuous ringing in my ears.

My throat is dry, I would like a sip of water. I try to speak, but find, unfortunately, that something closes my jaw, preventing me from articulating sounds. I blink rapidly so I can focus on the images, but I can still only see shadows and nothing else.

A cold hand touches my forehead, startling me. Suddenly, a light hits my pupils, which dilate immediately. First the right, then the left.

I try to move, but an intense pang cuts off my breath. I shake, I can't breathe. And suddenly, a flash: kicks, blows all over my body. My heart starts beating wildly.

All around me, everything is moving fast, only to suddenly shut down. I fall asleep again.

Later I manage to open my eyes again. Everything is very confusing, but my father's presence reassures me. He is gentle and looks aged to me.

He squeezes my hand and, after an even tighter grip, he stammers:

"Wait, I'm here, wait."

He runs into the room to call the doctor by name, shouting at the top of his lungs, with all the breath he has left, what has just happened.

Dr. Smith rushes to my room, inviting my father to wait for him outside, and begins the examinations to find out my current state of health.

After a few hours, which seemed like an eternity, spent in apnoea from anxiety, a mixture of happiness and fear, my father is allowed to enter the room, where, with great satisfaction, the doctor announces that our nightmare has come to an end, that from this moment on my life is no longer in danger.

I am upset, and sometimes confused, but I begin to utter my first words, stammering.

"Dad, Dad... Where am I?" I ask in a very faint voice, but just enough for him to hear me.

"My son, you've woken up!" He sighs without answering my question. "I knew it, I knew it would happen. You'll still have to stay in hospital for a while, for check-ups and physiotherapy."

The doctor, addressing my father, invites him to calm down because the worst is over. On the other hand, the bruises, contusions and wounds, due to the long period of hospitalisation, have had time to heal. Only a few weeks of therapy are needed before I can begin to lead a normal life.

In the afternoon, the doctor comes by again for a check-up.

"Tom, I want you to try to sit up now, but I warn you that the feeling of nausea and dizziness is quite normal for what you might feel; it was thirteen months in bed."

The young doctor tries to warn me about the possible dizziness and does his best to shorten the recovery time, since every extra day spent in hospital is a huge financial sacrifice for my father, but he doesn't take into account the emotional stability.

"Excuse me, thirteen months? But what happened? Why?"

I start to shake and fidget in bed. The doctor tries to reassure me by resting one hand on my back and calling out to my father with the other.

I notice my father's expression, which changes from happy to worried, he doesn't know exactly what has happened either. We both deserve an answer.

The young doctor decides to intervene.

"Mr. Carl, Tom needs to rest now. Why don't you go home and do the same? After all, the boy is out of danger. Come back tonight and you can talk calmly."

I realise that the doctor, for some strange reason, knows more than he lets on, and I decide to play along.

"Yes, Dad, go easy. You look ten years older. I'm sorry I put you through all this pain."

Dad knows I'm right.

During the time of my convalescence, my father barely managed to sleep more than two hours at a time, he is extremely worried and, above all, he feels that he broke the promise he made to my mother on her deathbed to take care of me. Also, things outside the hospital are not going well at all. But I'm alive, and that's what counts.

"All right, my son, I'll be back tonight. Please rest."

His words are accompanied by bitterness and pain, and those of us present realise that the real victim was in fact old Carl.

Once the doctor and I are alone, I bombard him with hundreds of questions.

"Doctor, I want to know the truth. What happened?"

The doctor looks at me with a compassionate look on his face and answers with another question:

"What do you remember? What is your last memory?"

I can't understand him, I obviously don't remember anything, but I try to please him and try to remember.

Wrapped in a white gown, with the doctor's help, I sit on the bed. I look at my arms and everything seems to be in place; then I take a look at my legs: I don't feel any pain that could remind me of what happened.

Suddenly, an image flashes through my mind like a bolt of lightning in a clear sky: a car, a knife, kicks, the sound of breaking glass…

Little by little, the images become clearer in my mind. I start to feel nervous and paranoid, I become hysterical again.

The doctor understands that it is now his turn, I have remembered enough.

"Tom, you were assaulted, on your way to work from home. Matt was on his way to the bakery when he came across the fight. The assailants lunged at Matt with a ferocious fury. I don't know how you managed to hit one of them with a bottle. He passed out and a few days later he recovered. But don't worry, Matt recovered after a few months in hospital.

The attackers didn't manage to finish the massacre, as people started to arrive and they fled."

I sigh in despondency and resignation, with many questions swirling around in my head.

The doctor looks at me, and continues:

"You were very lucky, Tom, you arrived in really critical condition, but thanks to... but thanks to a good person, you're here now, and Matt is fine too."

The young doctor realises that he has spoken too much.

"Thanks to whom? Who saved me?"

"A young man who did not want to leave his personal details. You know! With the times we live in... They found you with your trousers down, Tom. Rumour has it you've been attacked because you're gay, and do you know why they do that? Because to them it means you've been punished fairly, so there's no punishment for them. The boy who saved you, in an act of bravery, probably wishes to stay out of this story… And who can blame him?

The important thing is that you are alive and that, despite everything that is happening, there are still good Germans."

"At least now I know it was a German. But why did he say "despite everything that is happening"? Doctor, what happened while I was in coma?"

I'm really afraid to ask, I'm afraid of the answer. Things were already bad before the accident, who knows how they are now.

"It is useless to give you any more worries, Tom. Now is not the time. Think about getting your strength back, your father needs you. In a couple of days, you'll go out and see for yourself. We Jewish doctors can't practise in public hospitals; the walls around us belong to a private hospital.

We are financed and supported by the Association of Socialist Physicians, which distanced itself from the shameful Nazi politics.

Most of the doctors in the country support experimenting on human beings. Not only do they carry out experiments on rare diseases and gangrene, inflicting wounds on prisoners and making them infected, they also experiment with sterilisation, abortions and much more.

The number of doctors who have lost their minds and betrayed their oath to medicine is so great that the prestigious medical journal Deutsches Artzeblatt celebrated Hitler's rise to power by publishing a large swastika on its July cover. In that issue, it glorified the mission entrusted to Alfons Stauder, president of the

German Medical Association, to continue the cultural and spiritual elimination of Jews in the country.

That's why you couldn't stay in a public hospital. Who knows what they would have done to you! What experiment they would have subjected you to! Your father, who is a wise man, was right to leave you here, where the man who saved your life brought you."

Those words intensify the feeling of despair and despondency.

Private? Poor Dad! Let's hope that at least things at the bakery are going well. How could he have been able to pay for more than a year of a private clinic?

As I sink into my thoughts, a noise wakes me up and brings me back to reality. It is a hand knocking on the wooden door of the room.

"Excuse me… Am I disturbing you?"

A charming young woman appears. I see in her the features of my best friend: blonde, wavy, back-length hair, blue eyes: just like Matt's, a clear blue like the sky on a sunny day. She is tall.

I recognise her with difficulty, young people grow up too fast…

"Anna, what brings you here? It's been a long time since I've seen you, but it's always a pleasure to see you. Doctor, excuse me, this is Anna, my friend Matt's sister."

"Yes, yes, yes, I know. This beautiful young lady has been coming practically every day since you've been here."

The doctor shakes her hand.

"Really? Are you alone? Is Matt coming?" I feel a bit disoriented, it's strange to see Anna and not Matt.

"Anna, that's Grandma, isn't she?"

"Yes, Ben, she's that fantastic woman who continues to look after us every day. Now as then."

> The doctor glances at her, nods, as if to say "it's your turn", and then leaves.
>
> "I hope you can excuse me; I still have work to do. Talk quietly... I'll stop by again before the shift changes, to make sure everything is going well. Anna, Thomas."
>
> I'm finally alone with Anna and I start peppering her with questions.
>
> "Where's your brother? Why isn't he here too?"
>
> "Tom, I'm sorry, but Matt isn't coming today and probably never will." Anna looks at me waiting for a reaction, but realising that I'm still nursing my shock, she decides to continue: "Look, Tom, my dad's found out!"
>
> I open my eyes, stunned and terrified.
>
> "What did he find out?" I ask in a frail voice. I'm exhausted, I'd like to close my eyes and rest as if none of this had happened.
>
> "When you were admitted to the hospital, it was more than obvious that you were not the victims of a simple accident. At first, my father thought it was one of the typical attacks on Jews, but then why beat up Matt as well? It was obvious that he belonged to the Aryan race. Both had been beaten almost to death. Neither of you could speak."
>
> My father, in spite of everything, did nothing but look for answers. You know what Dad is like! When he gets something in his head, there's no stopping him. He couldn't watch his son dying without knowing who was responsible. Someone had to pay dearly for

the suffering inflicted on my family.

My mother cried day and night… Also, my father always had high aspirations for his only son. It's true that Matt dislikes him a lot, but my father always believed in him; he said that he was just a phase of adolescence, that sooner or later he would grow up."

I stare at her motionless, listening carefully to every word. She has grown up a lot, she is no longer a child. She speaks slowly, articulating her words perfectly, trying to find the right phrases.

"You know what my father is like, don't you? When Matt's condition was still critical and hovering between life and death, my father, instead of standing by his son's side and spending, perhaps, the last days of his son's life, sought to do him justice. Even for one like him, with his resources and contacts, it was very difficult for him to discover the truth. It seemed impossible, it was as if there was no evidence, no witnesses to what had happened, but, in the end, he got away with it." Anna pauses to fill her lungs and find the right words, then continues: "He interrogated the doctors at the clinic who were on duty that night, threatened to have the centre closed down and denounce them as traitors to German politics, until one, out of fear, spoke up. He said that you had been brought in by a German man who had intervened, much to his regret, because for him you had to be cured and forget about it, since the aggressors were right, because gay massacre is not a crime. Besides, you arrived with your trousers down and your belt unbuckled."

"Anna, I'm getting more and more confused. A German man who saves us, but then supports the attackers by claiming that we deserved what happened to us? Is he crazy or what?"

"Tom, he probably saved you, but he also tried to protect himself… And, in the end, you too. Imagine if my father had had the attackers arrested: they would have got away with this story of homosexuality that would have become public knowledge. Look, Tom, all is not always as it seems, even in the accusations and rejection of you by that young man, there may be an attempt to preserve your future and your life."

She is already a little woman, much wiser and more mature than Matt and I combined.

"Grandpa, I imagine that just in that year the political and social situation collapsed, or am I wrong?"

"I asked Anna the same question, I had also had that feeling."

"Yes," she answers with a lowered gaze, "it's a bit different now, but I'll explain it better later, I don't want to traumatise you even more after all you've been through."

"I don't understand anything, I want to know more, especially about the German who saved us. Anna, help me understand how I got here."

"Tom, I told you."

"But why would a German have to save me?"

"Maybe because not all Germans have had their heads eaten off, or maybe he recognised Matt; maybe he saw him once with Dad. I have no idea, Tom, really!"

"What about Matt? How's he doing?"

"Matt did quite well, he was only admitted for two weeks, which seemed like an eternity to us. Anyway, the doctors decided to let the wounds heal a little better before discharging him. This is where my father comes back into the picture. He couldn't go on living like that, it had been confirmed to him that you had been assaulted because you were gay, but for some strange reason he refused to believe it. Besides... he couldn't accept that his son would be cured in a Jewish clinic. I think it was really because he couldn't accept the fact that Matt was gay. So, after two weeks in the clinic, without medical consent, he took him home. The desire to avenge him, to spare him slander and accusations was so great that he didn't think about the welfare of his son. The doctors, who were Jewish, had to obey. My father, after all, granted them privileges they no longer enjoyed. But my dear brother did not want to be discharged, so he told the whole truth."

"The whole truth? I am more and more surprised. So, my father is also aware of everything?"

"Grandpa, you're always telling us that we have to tell it like it is, and that we don't have to be afraid to freely express our ideas and dreams, but you had secrets from your father too. And what secrets!"

"You're right, Ben, but those were different times. I was just a young man and I had no one to guide me in that jungle of terror and repression. Besides, it was also a way of protecting him, of not giving him any more pain and not getting him into trouble because of me. It's hard, Ben, and back then it was even harder."

Anna confirms that her father has found out everything.

"Yes, absolutely everything. Also, because Matt is in love with a young man, I knew practically nothing about."

I smile, looking back to those days that had brought us so much happiness.

"Yes, I know, Anna, the lawn boy." I smile again with my heart and my face.

"Well, that... Matt suddenly saw his beloved stranger right outside the door of his hospital room, playing the doctor who had saved his life."

"He saw who?" I interrupt her.

"The doctor! Apparently, he had fallen in love with the doctor. The young man on the lawn, do you understand? The boy he'd been looking for was there, in the white coat looking after him."

I can't believe it.

"What luck he had!" I exclaimed.

Only to Matt could such a thing happen. It's unbelievable! It's amazing how reality often surpasses fiction.

"Matt started talking when he saw his beloved. I think he did it to get his attention and to finally be himself. Life had given him another chance, and he wanted to live it to the fullest. You know how Matt is! Sometimes he can be very irresponsible. He talked to my dad, as if he were a normal dad. He confessed everything to him, as if Dad could understand..."

I feel very nervous, too much information, too much news. It's hard to put my thoughts in order, so I decide to ask:

"Sorry, Anna, I don't mean to bother you with hundreds of questions, but I need to know. Your brother, what exactly did he say about me?"

"Just that you are a true friend, that even if you don't share his lifestyle, you are a great friend to him.

The doctor hasn't mentioned anything either. I think this is the first time my brother has done something good by not talking about you. Sometimes he looks stupid, but he is actually a very loyal and thoughtful man, as long as it's not about himself."

"How right you are!" A smile escapes me.

"Matt's a really great guy, he'd never betray a friend, but when it comes to him, he just keeps screwing up."

"One thing is not entirely clear: if your father understood Matt, why did he try to cure him by keeping him locked up in the house like a prison?"

Anna, after a big sigh, answers me:

"At first it was like that, really, but a few days later, in the barracks, everyone knew what had happened. A month later, the rumours reached the higher echelons. You know what they're like in the SS!

Even if there was no proof, the fact that a German was assaulted and taken to a Jewish clinic was very sobering.

My father, an SS general, obviously couldn't afford to have a gay son, and, trying to turn the tables, he pretended that Matt was one of the attackers, but that unfortunately he had been beaten almost to death and, amid the chaos, was taken to the Jewish clinic. He had to hide the truth somehow, before the bomb exploded."

I can't believe what I'm hearing.

"SS General? But... if your father is a colonel in the SA, what does the SS have to do with it now?"

"Grandpa, Hitler discovered an attempted coup d'état and decided to arrest, or rather kill everyone. Ernst was the head of the SA and, moreover, a homosexual. It was said that the SA men were caught by executioners in the middle of a homosexual party with young aspirants. What did you think happened to Ernst?"

"Ah, I see you know your history very well, I guess I'll have to congratulate your teacher. That was just what Anna said, trying to quickly explain to me what had happened in the last year."

Clearing her throat, she explains:
"He was, but not anymore! Hitler decided to clean up his act and, after killing the SA leaders, brought the rest into the SS. With this change, my father even managed to rise through the ranks, from colonel to general."

Before continuing, she waits a few seconds for my reaction, which is not long in coming.

"I'm stunned. Hitler already knew about Róhm's homosexuality, it was practically common knowledge."

These events can only mean one thing: the execution of the dreaded paragraph 175; a law that has always existed, but has never been applied... Until now!

Anna, sensing my anxiety, decides to continue talking about Matt to distract me a little from the bad thoughts running through my head:

"So, as I was saying, my father was forced to invent a new version of events: he preferred to label his son as weak. In the meantime, he had to survive the shock and convince himself that Matt's homosexuality was curable. All this shames him greatly. The humiliations he has been subjected to day after day are truly terrible, but now his only mission is to cure Matt, and not because he believes he will succeed; if he does it, it is for himself. Continuing to be a general is the only way to keep his dignity high."

"Poor Matt, I feel so sorry for him."

Anna smiles and adds:

"Don't feel so sorry for Matt! You know what your dear friend is like, he gets away with it even under my father's dictatorship."

At last, it's time to reveal some good news, little Anna settles down next to my bed.

"How about this? A few days after Matt came home, he got a notice from the recruiting centre. My brother didn't want to go for the world, but he couldn't tell my dad, so he did one of his own. I think they call it reverse psychology. He told my dad that he was excited and couldn't wait to get away from home, and with all those men around, he was sure to have a lot of fun. My father fell into the trap and, not realising that he had been tricked, decided emphatically that his son would not leave for anything in the world."

I let out a big laugh that paralyses me for a few seconds in bed due to a slight discomfort in my chest. I know for sure that Matt would never ever go to war to fight in a battle he doesn't believe in at all, but that he has managed it so masterfully is a surprise. Little Anna laughs too, but after a few seconds she turns serious and adds:

"Tom, it's very difficult to be in that house. My brother is imprisoned in his room and my father doesn't know how to cure him. I'm afraid he'll try everything he can, but he won't succeed. He's a man who lives in torment!"

"Anna, I'm so sorry."

I tell her I'm sorry because I think a small gesture of

understanding might help her, but I'm not really sorry at all. Why should I feel sorry? The fact that straight people have problems with gay people is their own problem. The ones I do feel sorry for are Matt and Anna. Poor kids, they live with the enemy at home.

Just as I'm lost in thought, Anna adds:

"Don't feel sorry! Problems are only for those who create them."

"How amazing Grandma was...! It doesn't seem, or come to think of it, it's quite predictable. Go on, Grandpa, I'm listening anxiously."

I'm really surprised about Anna, Matt's sister. She's growing up so fast.

"Anna, how old are you now?"

"I'm fourteen now. I'm growing up!"

She blushes, after all, she's always been trying to get my attention.

Even as a little girl, she used to wander around me to get her special animal-shaped buns: butterflies were her favourite.

When my mother was still alive, she, Matt and their mother would come to the bakery; while our mothers spent hours talking, I would amuse her by giving her a small piece of dough with which she would amuse herself for a while. I would say, "Come on, now make a beautiful butterfly, so we can put it in the magic oven and bring it to life".

Anna was still very little, about five or six years old, but she still remembers perfectly well the shapes of bread she gave me, almost always irregularly shaped balls, but the big oven was really magical: once inside, those little balls were transformed into splendid butterflies; sometimes into bears; sometimes into dogs or cats.

"Just like she did with us when we were kids! Ben exclaims enthusiastically."

"Yes, Ben, but her real interest in me came at the age of ten, when on the day of her first communion she stopped by the bakery to greet the family and noticed, for the first time, a detail she hadn't seen before: she saw how, with a deft and swift gesture, I threw away the dough she had previously moulded and replaced it with another one I had ready and stored under the counter.

That day, a huge bouquet of flowers came out of the big oven. My goodness, how much work I had put in... Even the leaves were skilfully made. From that moment on, Anna, even knowing the truth, continued to play along with me, having even more fun because she knew I was thinking of her: I baked those splendid little breads just for her!

Unfortunately, it all ended after my mother's death. Anna's mother stopped coming to the bakery and, in the meantime, she grew up. For Anna, I was just a utopia, the boy who was always in her thoughts…"

Given the age difference, she, for me, was always "little Anna".

"But, Grandpa, what happened? When did you fall in love and get married?"

"Be patient, Ben, I've already lost the thread... Where was I? If you keep bringing me back to reality, I run the risk of really waking up and forgetting, once and for all, that past that I've been trying to forget for years."

"You were in the hospital, Grandpa, and Grandma, sitting at the foot of your bed, was filling you in on what had happened in the last few months."

"Oh, yes... That's how Anna found out about my homosexuality, and her slim hopes were dashed forever."

After so many stories, it's getting pretty late.

"Sorry, Tom, but I have to go now. You know: curfew." He kisses me on the forehead and adds: "Greetings to Peter."

"Peter? Who's Peter?" I can't make out who she means.

"Dr. Smith, Peter Smith: your doctor." She winks at me and continues: "And Matt's too." Anna now seems amused, clarifying: "It's Matt who sent me. At first, I thought it was for you, but every time I left the house he handed me a letter for the doctor, then he started replying, and now I'm his personal messenger. But please don't misunderstand me, I'm delighted to see you." Anna has said too much. Embarrassed, she gives me a little rest. "I must go, but I promise I'll come back and visit you tomorrow... If you want me to."

Blushing more and more, she leaves, leaving behind a sentence that I utter and makes her smile:

"Of course! I'm counting on it, come back and visit me. You are, without a doubt, a beautiful distraction."

10

Anna leaves and the young doctor approaches me. "You know everything now, Tom, or almost everything." He smiles at me. "I really love Matt."

I exchange his smile, I'm happy for them and, above all, I'm happy because I'll be discharged shortly.

In the meantime, I have nightmares that don't leave me alone. Everything is dark and cold. No smell, no colour, no sound that can reveal to me where I am. I wander through the unknown in search of a sign, and I hear a soft voice saying: "Tom, don't leave me, I love you!"

I try to follow that voice, but I cannot understand where it is coming from. Now I hear other voices. They seem to come from different places.

Terrifying images: a knife at my throat, a bunch of legs hitting my face, my head, kicks in the stomach, trousers pulled down....

Disjointed phrases from deformed voices: "Give me everything you own, you filthy Jew"; "Tom, Tom, you fucking Nazi bastards"; "Jew"; "Jewish fag".

I try to scream, but, as usual in nightmares, only a desperate rattle comes out of my throat. I feel the metallic taste of blood, and again garbled sounds, and sirens... And that voice: "Tom, Tom, don't leave me."

Suddenly I recognize it, my heart starts beating at full speed. It's him, I'm sure: "David, where are you? I beg you, answer me, tell me where you are", I cry out

in desperation, but all I can hear are confused phrases.
"Are you a Jew?"

This last sentence reverberates much more than the previous ones, I hear it from different points of the room. I tremble.

"Tom, Tom, wake up." The doctor shakes me.

I shiver and break out in a cold sweat, shake and keep screaming.

I have no fever and it is evident that this is a bad dream that keeps repeating itself.

"Peter... uh... Doctor, excuse me. I think I had a nightmare."

"Peter, call me Peter."

He allows me to call him by his name, but now he must exercise his role as a doctor and this time it is to tell me some great news:

"Let's see, in spite of your repeated nightmares, and even though you are still weak, both emotionally and physically, if you promise me that you will behave yourself, I will let you go home. On this paper is written everything you must do, medicines included. Don't forget them! I know you have refused physiotherapy, I don't agree, but I understand you. In these other papers, the physiotherapist has written down the exercises that you will have to do every day. If you have any doubts or problems, I'm here." He hands me the papers with all the details, and concludes: "Do you feel ready to face the world?"

I'm delighted with the wonderful news.

"Of course I'm ready, why shouldn't I be? The bakery and my father are waiting for me. I have to recover as soon as possible, I can't afford to be sick any longer, especially after my stay here in the private clinic. I will make my father rest, he deserves it; apart from needing it, he seems to have aged a hundred years."

Noting my enthusiasm, Peter fails to tell me what is really going on outside, and Anna's arrival saves him from further arguments.

"Good afternoon to both of you. How is our favourite patient today?"

"Perfectly fine, about to go home. And I don't want to see him here again."

The doctor's good humour rubs off on all of us.

"Peter, wait! Can I ask you if a boy named David ever came to visit me?"

Although I can already imagine the answer, I still dare to ask the question, hoping and wishing for good news.

Peter just shakes his head and adds:

"I'm sorry, Tom. I know who David is, Matt told me, but I haven't heard from him."

"It's all right. Thank you."

I finish the speech with a tone of apparent disinterest, but I am not indifferent.

A whirlwind of conflicting emotions tortures me, like a punch straight to the pit of my stomach.

Why didn't he come? Maybe he doesn't know? What if he found out and didn't come because he is ashamed? Deep down, I was and am a Jew.

And while I'm lost among a thousand whys, my father comes looking for me. He seems relieved that I am recovered, but he doesn't seem happy to take me home. I don't understand, something escapes me. Maybe he thinks I'm safer at the clinic.

Anyway, I've been discharged.

He has prayed so hard that I would come out of the

coma and come back to me.... But something is bothering him.

He doesn't know how to treat me, how to explain everything that has happened in the last few months. How did he cope with the work at the bakery? Or, even worse, the continuous laws against us.

"Grandpa, I don't understand it. I can't understand how a man can persecute other men. Why did it have to be so difficult for you and the other Jews?"

"Ben, I don't know. Even now I still live the memory of those years as a terrible nightmare, not as a reality; I still can't understand and accept it, how can you? We just need things like these to never happen again."

When I finally leave the clinic, I realize that I still can't stand up perfectly and that I get exhausted very quickly, so we take a break. We sit down on a bench, a bench that Dad knows in depth. It is the same one where we have sworn to always help and support each other, after the tragic event of my mother's death.

It was a very intense moment, one of those rare moments of true love and absolute sincerity that two people can share. Dad and I remember that day well. Mum had already been ill for some years with brain cancer. They both knew that she would not be cured, but they decided to tell me only when the situation worsened; after all, why feel such excruciating pain before the worst came?

On my sixteenth birthday, Mum decided to throw me a party to have some fun, giving me special and unforgettable moments. She turned on her record player and we danced for at least two hours, infecting

Dad as well. It was a beautiful day that, unfortunately, ended on this very bench where we are sitting now, waiting for me to regain my strength.

Perhaps because she was tired, or perhaps because her time had come, Mum fell to the ground that day. The trip to the hospital was quick, but not quick enough to save her. I, who had refused to go, sitting right here on this bench, tried to convince myself that my mother would once again walk out those doors to join me. I thought and thought that the only woman in my life could not leave forever without even saying goodbye. She would never do it.

But she didn't: Mum never left that building again. After what happened, heartbroken, Dad settled down next to me. He was not prepared for that moment, even knowing the condition his wife was in. He had avoided thinking about the consequences, so he simply talked about her.

He told me everything: how he had met her, why he had fallen in love with her, her desire to travel around the world, why she opened a bakery, her love for dancing; thousands of conversations, dreams, secrets and happy moments came to the surface in that instant.

I was in awe of all these stories, but in the end, I asked:

"Why are you telling me all these things now that Mum is dead?"

Dad, disconsolate, only understood at that moment why.

"Look, son, as long as you keep her memory alive in your heart, she will never die. The more memories you have of your mother, the easier it will be for you to remember her and have her among us."

"But now I'm digressing… Your friends and your teachers are not interested in the memories of a poor old man, except those concerning Nazism."

"Don't worry, Grandpa, they do interest me. When the video is edited, I'll remove these pieces, but first I'll keep a complete copy for myself."

Ben smiles and winks at me, barely concealing his excitement.

I take the time I need to regain my strength, and we continue on our way home. As soon as we enter, I realize that something has changed.

"I have been told that things are different outside, but no one has told me that they have changed inside the house as well, and honestly, I couldn't even have imagined it."

My poor father pales, he didn't expect the changes to be so evident. The time comes to give me some explanations.

"I'm sorry, Tom, it's true, everything is different now for us Jews, and this has affected us, unfortunately, also at home."

"Explain yourself better, Dad. I don't understand how this is possible."

He picks up two glasses, puts them on the kitchen table, takes a bottle of wine out of the refrigerator, looks at it and puts it back.

"Maybe it's not the best option with the amount of medication you have to take," he says, referring more to himself than to me.

He picks up a bag of milk, taps his hand on the chair, inviting me to sit next to him, and starts updating me.

"Tom, I imagine you've noticed that you've been to

a private clinic." I nod, and he continues: "This year, racial laws have prohibited Jews from benefiting from and using public hospitals, among other things. They have even denied us the right to insurance mutual. Therefore, I have been forced to face expenses much higher than our income.

We are living hard times, we only had Jewish customers, and lately you can count them on the fingers of one hand, so I had to sell some things. Little by little, the situation got worse and the Germans forced me to close the bakery, leaving us without the little that allowed us to survive…"

I'm speechless, what I'm hearing can't be true, although Peter had already told me something. I am the only one responsible for my father's ruin. I will never forgive myself!

A tear runs down my cheek against my will.

"I'm so sorry, Dad. I'll do anything to fix the situation. This is really terrible, and I'm the only one responsible. I'm so sorry! I'm so sorry, Dad."

Tears stream down my face. Dad understands my mood, and even though it's all been a consequence of the beating I got, he has never held me responsible for what happened.

"I beg you, don't apologize, you are not to blame for anything! The fault lies, perhaps, with those who decided to beat you up; perhaps with Hitler, who has put us in these conditions; perhaps even with our God, who seems to have forgotten us, but, in reality, things are going as they should."

I look at Dad. With his meagre studies, he is a great man endowed with great intelligence and nobility. Then I look around and see Mum's old record player.

"Thank you for not selling it."

Dad follows the trajectory of my gaze and, with bitterness, replies:

"I would never have thought of it, but you must know that to save your life I would have given my very life…, even that record player."

I know it's true what he says: I would have done the same for him.

Ben turns off the camcorder for a moment with the excuse of changing the memory card. In reality, he is just trying to hide his face wet from the tears he can't hold back and his sore throat from the sobs that are about to break out.

11

After a relatively short pause, Ben continues with his work, still moved and confused.

"Grandpa, where did we leave off...? The hatred of Jews..." He opens the book so that he can continue to hide the anguish portrayed on his face. "Good."

On 13 July, Hitler made a speech at the Krolloper, the famous opera house in Berlin, finalising the terms of the purge. Two days later, the great army manoeuvres took place, when the military confirmed their total loyalty to the Chancellor, greeting and honouring him. On 26 July, the SA were officially reconstituted, headed by Viktor Lutze, separating them from the SS, and on 2 August, when Hindenburg died, Hitler, as expected, bestowed upon himself the offices of Chancellor and President along with the title of Commander of the Reich armed forces.

The officers and soldiers were sworn in on 19 August; the Germans approved Hitler's appointment with 89.93% of the vote, propelling him to the German presidency. Hitler then proclaimed himself Führer of Germany at the opening ceremony of the Nazi party congress at the Luitpoldhalle in Nuremberg on 4 September. On the Night of the Long Knives, according to the data provided by the Reich Chancellor himself on 13 July, seventy-one persons were killed, but, in reality, the total number of victims is estimated to be between one hundred and fifty and two hundred; only eighty-five were identified.

From that date onwards, the Nazi persecution of homosexuals, which had hitherto been sporadic and moderate, became ever more systematic and brutal.

"Yes, Ben, I told you about the Night of the Long Knives. I was in hospital; it was Grandma who filled me in on what happened. Now, how about we take a longer break? I need something hot, and you need to sort out your notes."

Anna takes advantage of the interruption and brews coffee for Grandpa and hot milk for Ben.

12

"Grandpa, shall we go on?"

"Yes, Ben, let's go on; but as your little brother is asleep, and Grandma is here with us, I think it is only fair to give her the floor, what do you think? Or are women not allowed in your interviews?"

"Grandpa, what are you talking about? I chose you because you're Jewish, but Grandma's statements are just as valuable as yours. Come on, Grandma, it's your turn!"

"I understand that Grandpa told you about Matt; I experienced his drama first hand, he was my older brother and I loved him very much. I often saw him lying in bed, locked in his room. The time that passed, isolated within the walls of the house, must have seemed like an eternity.

He was lying in bed, on his back, staring at the ceiling, and I asked him if I could do anything for him, if he needed anything. He replied that the ceiling seemed to be shrinking bit by bit, that he had the impression that the walls would continue to shrink until they crushed him.

At that time, he had become very close to Christ. Our father allowed him to leave the house only to go to church, obviously accompanied by his henchmen. Father Garret had embraced, like all Hitler's devotees, a "positive Christianity", the doctrine of Nazi propaganda, devoted to a strictly Aryan Christ: A God who appears kind and gentle, even sometimes sympathetic, but who must redeem Matt from his sins. The Lord does not admit homosexuals into paradise."

"'That which contradicts nature cannot come from God' Hitler repeated with conviction, didn't he, Grandma?"

"You're right, Ben."

"He claimed, according to what the teacher taught us, that Christianity was an invention of sick brains, a collection of Jewish delusions manipulated by priests; it was the first religion to exterminate its opponents in the name of love.

It is intolerant, it deceives the people, it contradicts reason and scientific development; the hardest blow humanity has received is the appearance of Christianity. Bolshevism is its illegitimate child. Both are an invention of the Jews.

That was what Hitler said, and therefore religion was to be condemned as everything which revolves around an inferior race and which in any way can contaminate the Aryan race. Point 24 of the National Socialist German Workers' Party stated: "We demand freedom for all religious denominations within the state as long as they do not represent a danger to it and do not militate against the moral sentiments of the German race. The party as such defends the idea of positive Christianity, but does not commit itself in matters of creed to any particular confession".

But not only was this freedom never granted, but all those who belonged to other creeds were captured, interned in concentration camps and marked with a violet scarf."

"Exactly, Ben. In this case your books reflect the whole truth."

Matt, pushed by our father to go to church, has learned to pray day after day, but he prays to a God who is more Jewish than Aryan, a God who is merciful and forgiving: it is beautiful to know that one is not alone!

This is how my dear brother confides to his God his innermost secrets, his most terrifying fears and also his greatest desires; he knows that the Lord may not be on his side, but he must still confess everything to him, all things. His God has not only given him another chance, but has also allowed him to live this new life with his best friend and the man of his dreams.

Who is our father to say that all this is wrong? How can a miracle be wrong? Why has his God granted it to him and his father wants to deny it to him? Who does he think he is? It's not fair!

A thought torments his soul: "If God has created me, if we are all his children, why should I change the way I am? It would be like arguing with his decision or admitting that he might make a mistake and fail! If my father and the world do not accept the fruit of his creation, do I have to be the one to change?"

Matt has always believed that there is a God above all else, but he continues to question why he created him this way if he doesn't accept it.

Suddenly, one day he understood. He understood that God decided to give him a second chance; he understood it as he lay in that hospital bed and saw his Peter in front of the door.

It had to be a sign; it was a sign. He had to live as well as possible the time he had left in this world.

That's why Matt interruptedly prays: "Help me, I beg you. In this house, with this monster of a father, I'm not happy. Please give me a sign, tell me what I have to do. Amen! I thank you infinitely for giving Tom a chance too. Even though he is Jewish and gay, if anyone deserves it more than anyone else, it is him. Our Father...".

Matt wanted so much to see Tom again, he had so much to tell him. For a whole year, he did nothing but pray for his health, and now that his prayers have been answered, he feels like a prisoner at home; not to mention Peter, the love of his life. All this drives him into a state of depression, so he decides to do something. He doesn't know what or how, but he certainly has to do something.

"As your grandpa must have explained to you, Matt was very particular, he had to act all the time, no matter what. This is where I came into the picture."

"Anna," he says, "you have to do me a favour."
"Tell me, little brother."
After the accident in which I almost lost him forever, I swore to myself that I would do anything for him. Having experienced that feeling of loss and helplessness, which I didn't like at all, I swore I would always be by his side, so I agree to act as his messenger. After all, it didn't bother me at all, as I could see Tom. Now that he's been discharged and the bakery has closed, I have no more excuses to visit him.

Matt, with each passing day, is drowning more and more in a terrible depression that is slowly sucking him in, like quicksand. I am the only friend and accomplice he has been able to count on this year. He confesses to me that he wants to end his life, leaving me devastated inside. I understand how he feels: with all the tension at home, it's impossible to live.

I get him to promise me that he will always tell me everything, absolutely everything, even those things that seem unimportant. Whatever he decides to do, crazy things included.

I am frightened by his apparent calmness. I think he will soon do one of his own.

I'm at Tom's house in no time. Seeing the bakery closed makes me very sad. Tom sees me coming from the balcony.

"Look what the wind blew in!"

I raise my head and answer him:

"It's more than wind, it's Matt's hurricane that sent me! I have something for you."

Happy for the news, Tom heads inside, down the stairs to meet me on the doorstep.

"Wow, that's fast for your condition!"

"I haven't seen Matt for a long time, and if you've got anything from him, I can't wait to see it."

I reach into my bag and pull out a white piece of paper folded in two.

"Here, this one's for you."

"Thank you, Anna, it makes me really happy, but, if it's not too much to ask, I'd like you to wait for me for a moment. After I have read it, I would like you to give him my reply."

Raising my hands to the sky, with a great deal of irony, I reply,

"Man, of course! Otherwise, what kind of postwoman would I be?"

He laughs and hurries to read the contents of the letter so as not to waste any more time.

"At the time, Ben, I was dying to know what the letter said. But years later, your grandpa let me read them."

My dear friend,

I am very, very, very, very, very, very, very happy that you are alive. I have prayed so much for you, and it is not like me. I have done it only for you! I would have given my life for yours; I thank heaven every day for giving you another chance, and I am delighted with the results. Unfortunately, I did not wish the same fate for myself, but our God is great and, apart from fulfilling my prayers, he has also fulfilled those of my little sister. And here I am, a prisoner in the walls of my own house. I feel very bad, I think that out there is you, Peter and a whole world that I, because of my bastard of a father, cannot live in. A life that God himself has given me a second time. I need you now more than ever.

I'd like to see you and talk to you ad infinitum about everything that crosses my mind, I miss you, dear friend! I'm afraid of going mad in this house! I LOVE YOU, don't forget it.

As soon as he finishes reading, he looks up with tears in his eyes, tears that will not fall for anything in the world. I'm sure he doesn't mean to worry me, but his sudden change of mood unsettles me.

"Tom, what's wrong? What did he write to you in that letter?"

He tries to hide his emotions and, with a fake smile on his face, replies:

"Nothing, it's just the excitement. If you'll excuse me for a while, I'd like to send him the reply. Why don't you come upstairs? I'll invite you for a cup of tea. My father's here too, he'll be very happy to see you."

I think he's hiding something from me, but he hasn't seen Matt for a long time and he was so excited to read his words that I decided to believe him.

When I get home, I find Matt sitting on the front steps waiting for me.

"So, what did he say? How is he? Is he fully recovered or not yet? Did he give you anything for me?"

I look at him with wide, doubtful eyes.

"Let's see... Where do I start? He told me he misses you very much. It seemed to me that he's still the same. No, he's not bad, and yes, he's recovered... And besides..." I take out of my bag a letter folded in four and hand it to him. "This is for you."

Matt kisses me enthusiastically on the forehead and goes to his room to read his friend's letter.

Dearest Matt, my friend,
I know you are happy for my recovery, but from what I read in the letter, I doubt it was you who wrote those words. I know your father is a real son of a bitch, but since when do you let him get away with it? Those words conveyed despair, resignation and total surrender. What happened to that crazy, thoughtless young man I knew? The one who didn't care about anything, because life was a gift and we had to live it to the fullest.

If you really want something, you must fight to get it. You have been the one who taught me that, remember? And now you must wake up. Do you want to be with Peter? Then fight to be with him! I'm sure he wants you too, he's madly in love with you.

What are you waiting for? This is the first and probably the last time I tell you. Go back to being your old unconscious self and live your days as you think best; after all, if the alternative is to be imprisoned in your own house, I think there is nothing worse. As much as your father may be a bastard, he is still your father. Don't be afraid of him. Do you feel like you're living a nightmare? Become a Jew and then we'll talk. Your situation is nothing compared to what we have to put up with out here. Did you hear that my father was forced to close the bakery? Not to mention all those prohibitions. Listen, my friend, there's a war coming, and you've had a second chance, so be happy; the future, unfortunately, doesn't guarantee us anything good. I LOVE YOU VERY MUCH, DEAR FRIEND!

Tom's words shoot straight through Matt's heart like an arrow. His heart rate fails to slow down. Everything boils inside him. Suddenly, he makes another decision. This time, he will free himself from his father's abuse. He finally reacts!

He picks up the pen on the table again and writes another letter.

Then he calls me.

"Anna, do you remember the promise you made me make?"

"Of course, it was only this morning. Don't tell me you've already thought of something? You promised me you hadn't done anything yet."

I'm in shock, my brother seems to be back from that tunnel. He looks like the same old Matt, cheerful and unpredictable.

"Yeah, but things have changed a lot since this morning."

"Sure, in a couple of hours 'things have changed a lot!'"

"Do you still want me to tell you everything or not?"

"And I want you to! Besides, you promised me."

"Well, then, you should know that tomorrow I'll be leaving home for good."

"What? Have you gone mad? Where will you go?"

"I'm running away with Peter. I'd take Tom too, but he has his father, and he'd never leave him alone. Here you go, it's a letter to Peter, telling him my plan. Can you do me one last favour and give it to him? This will be the last time I ask you for a favour. It will never happen again... if everything goes well."

"If everything goes well?"

"Read it, please."

Dear Peter,

It's been two weeks since my last letter, why haven't I had any reply? Is it that you don't love me anymore? Is another man taking my place? You know I love you more than ever. If my fears are unfounded, I beg you, let's do something crazy. I know things have been going very badly at the hospital lately, and for me it's even worse. I beg you: let's run away together! Tomorrow at two o'clock in the morning, let's meet at the place of our first meeting. Just so you know: I don't mean the premises! I don't want to live another second away from you. All I want is for us to be close: to kiss your lips, to breathe in the scent of your skin, to caress you, to touch you, to make you mine... forever. I beg you, run away with me!

Yours forever,
Matt

"You've decided to escape and you don't have a good plan? Where will you go? And if Peter doesn't agree, what will you do? Assuming you manage to escape, Dad won't give you a break: he'll look for you at the end of the world!"

I am really worried. My dear brother hasn't changed

at all, he's even more stupid than before. He has made a drastic decision without a clear plan in his hands.

"I don't care about plans; I just want to escape. I don't care where the wind blows me, any place is better than this hell."

Matt seems to be sure, and I decide to please him once again by handing the letter to Peter.

For the last year I have been grateful to the Lord for giving me back my brother, but sadly that brother was not the Matt he always was. Now, that light shines in his blue eyes, that typical light that my brother emits.

"Fine, I'll give it to your doctor. But I want you to promise me something else."

"But it can't be: every letter, a promise! In the end I won't remember them all... Come on, unpack."

"In case all goes well, I want you to send me news of you, so that I may know you are well. Don't tell me where you are, it might be dangerous, with our father wandering about the house, but knowing that you are well is one way of not losing you again."

"Is that all? It won't be easy, but I promise I'll do it. I love you so much, dear sister. If it wasn't for you, I would have killed myself."

With a tear running down my cheek, I hug him, let out a sigh and ask:

"Matt, when did it all start?"

Matt knows exactly what I mean, but he's trying to play the fool. It would be really hard for me to know the truth.

"All? All of what? What exactly do you mean? Life is a continuous question mark: you never know what's ahead of you! Things go the way they go."

"I mean... when did you realise you were different? When did our God decide that your destiny would have such a tortuous path?"

I hug him. I am very serious and the tone of my voice reflects the deep suffering I feel for him.

Matt, determined to tell me everything, invites me with a gesture to settle down on the bed. His countenance transforms, his gaze announces nothing good and no funny story to share. He sits down next to me, takes my hands and begins to tell his story:

"Darling, do you remember when we were young and Uncle Ernest used to take us to the fields because he needed help with the cattle?"

I feel confused, at that time I was very young and I remember things vaguely.

"I remember that I used to go with Dad from time to time, and that you went every Sunday." I smile. "I was always whining because I wanted to go with you, but Uncle Ernest didn't want me in the way because I was a child, or maybe because I was too young. I'm sorry, I don't remember well. Wait a minute... Maybe it was you who didn't want me there. I was so young I barely remember, but what does that have to do with anything? You would have been about nine years old back then, what could you know about love?"

"Seven to be exact." Matt's eyes begin to fill with tears. "He didn't want you there, not because you were too young, but rather because he couldn't have acted with me the way he did without being bothered."

I'm still very confused, but my heart starts beating a mile a minute. Inside me, I sense the end of the story.

"Matt, but... What are you saying? Is this our father's brother you're talking about? And he was married at that time..."

"Aunt had died a year before."

Now, the tears start to flow involuntarily, wetting my face. Matt, with his hands, tries to wipe my face.

"Do you want me to continue?"

"Yes, please. I'm old enough to handle the truth."

"The first time he took the belt out of his trousers, I didn't understand and, overwhelmed, I let him. After a while, I tried to escape, but that damned belt was always there... and it was like that for five very long years."

I'm furious, with a trembling voice I shout:

"Why didn't you ever tell Dad? He would have stopped it for good."

"I was only seven years old… I was young and ashamed. Besides, Dad wouldn't have believed me. He would have thought I was making it all up because I didn't want to go and help Uncle with the cattle."

"Did he tell you that?"

"Yes, he told me that Dad wasn't good like him, that he loved me; honestly, I thought I loved him too. I knew it wasn't right, but after a while it started to seem normal to me."

Matt hugs me again. He keeps sobbing.

"I'm sorry, Anna, I would never have wanted to tell you the truth, but I think it's only fair that you should know what kind of a person the guy you've always idolised is."

"He was my favourite uncle! He always brought me beautiful toys, he said he loved me so much. Every Christmas, every Sunday, he was at home to make us laugh and play. What a bastard! What a wretched man! Now tell me, why did he stop?" After those statements,

I wanted to know more and more, I needed to know the whole truth.

"I started to grow up and his interest in me gradually faded. That's all. In the meantime, I started to feel attracted to men, because that was the love I had known. At first, when our uncle started abusing me, I felt inferior to others: defective. When I came home, especially in front of Dad, I felt a deep sense of shame coupled with a guilt that ate my soul until I retched.

Every time Dad, Mum or you looked at me, I had the feeling that you could read in my face what was going on. Over time I learned to hide any kind of emotion and to exorcise the tragedy I had to live through with irony and play. It was during that period that my desire to be an actor was born.

That attitude helped me even later, when I grew up, to overcome the fear of rejection, but relationships with others tended to be quite conflictual and disappointing. With Tom it was different, he has always understood and accepted me without question, just as I accepted him. We were like brothers, together we were invincible.

Believe me, it has not been easy to establish relationships with others and, above all, it has not been easy to feel comfortable with my body and my sexuality, or at least with the one our uncle had given me: the only one I knew. It has been really terrible to be burdened with the doubt about my sexual identity. You, today, take it all for granted, but for me it has not been like that, it has been a thorny, complex and difficult path. It is true that every time our uncle approached me, I felt terror, shame, discomfort and even disgust, but I must admit that I felt an aftertaste of hidden pleasure.

I was discovering, for the first time, my body's reactions to physical contact. The first few times our uncle forced me to discover his body, it was a tragedy for me: I couldn't stand the smell of it, I was repulsed by the taste, but little by little it began to seem normal to me; a forbidden normality in which a veil of pleasure was hidden.

If it is true that empathy is learned as a child, I was learning to read in our uncle's gaze, in his movements, in the trembling of his hands, the desire and the excitement.

The first time was in the countryside, after Aunt's death… I was only a seven-year-old boy! The following spring, seeing him again made me feel embarrassed and strange. That night I expected him, as always, he would propose an exchange of forbidden kisses: intimate, perverted, sick caresses. But nothing of the sort happened. Uncle looked at me with satisfaction. "You've grown up, Matt", he said in a firm voice. "You're becoming a man."

As he said this, he came up to me, turned me around, pinning me against the fence separating the animals from the barn. My heart was in my throat. I couldn't breathe. I felt his gaze stalking my nakedness, I felt his big, rough, farmer's hands touching me, exploring me, probing me, when suddenly I was startled by a sharp, unbearable, intense pain.

It was my first time, and it was terrible. Uncle's words are still ringing in my brain: 'Do you like it, Matt, do you like it? I know you like it; I'm starting to feel you get excited, Matt.'

The more I tried to remain rigid and immobile, the

more pain I felt, a revulsion and an atavistic feeling of pleasure that caused me to twitch slightly. And then, suddenly, an even stronger blow. Inhuman pain and drops of blood running down my body.

I was crying, but not from the pain.... Little by little, as the days and months went by, that pain turned into pleasure. Five years, five long years I was the object of our uncle's desire.

For the next few years, I was obsessed with sex, even when I masturbated, I followed very carefully the example he had given me and the pleasure he had taught me. But there was something that obsessed me even more: doing it with a young man of my own age.

Perhaps, that way, I would have found it all less dirty, and this new pleasure, oriented more towards love than sex, could replace, in time, those unhealthy pleasures, desires and memories.

I wanted a young man to love, I wanted to know what it meant to be a man, a fully-grown man. My first crush came when I was sixteen. At school, I was completely indifferent to female charm, whereas, if I caught a glimpse of a boy I was attracted to, I couldn't help imagining him naked and thinking about what it would feel like to sleep with him.

One warm spring afternoon, like many afternoons in the countryside with Uncle, I was at Burt's house, my bench and playmate. His parents were away on a trip and we had to prepare for our final exams. It all happened by chance. I jokingly took the notebook from him and he took it from me again; we got into a little wrestling match, as is often the case with the boys, and in no time at all we were rolling on the carpet. He was small and fragile, which is why in the struggle I managed to throw him off easily and end up on top of him. While we were laughing our heads off, our eyes met, and, in his eyes, I saw the same desire I saw in our uncle's eyes.

At that age, it was already difficult to woo a girl, so to do it with a person of the same sex was practically an impossible mission. But eyes don't lie, he also recognised the same desire in mine.

I was the one who interrupted the silence by whispering in his ear, 'I want you, Burt, I want you.' He blushed, looked down, and muttered under his breath, 'Me too.'

Without taking my eyes off him, I turned him on his side. Hiding his face, he said, "Matt, this is my first time." I stroked his cheek, wanting at least his first time to be full of sweetness, love and pleasure. I whispered for him not to move, began to caress and kiss him as I slowly undressed him. I felt his desire grow stronger and stronger, as did his anxiety about the forbidden. I turned him onto his back. Beneath me, I felt Burt tremble. 'Don't be afraid,' I whispered, remembering the terror I felt my first time. 'Don't be afraid, I love you, Burt, I love you and I want you.'

I kept looking at him, loving him; I felt him shudder, I stroked his back until Burt consummated his first time and we orgasmed together.

Finally, I felt like a man. He was my first love; you know the rest."

"Little brother, you don't know how sorry I am, I feel so sorry."

Matt takes my face in his hands and, pulling it gently towards him, murmurs:

"Don't be, things are just going the way they're supposed to go."

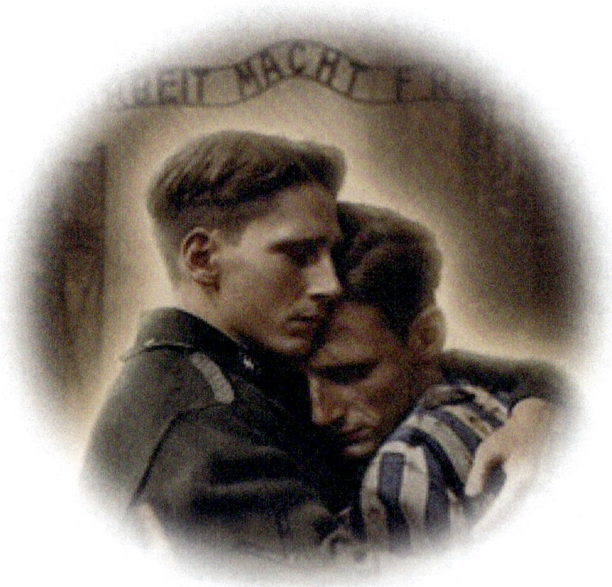
MACHT

13

"Grandma, do I look like a little boy if I tell you I'm very upset?"

"No, Ben, it's completely normal. I'm still horrified and angry… And you should still know that…"

"In the end, did Matt manage to escape with the love of his life?"

"Yes, Ben, but…"

Before he leaves, Matt realises that this time it's not a game; he realises that it's dangerous, that his life is in danger; he understands that he must be more cautious than ever.

He turns around and heads towards our parents' room, cautiously opening the door without making a sound. They sleep soundly. Matt, smiling sweetly, thinks goodbye, thinking that, with any luck, he will never see them again.

Before he leaves, he stops at my bedroom door. A strange sensation comes over him, he feels as if a hand is squeezing his heart. Matt knows that sooner or later we'll see each other again, and that we'll embrace when all this is over. That's why he decides not to go in, it could cost him all his plans.

"If he had woken me up, he would not have been able to leave. How many times have I reproached myself for not having been awake."

Night falls when Matt, equipped with a rucksack, jumps out of his bedroom window to escape from home.

He sets off for the countryside, thinking of that magnificent day after the Kleist binge, of that morning, on the wet grass and with the man who was then his mystery man. It's a pity he can't remember much, but the few memories he has are enough to make him long for something great, something new and eternal. Matt is brimming with passion; he wants to know if Peter feels the same way. What if he doesn't show up?

It's something he hasn't thought about, but his heart forces him to put the thought aside. They love each other, he's sure to show up! Maybe he has already arrived and is waiting for him. Matt is completely convinced; his heart is not wrong.

Peter has already reached the countryside when he notices someone approaching him. With some fear and excitement, he crouches down, hiding in the tall grass. Frightened, he shouts out, asking:

"Matt? Matt, is that you?"

Squatting, with goose bumps, protected by the tall green grass, he waits for an answer.

"Peter! Peter, it's me! Where are you? I can't see you."

They both run towards each other, letting the passion of that moment run free.

The love, the enthusiasm, the eros takes over, straight from their bodies with an ancestral force visible and recognisable to anyone. They embrace, cuddle and kiss.

Lying on the grass, they think of nothing but satisfying their carnal desires; they touch each other, continue to kiss and whisper sweet words to each other.

It all seems so perfect... Suddenly, Matt sees a strong, blinding light. It's pointed straight into his eyes. Faint at first, and then gradually getting brighter and brighter until it blinds him completely.

The boy, totally euphoric and excited, does not reason and does not realise what is happening. A few moments later, the two lovers hear a thick voice shouting at them:

"That's enough, you perverts, hands up! You're under arrest, you depraved fags!"

It is the SS, who have been controlling the area for some time now, following a tip-off received a few days earlier. In exchange for his freedom, a thief has revealed to them the place where the "forbidden lovers", as he called them, are usually found. He declared that infidels, homosexuals, Jews and Christians meet in that countryside to perform "disgusting and depraved" acts of love.

Matt and Peter, deranged, stand up, threatened by guns, barefoot, their clothes in their hands. They ask, at least, to be allowed to get dressed.

The SS members, having mocked, insulted and spat at them, lead them to the Gestapo.

The SS agents check the documents of the two young men. All Gestapo actions are not subject to judicial review; the Nazi jurist Werner Best himself declared: "As long as the Gestapo complies with the wishes of the leaders, it is acting legally." And so, the SS continue "legally" to interrogate the two young prisoners, who are sitting helpless and still naked. They interrogate them angrily, shouting at them and repeatedly hitting them in the face and on the genitals, until a soldier, suddenly changing his expression, shows the document of one of the young men to his superior.

A moment of silence pervades the room, it is Matt's document. Deciding what to do with the Jew is not complicated, but, as Matt Offman, they must first consult his father - after all, he is the son of their general.

That same night, the SS burst into our house. Dad wakes up startled, the Gestapo pounding on our front door firmly and decisively, as they always do.

Dad quickly puts on his dressing gown and goes to the door.

"What's going on? Why are you here? What's happened?" He is still drowsy, but seeing my mother and me panicking in the back of the room, he immediately tries to regain his solid composure.

"Heil Hitler!" says the officer in front of the house, raising his right arm horizontally in salute to his superior, and then he continues: "We've arrested your son, sir. We ask you to come with us so that we can decide what to do with him."

The tone in which the officer utters such phrases is loud, as if he wishes to draw the attention of the whole neighbourhood.

Dad, incredulous, decides to respond in an even louder tone to ward off such accusations and offensiveness.

"It's impossible! My son is in his room right now, sleeping. It's a mistake, a mistaken identity, I'll prove it to you."

Leaving the door open, he goes to Matt's room, accompanied by the two SS agents. After a quick glance, he addresses them in a threatening tone:

"You see I'm right, don't you? The young man in prison is not my son, my son is in his bed, right here in front of your eyes. You will pay for this inappropriate behaviour!"

One of the SS officers, determined to earn a promotion, is not intimidated by these accusations. He steps forward and stands next to Matt's bed. He leans back against the pillow, listens carefully, waits to hear him breathe, and then suddenly breaks the silence with a loud, cold, peremptory voice:

"Then your son must be dead for not waking up to all this fuss."

Dad, pale as a ghost, totally bewildered and more frightened than he could possibly be, approaches the bed and, with a great deal of rage and fervour, yanks the covers off. Two pillows are all that show: two pillows pretending to be the silhouette of a curled-up man.

Enraged by what had happened and by the insults he had received, and with great shame, Dad rushes off to the Gestapo

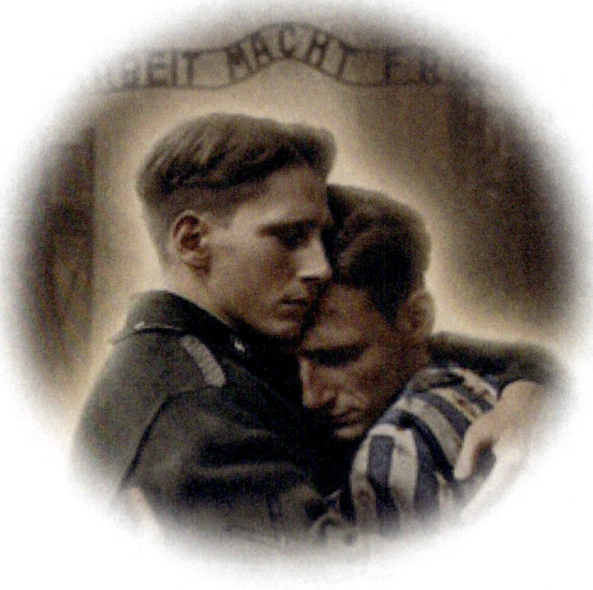
MACHT

14

"**M**y goodness, Grandma! This time, Matt's really screwed up this time!"

"Ben, if you think what I'm telling you is out of context, let me know. I wouldn't want to waste your time or make you do the wrong job."

"Grandma, are you serious? None of my colleagues would have thought of collecting the testimony of a German. Your story shows us that hatred and violence also caused suffering to the Germans themselves. Matt's suffering and pain are an example of how Nazism also claimed victims among the people it should have protected. Not to mention the suffering of your father… I can't imagine how he must have felt being between a rock and a hard place."

"Ben, I'm so proud of you, you're proving to be much more mature than your age."

"Thank you, Grandma, but now get on with the story."

"Good. So, as I was saying, Matt was captured by the SS."

> Around him, everything is damp and cold, the cell is large, but crowded with men and women waiting for someone to somehow put an end to this aberrant temporary detention. My brother continues to wonder what he is doing there, in that kind of waiting room. After all, he is not waiting for anyone. His Peter has been locked up who knows where. Tom can't

be aware of the facts and our father obviously won't go looking for him; in fact, he'll make him rot in there. Suddenly, a loud voice interrupts his thoughts:

"Matt, how could you? You were healing yourself, why did you do it? And with a Jew, aren't you ashamed of yourself?"

He instantly recognises Dad's voice.

"Dad…, I, I…"

A moment's hesitation, as that gloomy place prompts Matt to think that any lie, any repentance, could mean his freedom. He even thinks of explaining to Dad anything he wants to hear in order to get out of that cell, but his rebellious spirit and his desire to finally live the life he deserves, lead him to confess:

"The truth is that I don't regret anything. I am like that, a German, not at all proud of being a German, in love with a wonderful Jew."

His tone of voice, shy and fearful, far exceeds that of Dad. The firmness of those words, spoken in that tone, fills Matt with pride, but for Dad, surrounded by colleagues who listen with a deeply offensive expression, they wound him directly in the heart and, above all, in his pride.

"This is not my son!" A choleric shriek pierces his lips and, with his index finger pointed at Matt, he continues: "You will stay here now, rotting until you're cured. Do you understand? I know you're not really sick and, for your sake, I'll leave you here until you're completely cured."

Dad takes one last look at Matt behind the bars and, with a look full of hatred, contempt and, above all, shame, he leaves.

But the shameful day certainly doesn't end there

for him.

Two hours after Dad orders Matt's arrest, a notice arrives straight from the higher-ups into his hands.

The notice reads:

To the attention of General Alfons Offman:

We inform the above-mentioned that, due to recent events, we are obliged to take serious measures towards your son, towards your person and, consequently, towards your entire family.

Since, in our opinion, the work you have done has been exemplary for the Third Reich, we have decided for the time being to inform you of your immediate demotion. As of today, you will lose your rank of General, together with all the privileges you have enjoyed, and will return to the rank of Colonel. Please bear in mind that, if you continue to hold a high office, it is, above all, in order not to cause us further embarrassment. Take advantage of your position to change, even drastically, the situation. It is more than obvious that you belong to the Aryan race in your family, and your son is a splendid specimen, so be sure to keep your promises and cure your son as soon as possible, or get rid of him for good. Also, be warned that next time the consequences will be much more dramatic for your family. Understand that for you this is your last chance.

General Becker

Dad has never felt so humiliated in his life, not to mention the fear of the consequences for Mum and me. A whirlwind of emotions, among anger, fear, humiliation and a sense of failure, swirls around destroying even the shadow of future redemption.

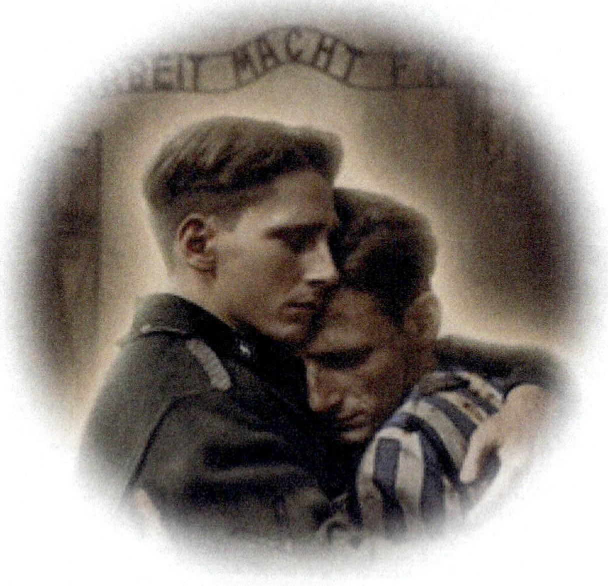
MACHT

15

"I didn't know that a general could have all those repercussions because of a son's sexual proclivities; I thought they were punished, even by death, only in the case of treason, and that for all other things they were protected, somehow, let's say... recommended."

"Those were hard times, Ben. We were at the dawn of the Second World War."

"Yes, Grandpa, I understood that. A war that not everyone was happy about."

Benito Mussolini met at the Borromeo Palace, on the Beautiful Island, with the top political representatives of France and Great Britain. The three were accomplices, united by a single desire and a mutual agreement: to maintain peace in Europe. It was the most important European effort to stop Hitler's madness before the outbreak of the Second World War.

They debated uninterruptedly for three days and, in the end, signed an invaluable agreement: the Stresa Front. But, as often happens when selfish and personal interests come into play, when one is only interested in one's own microcosm, forgetting all the rest, the agreements were short-lived. In June, Ethiopia, fearing an invasion by Italy, asked the League of Nations to send neutral observers to its borders. Its fears were far from unfounded.

In October, Italian troops stationed in Eritrea, without a declaration of war, crossed the border into Ethiopia, giving the green light to hostility. In Italy, a policy of autarky was launched, along with a major propaganda campaign aimed at denouncing the inconvenience caused by the "unique economic and financial sanctions" that the assembly of the United Nations Society had applied against it because, by becoming an aggressor state, it had failed to reach agreements.

"Congratulations, Ben! The history of those days seems to be more familiar to you than to us."

In those years, the atmosphere was infested with the smell of war, which is why compulsory military service was re-established, even for Germans, and they announced the creation of an air force, violating the clauses of the Treaty of Versailles, the pact that made the end of the First World War official, stipulated as part of the Paris Peace Conference signed by forty-four states.

Thus, the Wermacht, Germany's armed force, was born. The army that, in the early years of the Second World War, came close to conquering the world. Hitler felt ever stronger and, despite foreign fears and tensions, Germany did not lose sight of its mission: to exterminate Jews, homosexuals and anything else that would in any way sully the Aryan race.

These were difficult times for the Jews, who suffered the effects of thousands upon thousands of decrees and regulations that restricted their lives in every aspect, whether in the public or private sphere. Numerous officials throughout the country conceived, discussed, wrote, adopted, implemented and upheld anti-Semitic legislation. In Germany, no corner remained immune.

Jewish writers were forbidden to write; musicians were forbidden to play; merchants were forbidden to sell and buy; and everyone, absolutely everyone, was forbidden to sit on public benches, unless they were marked with a yellow symbol.

Jews were not allowed to walk in groups in the street. Woe betide them if there were more than twenty of them! In front of the shops, they displayed a sign: "No Jews allowed", in the same way as it was used for dogs. Although arms and men were needed to stop foreign attacks, they were considered unfit for military service.

Before coming to power, Hitler had, on more than one occasion, declared: "The racist state must declare the child to be the most precious treasure of the people".

That is why, in October 1935, the law for the prevention of genetically diseased offspring was passed; and, in December, in accordance with what had been declared and planned, the SS-Lebensborn, the Funtain of Life project, one of the many projects of the Nazi hierarch Heinrich Himmler, was launched through different clinics, promoting "racially correct" births and the eugenic theories of the Third Reich on the Aryan race.

Ben delivers it in a solemn tone, knowing that his speeches will be part of the video and the teacher will be proud of his preparation, not to mention that the following year he will be able to use this material for his final exams for university entrance.

"Obviously, Ben, as you can imagine, my father and I also experienced that hatred; our lives ceased to flow smoothly, submitting to the atrocities of a hatred that spared no one, not even Matt, Anna, Peter and the general."

16

Without the bakery, Dad and I are struggling to make ends meet. Dad knows that time is not his ally; it is clear that, in the state we are in, the situation can only get worse.

With my approval, he decides to sell his few remaining possessions. Sooner or later, the Germans will take over everything anyway. We'd better take advantage of them now so that we can survive. The only thing that drives me forward is to live for each other; it's the only way we can overcome this period of tyranny for our race.

This morning, the mood is particularly bright because I'm meeting Anna. Outside there is no trace of serenity, but Anna always brings a light breeze of love and calm. Our talks are always very long and well argued, we have established a great friendship; we tell each other and share our confidences. Anna updates me on Matt's state of health, or at least on what little she knows, since her father is very cautious when it comes to speaking in public about the shameless son who has touched him, although, if the public is his daughter, it is strictly forbidden to pronounce the name of that degenerate. The general has made a tacit agreement with his conscience, terrified that the whole family will be covered in shame.

What little Anna manages to find out she gets by eavesdropping behind the thin wall of her bedroom, when her father whispers to his wife during the night.

I, on the other hand, tell her about all the abuses I am forced to endure just because I am a Jew, and together we imagine solutions for a better world. We dream, with fantasy we travel to an imaginary world.

"Anna, we live in misery. We no longer have anything of sufficient value to sell, and every day we find it harder and harder to find something to eat. And my poor father is getting more and more tired and weary, unable to do anything. In these conditions, I don't know how long he can last. I am very worried."

Anna listens to me carefully.

"Indeed, the situation is not at all easy to resolve, but... Maybe there is a solution!" She hesitates for a few seconds before suggesting an answer. Something has occurred to her and she decides to share it with me. "Tom, it won't be easy and it's probably very dangerous, but I have an idea."

"An idea? Tell me, come on!"

I couldn't even imagine what Anna had come up with, but I encourage her to keep talking, keen to examine and evaluate any solutions.

"I'm already regretting telling you, because I know it will be very dangerous, but it occurred to me that you could continue to sell bread to all those who, like you, cannot buy it freely. The city is full of shops that refuse Jewish customers, many of them have already put up the sign: 'No dogs or Jews allowed'. Well, as I was saying, you produce a staple food and it could mean salvation for many people like you."

Anna looks at me as if she wants to read my thoughts, but my questioning expression suggests that she hasn't made herself clear, at least to me.

"Now, my boy, do you remember what you were able to do when I was young?"

Without replying, I shrug my shoulders. Anna continues:

"I'll get straight to the point. You are capable of transforming bread into anything you want. Do you remember the butterflies, the bears, and the bouquet for my first communion? You work magic with bread. So why not make loaves with shapes that are easy to hide? Shapes that stick to the body so that they can be hidden under clothes and can be transported directly to the homes of people who can't buy bread in the shops now.

I know it's a stupid and dangerous solution, but I wanted to provide a solution. Sorry, it's ridiculous."

She looks down and grimaces with her mouth. I know she really wants to help me; I know I'm a very special friend to her. I realise I've embarrassed her, so I decide to intervene:

"Anna, that's a fantastic idea! Thank you! Those bastards have forbidden us Jews to trade and, as if that wasn't enough, to enter their shops as well. I'll do something about it. After all, I haven't been banned from leaving the house before curfew yet... At least for now! It would be enough to modify the typical loaves a bit so that I can hide them easily."

That's a great idea, Anna, you're a genius!

She looks at me with satisfaction and replies:

"For every law there is a loophole. But be very careful, Tom, it won't be easy."

Excited by Anna's idea, I feel alive again, ready for a new adventure, convinced of improving my dad's life and mine. I am sure that, in the worst-case scenario,

I can solve at least part of our problems. I run to my father to tell him the news, hoping to give him back a spark of hope. Poor Dad, he has sacrificed so much for me.

I return home and, full of enthusiasm, explain the plan to him, but he is not at all elated. He is very worried about what might happen if I am found there, although deep down he knows that Anna's suggested plan is the only possible solution.

"Tom, I don't like this idea at all. Besides, I promised your mother that I would take care of you, and this is not at all the way to honour my promise."

"Dad, you have taken care of me for too long; and if we are in this situation, it is my fault. If it hadn't been for that accident, you wouldn't have been forced to get rid of your property before its time."

I feel a great embarrassment as I speak to him, so I bow my head, avoiding a cross look. Now it's my turn, I have to make up for my mistakes and, above all, repay my father for all the sacrifices he has been forced to make for my sake.

"Let me take care of it. I'm capable of taking care of everything myself."

Dad doesn't believe it, his body and mind are exhausted, but deep down he knows I'm right. How is he going to care of me in this condition?

The future doesn't bode well, so taking a risk is not a bad idea.

"No, my son, I want to help you!"

I can't believe it! Dad has accepted.

I'm really excited, but I can't involve him in this crazy idea which I know how dangerous it could be: it could even cost us our lives.

"No, Dad. It's my turn now. You've done too much already and my time has come."

I am convinced of my words. Dad is only fifty years old and has a distorted view of reality. He's a great baker and has been a great teacher, but now it's up to me to act, to do something for my father.

"All right, but remember that everything you know how to do is because of me."

I look at him smiling, kiss him on the forehead and add:

"That's why I will be grateful to you for the rest of my life, Dad. Even though I consider myself a great helper, you are and will always be the best baker in the world."

"Of course, of course…" old Carl shouts at me as I head for the bakery.

Now my time has come, I'll have to do my best not to get caught and not disappoint my dad, I think to myself as I stand in front of the big oven, which has been turned off for a long time.

There is only one problem, turning on the big oven means attracting the attention of the whole neighbourhood, given the smell of bread and the smoke it emanates.

It's dangerous, because of the SS. So, I decide to meet little Anna, a source of inspiration and a generator of brilliant ideas. Sooner or later, we will be considered lovers because of our secret meetings in the park of "forbidden lovers". On the other hand, for an Aryan girl, meeting a Jew is more than dangerous. For this reason, I will never be grateful enough.

"Hi, Anna."

"Hi, Tom. So, have you talked to your father about

our plan? What does he think? Tell me all about it!"

Anna feels like a member of my family and an active player and protagonist in this ingenious and dangerous plan that could help us get ahead.

"Yes, I spoke to my dad and..." I pause to build suspense, then continue in a cheerful tone: "Yessssss!"

Little Anna impulsively hugs me, delighted that her idea has helped. I give her a fleeting hug, but when I remember that I am in the middle of the street, under the prying eyes of passers-by, I reject her. The last thing I want to do is make trouble for her.

Anna quickly pulls herself together.

"Listen, Anna, I'm actually here because I have another problem."

She looks at me with concern.

"Tom, tell me, what's wrong?"

"I have no idea where to bake the bread. It's true that I have the oven and everything I need, but unfortunately, I can't use it... because of the smoke and the smell."

"That's a problem. If smoke was seen coming out of your bakery, it would be all over the place, and that's not good, but I think I have a solution."

I gape at her, hoping to find out the possible solution. This girl is an idea generator. Anna continues:

"Just on the outskirts we have an old property. It's one of the many that my grandfather left us when he died. You can use it if you want, my parents have never been there. It's very small, but you can build an oven, and I'm sure it will be perfect."

"I can't believe it! Why are you doing all this for me? It's dangerous! Besides, are you sure your father won't catch me in the act? I'm sorry, but I can't accept it. The idea is really great, but if your father knew about it, he wouldn't even show you mercy. After all he's done to Matt, I couldn't take any more. I shit on my future, I'm nothing but a dirty Jew who stinks of garlic, but you're a fantastic German woman with a wonderful future ahead. Who knows! Maybe you'll have a well-to-do husband and a few beautiful children."

A smile comes to Anna's lips, flattered by the kind words and the concern I feel for her.

"Don't worry, Tom, we've had that property for at least nine years, and I've never seen it. The descriptions I've given you come from my grandfather's stories. Besides, it's owned by a German. If they saw smoke coming out or noticed the smell of bread, no one would give it a thought."

I realise that this is my only solution, so I decide to change my mind and accept my young friend's proposal.

"Thank you, Anna, I accept your offer on the condition that you don't get involved. In case I get caught, I will say that I have occupied that house clandestinely. I still don't understand why you are doing this for me, but I just say thank you, thank you and thank you a thousand times over, from the bottom of my heart."

"So, the complicity between you goes back to your adolescence? But, Grandpa... what happened with Matt and his father?"

"Ben, you must be patient, I've warned you that it's a long story, and Grandma and I don't like to summarise things."

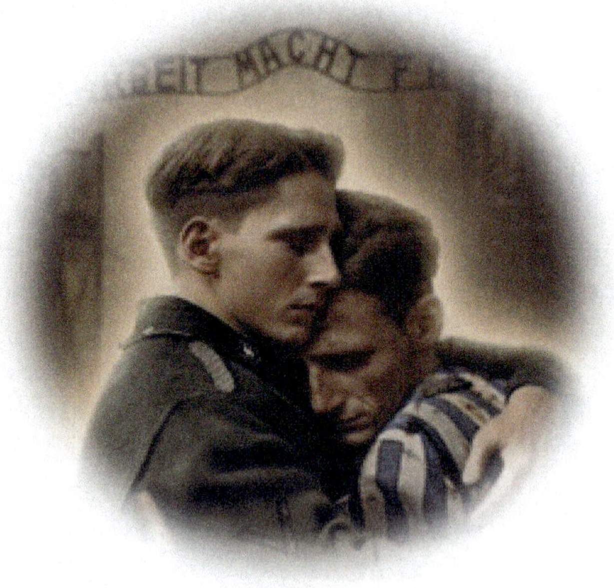
MACHT

17

SS Colonel, Alfons Offman, father of Anna and Matt, is at the barracks as he is every day. The SA are already an old memory. Since he joined the SS, his job is no longer the same. He used to be in charge of maintaining order in the city, whereas now the only goal seems to be to eliminate all Jews, who have already been deprived of all their rights.

"Yes, they were deprived of all civil and political rights. The Reichstag unanimously adopted the Nuremberg Laws at the Seventh Congress of the National Socialist German Workers' Party (NSDAP) on 15 September. It was a great paradox, since the law was supposed to protect individuals, and only those with German blood could be considered "citizens of the Reich" (Reichsbürger) and, as such, benefit from full civil and political rights; all others were mere subjects. Nuremberg also stipulated the law for the "protection of German blood and honour", which prohibited marriages with Jews, punishable by severe imprisonment. It forbade extra-marital relations, although in this case the penalties were less severe, but the height of paradox was reached with the discrimination of animals owned by Jews. In all honesty, it is utterly ridiculous."

"A lot, although I would say it is tragic."

Offman, at the barracks, does not have it easy. His colleagues continue to taunt him about his son, but he is sure that he will succeed in curing him, there is no doubt in his mind, even though he knows that achieving his goal will be far from easy.

It is now six months since Matt's arrest, and he shows no sign of improvement. Colonel Offman realises that he has done little or nothing to cure him, believing that his son is just going through a passing phase.

A terrible sense of anxiety comes over him as he thinks that Matt may never be cured.

What if he belongs to the other category of gays, what if he is one of those incurables, one of those who can't be cured? He thinks over and over again with his head in his hands and his elbows resting on his office desk.

"Colonel, are you unwell?" The voice of one of his officers at his service brings him out of his thoughts.

"No, why?" Colonel Offman lifts his head and can't understand the reason for the question.

"Excuse me, I saw you with your head down in your hands and I thought that maybe..."

The colonel abruptly interrupts the young man, not letting him finish. Seeing him standing there in front of him, a shiver of excitement runs through him; in the end, it's all clear to him: he knows what he has to do.

"Aaron, do you remember how many years you've been working with me?"

The young man immediately notices the change in his superior's mood, but he struggles to understand what he's getting at. But, accustomed to executing and obeying orders, he responds in a heartbeat:

"It's six years, sir."

"Well, I'm glad you remember, and I want you to

know that in six years you've never let me down. You know, son? Every time I look at you, I see your late father, he was a very special man! We were great friends; we knew everything about each other and we understood each other with our eyes before we started talking."

Aaron is increasingly confused, he doesn't understand what the revelations are about, but, knowing what a sad and difficult time the colonel is going through, he decides to comfort him.

"I know perfectly well! My father had great esteem and respect for you. It is for that reason that I will always remain by your side. After the death of my beloved father, you have been the only one to take care of my mother and me, and I will always be grateful to you."

Alfons takes a few seconds before continuing, inhales and continues:

"You're aware of my family situation, aren't you, Aaron?"

The young man, soundless, crestfallen, unwilling to look him in the face, nods.

"I'll be honest with you: I need someone I can trust to help me cure my son. Can I trust you?"

Offman continues to stare at the young man in front of him; he doesn't need a person who will carry out orders out of obligation, but someone who really wants to help him. Aaron is a great guy. He knows that the colonel is not a kind-hearted man to everyone, but thanks to the fantastic friendship he has built with his father, he has always been on his side.

"Of course, you can, sir. You can trust me!"

"Good boy, I'm proud of you. That's just what I wanted to hear."

"Where shall we start?"

The boy's excitement at hearing that he might be able to help his superior, but, more importantly, that he might be able to exchange some favours, is evident from his somewhat impatient tone of voice.

"Let's get straight to the point. My plan is to get a woman of little virtue into my son's cell, and let her seduce him into yielding; she must conquer him over and consummate the idyll. I'm sure that, having tasted the true pleasures of life, he won't turn back."

"It's a great plan, but are you sure the best cure is a woman? I mean, why would he ever have sex with a woman if he's not attracted to her?"

Aaron thinks it's a good plan, but deep down there's something that doesn't convince him.

"Because he'll be forced. He'll be forced, or rather, they'll be forced to do it in order to obtain what they want most in the world: freedom!"

Offman seems convinced of his words and very proud of his plan.

"Sir, let me take care of it. I already have the right woman in mind. I promise your son will be out of prison in a week at the latest."

"Perfect, go ahead. And remember, if you keep your promise, I'll owe you a debt and you can ask me for anything you want."

A slight smile of satisfaction spreads across Colonel Offman's face. He is completely convinced that everything will fall into place.

Aaron heads for the women's cells, where he immediately spots Adna. Her image, her face, her features, even her vulgar way of behaving towards others are indelibly etched in his mind because it was he who arrested her. He remembers that day perfectly.

It was a hot July afternoon; the workload was too strenuous. Often, he felt the need to rest, not physically, but rather mentally. At such times, he loved to relax in the Volkspark Friedrichshain, he loved to lie on the edge of the Marchenbrunnen fountain, which, in its neo-baroque style, with pools of Tivoli stone decorated with turtles and characters from the fables of the Brothers Grimm, seemed to tame the heat by splashing water. It was his moment, the water caressing his feet as he immersed himself in a good book. That day, he was interrupted by the cry of a baby just over a year old.

Aaron saw the baby, alone, crying under the shade of a large pine tree. The young man, gifted with uncommon sensitivity, rushed towards the baby, leaving all his personal belongings unattended in front of the fountain. He wondered who would have been so irresponsible as to abandon a child. He was worried. He looked around him and he didn't seem to belong to anyone. A small white cotton sheet, with light blue roses embroidered on the edge, was the only thing wrapped around him.

How can a mother abandon her own child in this way, thought the soldier. He is so small!

Aaron held the baby in his arms, hoping that human contact would calm and soothe him. As he clutched the baby to his chest and thought about what to do, a female voice called out to him:

"What is my son doing in your arms? Help! This man wants to kidnap my son."

The young man, taken by surprise, remained motionless with the child still clinging to his body, watching the woman screaming like mad. He didn't understand what was happening, he had to be the one to yell at the woman, the uncaring mother who had left the child unattended. She was the one who had made a mistake. Before he knew it, people began to approach to help the woman; his heart was pounding. Frightened of what might happen, he impulsively decided to leave the child where he had found him and, after retrieving his personal belongings, run away. When Aaron reached the exit of the park, a sense of panic assailed him, he leaned against the gate, trying to take a deep breath. After oxygenating his brain, he reasoned sensibly.

I am an SS officer! I can't escape like this! *I have seen a child alone and, believing he had been abandoned, I acted rightly to try to help him. I am not the one who should run away.*

He had two possibilities: go back to the park and face the situation with all the possible consequences, or keep running away and pretend that nothing had happened. For someone like him, the solution was more than obvious, to face up to what had happened, even if he had to apologise to the woman.

After a deep breath, he turned around and started looking for her. The real problem was that it would be easier for him to recognise the child than the mother, since the encounter with the woman had been so traumatic that he had not wanted to look her in the face. But he was lucky, for behind his beautiful fountain, he spotted a child wrapped in a pretty white sheet with little light blue flowers embroidered on the edge, in the arms of a woman sitting on the floor.

Aaron approached them, this time very carefully: he didn't want to frighten her. The water of the fountain was so noisy that the boy realised that talking would have been useless, she would not listen to him. He decided to touch her back to get her attention and turn her around, but just then he saw that the woman was holding something very familiar to him. Surprised, he checked his jacket pockets and his trouser pockets. He couldn't believe it! The rage began to grow and grow, his face was as red as fire.

The woman had planned everything to steal his purse and the pocket watch he had inherited from his beloved father, and worst of all, he had fallen into the trap. That's when, instead of touching her back, he grabbed her hand so hard that the woman let out a shriek; the child, still in her arms, began to scream, again attracting people's attention, but this time Aaron began to shout, looking around, wanting to be heard by everyone:

"Stay away! This woman is a thief and is now under arrest."

How could he forget that woman who had dared to mock him, a member of the SS…

"Why are you laughing, Ben?"

"And how can I not laugh? I can imagine the scene: an SS soldier, fearsome, unbeatable, suddenly tricked by a tart." He couldn't stop laughing. "Imagine if the rumours had reached the army."

"Ben, it's easy to play hardball with someone weaker than you, but violence almost never goes hand in hand with intelligence or cunning."

Continuing the story, our Aaron, with a smirk and a

mixture of mischief, irony and revenge, approached her cell.

"Well, well, we meet again, Adna."
"What do you want from me? Did you come to free me in the end? Did you realise that you're a bastard? Did you realise that you stole a poor child from a mother?"

The woman is really furious; every time he sees that face, the blood rushes to his head and his face turns green with rage.

Aaron, still smiling, adds in a serious tone:
"Actually, if I remember correctly, you're the thief. You were the one who stole my belongings and, you were the one who took advantage of that poor creature to get away with it."

Adna doesn't respond, but taking advantage of the small distance between them, she spits in his face. The soldier doesn't lose his cool and, keeping the same tone of voice, continues:

"Believe me, the child can be fine if he is away from you. You are just a thief taking advantage of him for your dirty business. How can you think he needs such a wretched mother?"

Adna bursts into tears.
"I beg you, let me see him, I need to see him again. I'll do anything. I beg you, please, please, I implore you."

The sobs block her breath, tears stream down her face. Aaron tries to hide the compassion he feels deep down.

"I'm glad you said that, because I have a solution to all your problems. If you do exactly as I say, you can see your son again."

"I'll do anything you ask!"

Adna continues to whimper with a modicum of hope in her heart, she is aware that nothing simple or easy awaits her, indeed, she knows perfectly well that it is something dirty and humiliating, but for her son's sake she must do it.

In Aaron's words, Adna sees the truth, she has not been a good mother at all and now she has to get out of this prison in order to make up for all the mistakes she has made. She knows that the longer she stays inside these walls, the less likely she is to get her son back.

MACHT

18

Behind those bars, everything is extremely dull and disgusting. The bed is beginning to give him serious problems. The mattress is flat and old; and, as if that wasn't enough, lumpy almost all over because of the springs of the box frame that run across it, giving Matt many a sleepless night. The water stinks rotten and the food makes him vomit almost every day.

On the bright side, he has made friends with the little mice that visit him from time to time, something Matt has found difficult to do, as he has always been terrified of them.

Worst of all is the extreme loneliness. Placed in isolation by his father's will, he feels himself going madder and madder with each passing day.

He misses me, he misses our talks, our helping each other, our way of smiling at life.

He misses his great love, Peter, not to mention his sister; and to his surprise, he begins to miss his mother.

Enough! He thinks. He turns the matter over a thousand times. *I'm really fed up. I'd rather die than go on living like this.*

While he is deep in thought, a voice catches his attention.

"Good afternoon, Matt!"

"Hi, Aaron, what's on the menu today?" he asks sarcastically.

"Today, my friend, on the menu, there's a beautiful

surprise for you."

Matt can't understand the meaning of those words. He looks at him in bewilderment; he doesn't know what to expect. That terrifies him deeply.

Aaron encourages the surprise to take a step forward. A beautifully groomed woman, dressed in a prisoner's uniform, materialises in front of Matt's eyes.

"Hi, I'm Adna, nice to meet you."

An unenthusiastic female voice, lacking in culture and elegance, but very sympathetic, and a little resigned, comes from those cracked lips due to dehydration, badly painted with cheap lipstick.

Matt, still puzzled, looks at the woman who is about to enter his cell. Short, slim build, very slim. Perhaps she has been in there for a long time too. She has a fair complexion, and is accompanied by dark blue eyes: she is undoubtedly Aryan.

"What do you want? What's she doing here? What's going on, Aaron?"

Matt wants to understand, he wants to know everything, he is tired of being patient. His heart starts to beat faster and faster, and he doesn't like that feeling at all.

"Matt, aren't you sick of being here? What a stink! And, moreover, all alone, what a bore! But today is your lucky day, my friend. This is Adna. You'll be able to enjoy her company every day after sunset... Aren't you happy?"

Aaron seems excited and happy to be able to help his superior and perhaps start a career in law enforcement. Someday, I'll be a colonel too, or better yet, a captain, and everyone will carry out my orders, the soldier often fantasises. The environment in which Aaron works makes him quickly lose the innocence that his father so lovingly instilled in him.

Matt, without further explanation, understands everything. She is the woman who must cure him! Beautiful, yes, but she's not his type.

"Aaron, I'm more than fed up with this situation. Couldn't you tell my father that I'm cured and forget about this story once and for all?"

Matt knows the answer perfectly well, but it never hurts to try. The burly man in the uniform bursts out laughing.

"Yes, of course! I'll go running..." Then, raising his voice, this time much sterner and commanding, he comes within an inch of Matt's face and continues: "Fuck her! If you're really cured, I don't think it's going to be a problem, after all, you've been abstinent for a long time. I expect wonders from you."

"Son of a bitch!" shouts Matt.

Aaron walks towards the exit of the cell, takes one last look at him, smiles and, in a cheerful and jocular tone, adds:

"And I was expecting at least a thank you… Yes, yes, of course... Cured. Cured my ass!"

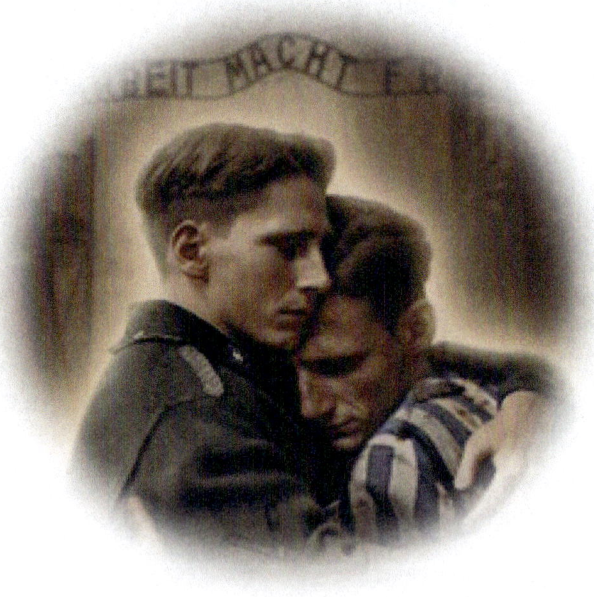
MACHT

19

"Grandpa, I'm sorry, but... Matt, for once, couldn't he make a sacrifice and have sex with a woman?"

"Ben, when you have your first relations, you will discover that the body is sacred, dignity is important and, above all, that involuntary sex is not possible for a man. In any case, the cell is too small and cramped for one person, and it stinks. So, there were two of them, and that shit stank even more."

Adna knows perfectly well that she drives men crazy, she is attractive and very well endowed. Thinking it would be a piece of cake, she gets straight to the point.

"Well, Matt, I understand we're both sick and tired of being here, so why don't we get this story over as soon as possible?"

As she utters these words, she begins to undress quickly. By the time she reaches the end of the sentence, she's wearing only her underwear.

Matt looks at her with wild eyes, then shakes his head, as if trying to shake off what he has just seen, and answers her by moving away and standing on the other side of the cell.

"Look, pretty girl, I'm not going to touch you, let alone fuck you. No offence, but you disgust me: literally! You're not bad at all, but, believe me, you're not my type, unless you're a woman in appearance only."

The woman dies laughing, folding herself in two, almost in tears.

"It's the first time I've ever been told something like that while undressing for a man."

"You've taken it well, I see."

"Thank you, I haven't laughed like that for a long time. But..." She pauses to take a breath and collect herself; her countenance becomes a little more serious and melancholier. "But I tell you, sooner or later I'll fuck you."

Matt looks at her with a serious expression, wondering what she has been promised in return. But he doesn't really want to know because he probably feels sorry for her and won't be able to do anything to help her, even though he knows she's his only chance to get out of that place and be a free man.

The days go by and, as arranged, Adna arrives at Matt's cell after sunset and stays for at least three hours. The two joke, talk and play, but the woman never stops trying to seduce him. Every occasion is a good one, and every one turns out to be a failure. She invents everything, surpassing herself in audacity, seduction and vulgarity. Anything to embrace her little boy again.

As Matt sits on the bed with his arms relaxed at his sides and his palms up slightly open, she can't resist, looking at him and thinking to act immediately. This time, she is wearing only her striped shirt and panties; she sits on the palm of his hand, letting it wrap around her ass, and begins to move slowly among his fingers, making herself touch, rub, penetrate her private parts; but nothing, no response, except to be pushed away by a sharp movement of Matt's arm as he withdraws his hand.

Not only does Matt feel no attraction towards her, he is repulsed by her private parts. He has the feeling that this body, dug inwards, will sooner or later swallow him up.

Disgust. That is the correct term. Matt is disgusted by female intimacy.

Adna, who has grown up surrounded by men whose only desire was to take her to bed, can't understand Matt's position; it's special after so many months of sexual abstinence. Normally, she leaves her ample shirt unbuttoned down to her sternum, so that, with every movement, she reveals her naked, turgid breasts; she moves them casually near Matt's indifferent face, but gets nothing.

Even with Aaron's help and complicity, Adna wears a mini skirt with stilettos that can drive anyone crazy. She's sexy to the extreme, but the day ends with laughter and games, and Matt dressed up in Adna's clothes. For a moment, they feel alive, free and out of that filthy hovel.

In a moment of intimacy, she tries to embrace him, drops her hand between his legs and starts to masturbate him. Matt lets himself go, closes his eyes, tries to imagine that those hands belong to his beloved Peter. Excited, he agrees to let her do what she wants. When Adna notices that Matt is ready, she moves on top of him, but he pushes her off roughly, breaking the spell of that moment.

Back to reality, Matt stresses that he only wanted that from her, nothing more intimate, he wouldn't stand for it! In desperation, Adna bursts into tears.

"Matt, can you understand that I need to get out of this sewer?"

The young man, who has so far refused to listen to any information, takes her chin in his hands and begs her to confide in him. Adna, resigned, blurts it all out. If she hasn't been able to achieve anything with her great sensuality so far, who knows? Maybe compassion will pay off.

"Well, all right. I confess that I'm very well with you, I enjoy myself, and if I really have to be in here, I prefer your company to that of the other women. But you should know that I have a son I haven't seen for four years, and I've been promised that, if I manage to cure you, by fucking you, I'll be able to go back to my little Lucas. Matt, I'm afraid of losing him forever. After all this time, I imagine he already has another family or, even worse, maybe he calls another woman his mum."

Matt, wiping away her tears, promises her:

"You'll go out, at the latest, tomorrow. You will go out and hug your son: it's a promise."

Matt waits for Aaron to come back for the woman to take her to her cell. They are both lying on the bed. As soon as the woman falls asleep, Matt undresses completely and lies down behind her. As soon as he hears Aaron's footsteps approaching the cell, he embraces Adna, still asleep, and pretends to sleep.

"Well, well, I see you've made progress!" Aaron smiles, half-satisfied.

Matt pretends to wake up, stretching out in bed, and talks to the young man:

"I hope you're happy, what you wanted happened. Now you have to release us as you promised."

Adna, who had just woken up, upon hearing those words and seeing Matt's naked body, immediately grasps what is happening and plays along.

Aaron, who is not that stupid, lets out a smirk.

"Are you kidding me, Matt? Do you really think the sight of you crouched down is enough for me? Who's telling me that's true?"

The woman's heartbeat quickens to the point that even Matt is able to feel it, to which she responds:

"What do you want us to publish it? He's cured, I assure you. That's what counts, isn't it?"

Aaron's countenance suddenly changes. He becomes serious and, determined, adds:

"Do it now, Matt. If you're already cured, it won't be a problem. Fuck her now! Right here, right now, in front of my eyes."

"Are you crazy? In front of you? Disgusting!" Matt responds in a loud, accusatory tone.

He knows he is in serious trouble. He longs to get out of that prison and, above all, he wants Adna to return to his little boy's arms as soon as possible, but… At what cost? The woman looks worriedly at Matt, her trembling eyes pleading for mercy.

Aaron intervenes:

"I knew it! You're just a liar! You're not cured. Come on, Adna, we're going back to the dungeon, the same dungeon where you'll rot for a long, long time yet!"

The woman dresses slowly, crestfallen, without looking at either of them, disappointed and saddened by the results. As she approaches the cell door, Matt grabs her by the arm and, with his eyes closed, pushes her against the wall and kisses her.

Adna is stunned.

Aaron closes the cell and nods in amusement.

Matt kisses Adna's neck and whispers in her ear:
"I do it only for your son."
The woman lets her body relax and helps Matt to do the same, returning the kisses on his ear, slowly licking his earlobes, pressing them between her lips as she whispers:
"Forgive me, forgive me, but... Thank you!"
Matt has a hard time getting an erection, especially since he knows he is being watched by a gloating asshole.

He tries to help himself; he knows he can do it. He closes his eyes and suddenly it's not Adna on her knees in front of him, but his Peter. It's been a long time since he's felt that sensation. It is pleasure, delight, excitement that for the first time a woman is giving him, even though, in Matt's secret fantasies, it is a young Jewish doctor who is giving it to him. When he achieves a full erection, Matt penetrates her. A round of applause accompanied by a laugh from Aaron marks the end of the games.

20

"You see, Grandpa, with a little fantasy, you can have sex with anyone," he jokes.

"Ben," Anna calls him to attention in a rude tone, "stop it! This is my brother we're talking about."

"All right, all right, I'll shut up, but don't get angry. Grandpa, has she always had this temper?" He smiles. "In the end, her plan to get you back to work, did it work?"

"Of course, or at least in the beginning all my time and effort were focused exclusively on the construction of the oven, or rather, its extension. In that house, there was a small one that they used on holidays, when they decided to celebrate an evening in the countryside and in company. Unfortunately for me, it was small, but it certainly served as a basis for me to enlarge it and thus create a suitable and dignified structure. Then I started to work at full speed."

> Anna's idea was really extraordinary. I don't like to use a German's house for my business at all, but, in the end, it is my only escape while waiting for better times to come. I have to be very careful not to wear "the star" while going in or out.
> Once on the corner, I put it back in place and make my way as quickly as possible to the house of my old customers, who have not at all forgotten the pleasant taste of my bread and continue to buy it; among them, some old German customers who do it partly for the

bread and partly to help me and not to abandon me.

Anna tries to help me as best she can. She has worked miracles for me, even sewing me some bands with pockets so that I can stick the bread to my body more easily. I'm pretty good at shaping the bread into just the right size. Every morning, at seven o'clock, I get to mimic the custom-made loaves.

Today I would be taken for a kamikaze ready to immolate myself. I am well equipped to do this job.

I'm late. I don't like going out of the house when it's light, a lot of people know me and surely no one remembers me as a chubby boy, especially now that things are going so badly, someone might wonder what's going on, putting me and my dad in danger.

I'm just finishing getting ready when someone tries to enter the house. I know it's not Anna, because she knocks four times before doing so. Frightened, not knowing who it might be, I quickly undress and try to hide inside the oven, which fortunately has already cooled down.

"Tom, Thomas... Are you here? It's me, Matt."

I can't believe it, it's him, my best friend, who has scared me to death. I come out of hiding. My legs are still shaking. I'm so excited to see him again that, instead of slowly crawling out of the oven, I dive headlong out of it. Matt screams in horror, although he knew I was here, he had no idea I'd come out of the oven. There is no doubt that we both got a big scare.

We laughed like crazy, like we hadn't laughed for a long time, and we embraced each other: at last, we are together again!

"My friend, I'm really happy to hug you again, now things can only get better."

Matt is elated and happy that the recent tragic events have not changed me. I'm the same as ever, maybe a little thinner and a little dirtier, but I'm still the same: his best friend!

"Matt, how can you be so naive? Things can only get better? What do you think I'm doing in this house? It belongs to Germans! Have you seen where I've come from?"

This time, Matt's tone is much more serious:

"I'm sorry, you're absolutely right, I'm really sorry, my friend. I promise I'll do my best to help you. Now that I'm back, no one will separate me from you."

I know his words are sincere, but perhaps Matt is unaware of everything that's going on, or worse, as irresponsible as he is, he knows exactly how things are going and minimises them.

"Thank you, Matt. I know you mean it, but you don't have to put your life on the line for me. It's dangerous enough what I do, and I'm sorry I needed your sister's help to the point of getting her involved in this situation so I could sort some things out, but now I'm the one who has to deal with it... Only me!"

"I'm sorry, no way! I've been away for too long, now I want to help you no matter what."

We embrace again. The emotion is so intense that our faces are wet with hot tears.

"Dear Matt, how have we survived all this time apart?"

At that moment, Matt says a few words to me that I will never forget.

"If we made it, it's only because we knew we'd see each other again."

I know it's the truth, I know Matt will never let me

down... at least not willingly.

While we're still cuddling, I feel Matt laugh.

"What's going on? Why did you decide to spoil this beautiful moment?"

"Sorry, Tom. You're right, but I was thinking about when I came in." He laughs out loud. "I can't stop thinking about when you came out of the oven... all full of flour! You looked like a ghost, you looked ridiculous."

I get serious.

"You got out of prison yesterday and you're already talking like one of those sons of bitches. If you saw me in that situation, which you think is funny, it's because of you."

Matt realises he's screwed up, and this time his face shows concern.

"I'm sorry, Tom. Don't get me wrong. I wanted to take the edge off. I know it must be very difficult for you, but if one of those bastards actually came through that door, you should know that the oven isn't the safest place to hide. Don't you think they'd look inside first? Sorry, I'm really worried about you."

My serious gaze takes in Matt's serious face, when I suddenly burst out laughing:

"You should see yourself, Matt. You're all red in the face. I know exactly what you mean, but I wanted to tease you a bit, and as usual, you fell for it..." He laughs nonstop. "Apart from being straight, have you gone dumb?"

I know I am bothering him, and I know what his sore point is, but this is what I want: to play with him as when we were free.

"What? Straight, me? Who told you that? How disgusting! Don't even say it as a joke."

Matt doesn't know how to justify himself, but it's more than obvious that I know more than he imagines. And so, increasingly amused and happy to relive old moments that seemed to have vanished forever, I tell him all about it.

"Your sister, obviously, who else could tell me?"

"Hey, hey... Are you and my sister that close? You're not the straight one now, are you? To me, you're a brother, and Anna is my real sister; imagining you two together... it makes me sick. For me it would be like incest."

Matt is not at all serious when he utters those words.

"You should know that if I ever became straight someday, your little sister would be the only woman I could marry." And as I say it, I hit Matt with the slice.

After a few minutes of banter, Matt comes back to reality.

"Seriously, you and my sister are the people I love most in this world, so seeing you two together would be a wonderful thing, but you have your David, so that's just a dream. Who knows what bastard my little sister will marry?"

After those words, melancholy assails me. David? I think about him, but I decide to keep quiet. It's not about me now, it's not about David, it's not about my problems or ours: it's Matt who deserves all the attention now. I can't believe how much the experience he's had in prison has benefited Matt's maturity.

"Don't worry about Anna. She's mature enough to know how to choose a good future."

Matt hugs me, aware of how lucky he is to be surrounded by people like Anna and me. We love him, and we are an encouragement in his development.

And it is precisely the love and deep affection he feels for me that brings him back to the opening scene: my sudden exit from the oven.

"Listen, Tom. I wonder, if someone comes in attracted by the smoke, what are your plans? Where would you hide?"

I pull myself together and take Matt by the arm, show him that underneath the oven there is a small hole covered with firewood. I remove it and add:

"I still have to modify it, but I think it will be enough for me and my father. As he enters, he goes to a small space at the back of the bakery. This oven is much smaller than the one I had in the bakery, but two people can sit in it comfortably. We just have to hope that the oven isn't too hot at the time, otherwise I don't know how long we can hold out."

Matt looks at me with admiration and says:

"Well, I'm very proud of you. Tell me how you plan to modify it and we'll do it together, like everything else. I'll always be by your side now."

"Well, my friend, that's just what I wanted to hear. Start by delivering this bread."

We look at each other and laugh.

"Of course, your friendship with Matt must have been the most precious thing you've ever had... I've always dreamed of having a friend like him, but I haven't been lucky enough to find one."

I smile at Ben and ruffle his hair with my hand.

21

I returned home about half an hour ago, at about seven o'clock in the evening, pedalling my bike. I'm in the kitchen preparing dinner for my father and me, trying to peel the onions but, in my mind, there is only room for one thing: my sweet David.

I think of the sound of his voice, of the soft perfume he exudes, but above all I think again and again of that kiss. There was something special between the two of us, something unique and, if God had willed it, that encounter could have been the beginning of a great love story.

I finish with the onions and start with the potatoes, and suddenly my thoughts are interrupted by shouting from the street. I don't even have time to peek out of the door to find out what's going on, when someone pushes the door open so hard that I'm knocked to the ground.

I"s two SS agents shouting:

"Jews, you are obliged to hand over to us all the electrical appliances you have at home. Come on, it's an order."

"Sirs, we haven't owned anything for a long time. I'm afraid you'll have to leave this house empty-handed," tries to explain old Carl, who stands beside me in a low voice, feigning pity.

The oldest of the SS guards, hearing this, becomes agitated and, in an even more furious tone, shouts at him:

"How is it possible that you have nothing? I've heard this excuse a hundred times today, but, having checked it myself, I've found everything, so don't waste our time. Come on!"

My father glares at the two officers to go in and search while I stand beside him in silence, as if paralysed with fear.

The soldiers enter without delay and begin to tear the house apart, while my father explains to them that he has had to sell all his belongings in order to get through this difficult period.

The youngest SS officer, after having searched most of the only room, stands right in front of my paralysed eyes.

"How is it possible that you have nothing? Not even a radio?"

Still very disturbed, I just shake my head, but the SS agent, not at all satisfied, looks me in the eye, and, after drawing a smile on his face that doesn't bode well, unexpectedly starts to beat my father savagely.

I can't believe my eyes: my father lying on the floor, after a punch in the stomach, a kick... then another and another, and another, and another until I finally decide to react.

"Stop it, stop it, I beg you, stop it. We do have something..."

The two agents exchange complicit and satisfied glances as I head for the attic to get my mother's record player.

Once downstairs, I look the guards straight in the eye, with an air full of hatred and anger, and ask:

"Why do you do it?"

Though deep down I think I know the answer.

"War is expensive, boy!" one of them replies.

Hearing those words, my heart seems to stop. They take my breath away; staring blankly, I think: I can't believe this is happening. I just gave up my most precious asset to finance a fucking war. And not just any war, but a war against me and my people. This is all terrible!

"Just this? Nothing else?"

Still staring blankly, I shake my head slightly. The two soldiers, disappointed with the loot and angry at the lost time, decide to punish us by pouncing on us and pummelling us with punches and kicks. Although I am still confused by the beatings, I manage to catch what the SS officers say to us as they leave the house.

"This is how they will learn not to bother us, as if we were stupid Jews."

With our bodies and souls wounded by so much violence, we fall asleep on the floor.

The next morning, I am the first to open my eyes. I look around me, glancing at my father who is still curled up asleep. It only takes me a few seconds to realise what happened: unfortunately, it wasn't a nightmare.

I wake my father up and make sure he's okay. Luckily, apart from some painful bruises, we both manage to get to our feet.

Suddenly, I relive, in a déjà vu, the gratuitous violence that I had been given some time ago and that had cost me ten weeks of recovery and nightmares that still ravage my brain.

"Dad... why all this?"

My father has no answer. He looks down and gives me a big hug.

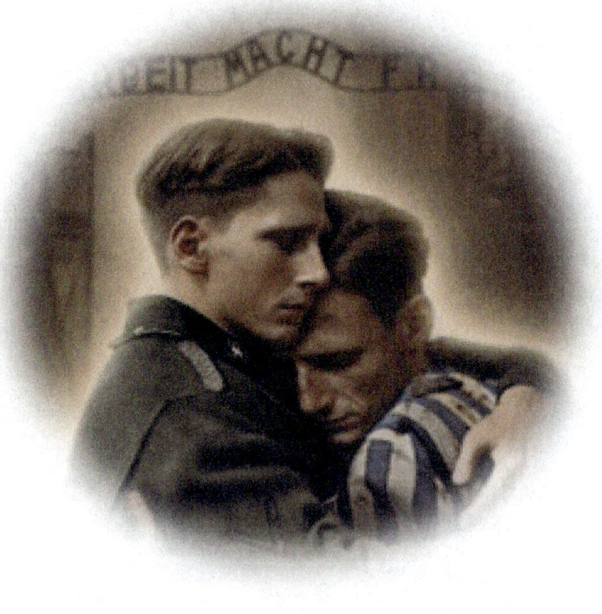
EIT MACHT

22

For my father and me, the winter of 1936 was very hard, as was the following spring.

But summer comes with all its heat, and working in the oven is even harder, but I don't give up, I can fight against the heat of the fire, against the heat of summer and against the bands that squeeze my body holding the freshly baked bread.

"Grandpa, the Winter Olympics were held in Germany from 6 to 15 January, weren't they?"

"Yes, Ben, but, as you can imagine, we Jews had much more serious problems to think about, we had to fight to survive; the Olympics didn't matter to us."

"I know, but it's history anyway, and I need it for my research."

In 1935, the municipalities of Garmisch and Partenkirchen, in the southern part of Bavaria near the Austrian border, joined forces for the Olympic Games. On the other hand, this had already been decided in April 1931 in Barcelona.

As it was written, even the Olympics, a seemingly playful event that should have brought peace and an end to every act of war or violence, were part of a much larger plan that was gradually taking shape in Hitler's mind and translating into a new barbarism. Festive and lavish ceremonies served to sow an idea of peace and brotherhood, when in reality an uncompromising intolerance dominated in Germany, which was concealed during the Olympic Games.

During the Summer Olympics in 1932, the People's Observer, a Nazi party newspaper, pointed out that black athletes should not have aspired to the Olympics, which is why they did not participate in the Winter Olympics.

During the traditional visit of the delegates of the Olympic Committee, led by its president, Count Henri de Baillet-Latour, who travelled to Garmisch to supervise the state of the construction work, he noticed, to his horror, a sign at the entrance to the Olympic Village: "No dogs or Jews allowed".

The Count, indignant, asked for an interview with the Führer, who responded in his own way to the request for the removal of the sign: "When you are a guest in someone else's house, you must respect the rules." The Count reminded him that when the Olympic flag was raised, the roles would be reversed, so Hitler had no choice but to comply with his brave request. The impressive opening managed to hide almost everything, but the Olympics did not run as smoothly as desired.

The only authorised photographers were Germans, and the area was constantly patrolled by more than six thousand SS agents. As can be seen, Hitler's every action was aimed at the fulfilment of his repugnant plans.

"That's right, but nobody lifted a finger to help us. Our extermination happened under the eyes of the whole world, and nobody did anything. Anyway, coming back to us, mine is the only story I can tell you. On that summer day, Anna came prancing in, wrapped in a light that emanated joy."

Who knows if it's because of heat, fear or uneasiness, I don't react well to her enthusiasm and, in a curt tone, I remind her that I'm working, that I can't afford to be happy and that it would be better if we met some other time.

Anna bows her head in shame. She is still a child who had to grow up before her time, and she too has the need to dream, to have fun, or simply to distract herself by losing herself in an everyday life that is brushed with normality.

For her, I am like a blood brother, and for that reason, she often forgets that I am Jew and that we Jews today have very serious problems, which erase any trace of nonchalance and serenity.

Anna is often tortured by a feeling of helplessness, not only towards me and all those in my situation, but also towards her brother. Her expression changes, she feels ashamed and sad, and she apologises.

"Forgive me, Anna, my attitude has been embarrassing. From time to time, talking about other things would be good for me, but it's impossible for me to do so. I imagine that, although your family is in a privileged situation, it must be difficult for you too, probably more so than for Matt, as his character helps him. If your father realised that behind his behaviour lies pain and anguish, maybe..."

"Tom," Anna sighs, "how will my father understand? On 11 November he witnessed a speech by Hitler about the racial and biological dangers of homosexuality, and less than a month ago he went to Heinrich Himmler's anti-homosexual speech at the opening of the *Reichszentrale zur Bekämpfung der Homosexualität und Abtreibung*[3], a criminal police institution under the SS. His work does not help him at all. These maniacs work with real 'brain washers'. For my father, there can be no greater humiliation than having a son like Matt."

I smile, holding back.

"No wonder, Anna, he's gone so far as to force his own son to have a sexual relationship with a prisoner. Any other man would have been delighted." I laugh so as not to cry. "Poor Matt, I can just imagine the scene."

Anna bows her eyes once more.

"I'm on your side. You know that, don't you? But I can't help but feel pain and sorrow for my father. Deep down, he just wants to cure him."

"Cure him?" I reply, upset. "Cure him of what?"

"Come on, Tom, you know what. For them, homosexuality is incompatible with their own ideals. For them, the purpose of sexual relations is reproduction for the preservation and continuation of the existence of the Volk, that is, of the people, rather than for the pleasure of the individual."

I knew it, but to know does not mean to understand, does not mean to comprehend, does not mean to support it. There are many things I do not understand or, perhaps, simply do not accept.

---

3 *Reich Central for the fight against homosexuality and abortion.*

23

Several months have passed since Matt's release from prison. His life is not the same as before, but he doesn't complain. Between one pretext and another, he always manages to get permission to go out. We see each other whenever we want, he helps me with the bread deliveries and, most importantly, he gets to see his beloved Peter again. He does it very cautiously and secretly, but all that matters is that he gets to see him. Luckily, like Matt, Peter has been released from prison after his arrest in the "love countryside". For him, despite being gay and Jewish, getting out of prison was much easier than for Matt.

A colonel, during an improvised inspection inside the prisons to monitor the work of the guards, collapsed and fell to the floor. He was completely rigid and began to tremble, as if he was being electrocuted. The soldier's face turned blue; he was drooling from his mouth: he was drowning! All the officers tried to help him, but the man was getting worse and worse. One of them, turning to the guards, shouted: "Call a doctor immediately! Hurry!".

Peter's cell was just there, a few steps away. The young man was witnessing the whole scene when, realising that the colonel was about to suffocate to death in a few minutes, and that the doctor who had been called was not in time to save his life, he decided to intervene:

"The tongue! Get his tongue!"

One of the guards present hit him in the face with the handle of the machine gun that he managed to get through the bars.

"What do you know? You're just a stupid Jew!"

Peter, feeling a lot of pain and clutching his nose, which was probably broken, with one hand, replied in a very low tone:

"I'm a doctor..."

One of the officers present looked him straight in the eye and ordered the guard to open the cell.

For a moment, Peter thought the officer wanted to continue what the guard had started, but he soon calmed down.

"Come closer, quickly!"

Given the colonel's condition, which appeared to be extreme, the officer decided to let Peter intervene. The young doctor, who had already understood that it was an epileptic seizure, did his best to save his jailer's life. After the moment of unconsciousness, when he regained consciousness, the colonel, willing to repay his debt to Peter, decided to pardon him by making him promise that he would not allow himself to be caught again.

This is how freedom allows him to find his love and among a lie, an excuse and a cover-up, they manage to resume their relationship.

"And they lived happily and contentedly..." says Ben, smiling.

"Sadly, no, dear Ben..." interrupts Anna, taking the floor. "Soon after, for us, the gates of hell opened."

"What do you mean, Grandma? Come on, tell me."

24

One day when Matt returns home thinking about his one great love, Peter, while chaining up his new bike, he is surprised by a sweet female voice.

"Hi, Matt, remember me?"

He turns around and sees the once little Margaret Fisher.

"Margaret? You've grown up! What brings you here?"

She looks at Matt with amusement and, pleased by his words, replies in a captivating tone:

"I'm here for you, it was your father who invited us. Didn't he say anything to you?"

Matt looks at her in bewilderment and simply replies with a 'no'.

Margaret, oblivious to everything, unaware that Matt is gay, and that his father wants to cure him at all costs, full of enthusiasm and with her eyes shining with happiness, clarifies everything:

"We are here because your father has approached us about the possibility of an arranged wedding. My father is currently arranging for us to get married at the end of the month."

"Excuse me? Who's marrying who?"

Matt breaks out in a cold sweat, he knows he's got it right, but his heart starts pounding so hard that he thinks panic is playing tricks on him. Margaret answers with a big smile:

"You and me, you fool!"

He is speechless, staring blankly, as if paralysed.

The girl notices his state of shock and the bewilderment on her future husband's face. Surprised by his reaction, she tries to cheer him up.

"Matt, I know it's probably not what we've dreamed of, but there is no other man in my life. Even if I don't love you now, I'm sure I'll learn to, the way my mother did with my father. I have known you since you were a child, I think I know what could make you happy and what could not. Everything I don't know about you I will learn and respect. My only wish is to make you happy, to take care and raise our future children well. Love will come in time, when we learn to know each other intimately."

Matt finishes hitching up his bike, hurries into the house, leaving Margaret outside. He immediately heads for the kitchen, where he assumes his father is. His mother and Mr. and Mrs. Fisher are also there.

As soon as he enters, everyone in the house looks at him with smiles and a festive air.

The owner of the house stands up, puts an arm around Matt's neck and announces loudly:

"Here's the groom! My son will make your daughter the happiest woman in the world."

Matt looks at him dumbfounded and, at the same time, terrified. Without saying a word, he grabs his father by the arm and drags him out of the house.

"Dad, why are you doing this to me?"

His voice trembles, he wants to say so much more, but the words die in his throat. Dad, seeing that young Margaret is standing there looking at them, invites her with a slight smile and a polite wave of his hand to enter the house; immediately afterwards, he answers his son in a strong, stern and authoritative tone:

"Matt, remember the promise you made me when you got out of prison?"

My little brother, mute, looks at him with eyes begging for mercy.

"Hey, why don't you answer me? Since you don't remember, I'll refresh your memory. You promised me that you would get married and find the perfect woman for you. I've given you six months to do it, but since you haven't managed to find a woman on your own, I thought I'd give you a hand. Now you go into the house and tell everyone present that you will marry this girl and that you are willing to give her children: that's what any man wants!"

Those words go straight into Matt's ears, as if they were a hammer blow. Furious and full of rage, he decides to enter the kitchen escorted by Dad. With a serious look on his face, he asks for a moment's attention. Dad, satisfied, smiles at those present, sure that he has convinced Matt.

"I'm very sorry that you have had to make this journey for nothing, but I will not marry your daughter or any other woman." He looks at the sweet-faced, sad and disoriented young woman, and with great regret continues: "I'm very sorry, Margaret, you are a good woman and also very beautiful, but you are not what I desire."

And, leaving everyone speechless, he heads for his room on the top floor of the house.

His heart pounding at the brave scene he has just played, he listens to the voices coming from downstairs. Mr. Fisher must be really angry about what has just happened, his shouting is quite heated:

"Now I understand why you haven't yet asked for my daughter's dowry, because he is the problem. He's still sick!" Then he grabs his wife and daughter by the arm and, without saying goodbye, leaves the house, grumbling about what has happened.

Matt hides his head under his pillow, he just wants to stop listening to that nonsense, but he knows he's going to have to face our father's speech soon.

Downstairs, Alfons' screams can still be heard, and it seems they won't be quiet for the time being. Matt is in bed, about to fall asleep with his head under the pillow, when Dad bursts into the room with demonic eyes.

"This is the last time you humiliate me." With a deft gesture, he unbuckles his trousers and, filled with hatred, approaches Matt's bed. "Because of you I have had to endure multiple humiliations. You are the shame of this family! You disgust me!

With the belt in his hands, he starts to whip him hard, hitting him all over: first on his face, then on his back and also on his private parts. To somehow defend himself from the blows that are causing him excruciating pain, Matt decides to turn over and lay on his stomach. Dad continues to pummel him relentlessly, amid Matt's cries, stifled by the pillow. He is aware that his lashes will leave wounds, but his wish is that they won't heal quickly, as proof of how much his despicable son is making him suffer. Exhausted from his ferocious rage, he decides to conclude.

"I will tell you one more thing: from this day forward, you are absolutely forbidden to leave this room! You will rot in here until the day you stand at the altar in the company of Margaret Fisher. Do you understand, Matt? Do you understand?"

And, without waiting for an answer, he leaves Matt in tears and bleeding wounds, staining his clothes red.

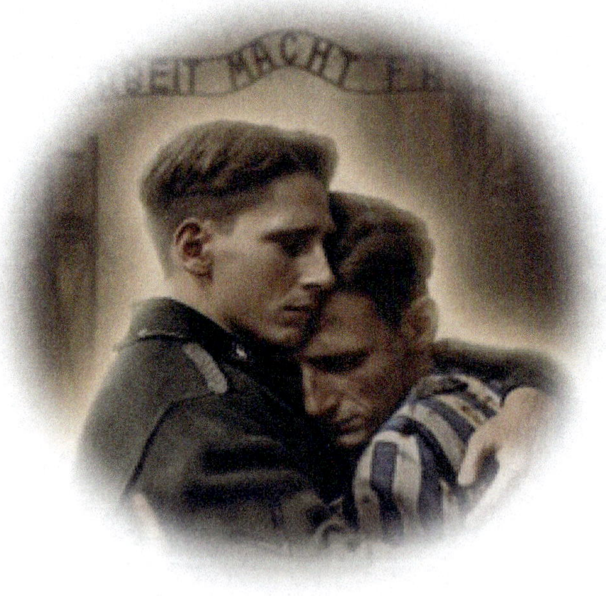
BEIT MACHT

25

Ben is speechless, his mouth open, like that of a boiled fish. He is confused and upset. One thing is the story as it is told at school, and a completely different thing is how the people you love have lived and live it.

"Grandma, could you make me a cup of hot chocolate? I think I really need it. In the meantime, I look where I was going, historically speaking..."

Months go by, but nothing seems to change in Berlin. The outrage against Jews and homosexuals grew more violent by the day, even though the Vatican, and in particular Pope Pius XI (Achille Ratti), with his encyclical Mit Brennender Sorge of 14 March 1937, harshly condemned Nazism. It was one of the harshest condemnations of a national regime that the Vatican has ever issued.

The Pope, opposed to any kind of dictatorship and totalitarianism, tries to do everything possible to stop the application of German doctrines. Hitler, taken by surprise, is completely bewildered. Furious and in a violent press campaign, he has defined it as a worldwide criminal attempt against the National Socialist state and the German people.

The Führer's hatred and rage explode with greater conviction, and on 15 July one of Nazi Germany's largest concentration camps, Buchenwald, is established on top of the Ettersberg hill in a dense oak woodland about eight kilometres from Weimar in eastern Germany.

"And as events fall apart," I interrupt him, projecting myself into the past, "within the walls of Matt's room, time passes very slowly."

 The months spent in the family home seem like years. Matt would prefer prison a thousand times over, where at least he was away from his father, as he visits him all too often armed with his belt. But at home there is also little Anna. Actually, the only thing he cares about is her. Thanks to his little sister, Matt can exchange letters with Peter and me. It's his only way to get news from the outside world and break through the wall of that heartbreaking loneliness.
 It's not yet dawn on this Berlin morning. The temperature has dropped below zero, and everything seems gloomier and more melancholic. Matt has already experienced a similar situation. In solitude, wrapped in his thoughts, he thinks about when his father discovered his homosexuality, about the captivity in his own home and how he has coped with the situation. He decides that this time he has to do something too, but that now he must learn from past mistakes and make it all work out, and this requires a well-articulated plan.
 In this long period of captivity at home, in his own room, he has certainly not lacked time for reflection. He has imagined so many times what he should do, but has never had the guts to do it for fear of making things even worse. However, he has come to the con-

clusion that he has nothing to lose.

It is seven o'clock in the morning when he decides to go and talk to his father. The man is in his room about to get dressed. Matt stares in disgust at the brown uniform on the bed, although he is now convinced that it is the perfect outfit for him.

He thinks that only a man like him is capable of wearing it, although deep in his heart he knows that this is not the case. He has met many of his father's colleagues over the years, some of them with big hearts and worthy of respect. So why do they do this job? Why do they carry out, without complaint, whatever Hitler orders, even though it is against their moral principles?

A bunch of imbeciles manipulated by a Führer, a self-proclaimed leader.

Matt plucks up his courage, hates his father and has to use his acting skills to be credible.

"Hi, Dad, can I talk to you?" A whisper escapes his lips so as not to wake his mother, who is still asleep.

His father, without worrying too much about his sleeping wife and Anna, in a high tone, after coughing, replies:

"At this hour? What do you want, Matt?"

The young man, with a dazzling smile, starts his big show.

"I wanted to tell you that, after all these months, I have had an enlightenment. Tonight, I saw before me the wife you had found for me. I imagined her, I saw all her beauty. I imagined that I was kissing her, and that I had her by my side. I have done nothing but dream of Miss Fisher all night, and at last I realised that it is the right thing for me to marry her, because, after all, I like her, I seem even to love her already.

The way she welcomed me, the enthusiasm that flushed her face. The sadness and composure when I rejected her, even before I made her my wife. Such a companion is worthy of a life. I want to marry her, Dad."

Offman, who is about to tie his tie, stops, looks his boy straight in the eye, raising both eyebrows.

"Are you telling me you're cured?"

Matt, thinking for a moment that his father has figured it out, merely nods. He looks down and wonders if he has a future as an actor.

The Colonel omits any details, what counts is his son's recovery. At last, after all this time, he has finally heard the words he has been longing for. Matt wants to marry... to a woman!

He knows that if his son is cured, it is only thanks to him. Of course, there was a period when he began to think that his eldest son probably belonged to the other category of gays, those incurable ones, but now he knows that this is not the case and that his healing method is infallible, so, without changing his tone of voice and without being too enthusiastic, he replies:

"Perfect. I want you to know that this whole story has been more difficult for me than for you. I'll get back to organising everything."

Matt backs towards the door and, without turning around, turning his back to his father, continues:

"I'd like to ask you one last favour."

His father looks at him perplexed and fearful. The young man, after taking a deep breath, continues:

"I have wasted too much time with my illness. Now that I am well, I want you to organise my wedding as soon as possible. I want to get married, have children and, who knows... maybe become like you."

The colonel, for an instant, on hearing those words, has the feeling that his son is pulling his leg, but then, analysing everything that Matt has been through, the humiliations, the reclusion, that despite being at home he continues to suffer, he understands that his haste is completely natural. Maybe he doesn't love her as he says he does, and maybe he doesn't have all that desire to have a bunch of kids with their snot hanging out, but whoever is tired of living a life that isn't a life has this immense need to turn the page. He approaches his son and reassures him, aware that what really counts is not what he feels, but what people think he feels.

"I'll see what I can do. The only problem is to convince the Fishers again, but I'll do it."

Matt, amazed at the great feat he has just accomplished, congratulates himself with an imaginary pat on the back, and immediately comes to see me.

I smile happily at him, nodding my head. His future as an actor is guaranteed. He can't imagine that his father doesn't care how he feels, what he wants is for him to get married and be able to appear normal to others.

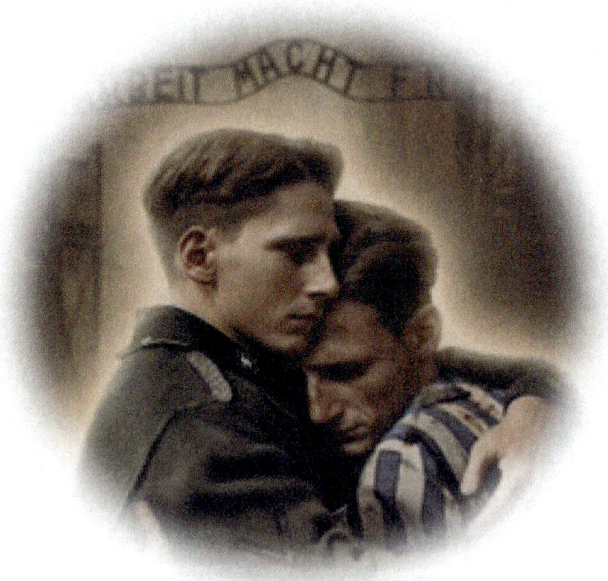
MACHT

26

"**G**randpa, I can't figure out whether the colonel was an asshole or a son of a bitch."

"Ben, there are people who are so sure of their own ideas and convictions that they fail to see reality, or perhaps they simply don't want to see it because it suits them."

"In the end, did he manage to organise the wedding?"

"Of course, he did, Ben, the colonel always got what he wanted."

The day of the wedding arrives, everyone is at the church, only Matt is missing.

Colonel Offman, together with his family, leaves home early so that Matt can prepare himself calmly. His heart is full of melancholy. He remembers his big day vividly. So many years have passed, but the emotion still lingers in his mind: that morning, the woman who would become his wife was waiting for their firstborn son. She was radiant at the altar, as beautiful as he had never seen her before, and she was carrying her little baby in her womb.

The colonel is aware that he is a lucky man because, for him, his wife is not only his love, but also the companion of a lifetime; she has always accompanied him at all times, whatever they may be, and now it is the turn of his son.

It has certainly not been easy to achieve that goal,

but he considers himself a great father and, at the end of the day, he has

considered himself a great father and, in the end, everything is going as it should.

Waiting in front of the church, among the congratulating relatives, time flies. Margaret Fisher is the most excited. She will finally fulfil her dream: to get married, have children and take care of her family. She has studied hard for it, giving birth to little 'thoroughbred' Aryans is a great satisfaction for her.

Margaret's father, hoping that his daughter would marry some SS bigwig, prepared her adequately, as the regime intended. In fact, the young girl studied at the famous and highly secret Reichsbrauteschule, a school for brides of Nazi officers and hierarchs. There she was taught "neo-pagan" indoctrination and the cult of the Führer.

The students, divided into classes of twenty, should attend the institute preferably two months before the wedding, to prepare for 'the joys of married life', but Mr Fisher has done so much earlier, wishing the best for his only lovely daughter.

The six-week course cost him one hundred and thirty-five marks, but it was worth it. Margaret has learned to cook, to garden, to wash, to iron her husband's uniform, and even to hold a conversation at occasions such as cocktails and parties, and, of course, to take care of her children. Although Matt is not a member of the Führer's army, he is still the son of a colonel; she will carry a prestigious name that she will pass on to her children.

On this important day, Margaret is wearing a plain white dress that marks her waist. A very long veil is lowered from a dark hat with white lace á pois. In her hands, a beautiful bouquet and in her eyes, romantic dreams of love.

Contrary to tradition, Margaret arrives on time and now she has no choice but to wait in the car, a few steps away from the church, waiting for her future husband. As soon as he arrives, the driver will start the engine and very slowly they will approach the church. Waiting for her will be her father, who will take her by the arm to the altar where Matt will be waiting.

"Alfons, Alfons, where's Matt? I'm tired of standing out here waiting."

Amidst the commotion, a little old woman begins to complain, annoyed by the husband's long-waiting imprudence.

"Mum, Matt is coming, he's a man heading for the gallows, have mercy!"

A burst of laughter breaks out among the guests. They all laugh in amusement, especially the Fishers, who, until that moment, had been distressed by Matt's absence. Mrs. Offman pretends to be angry, even though the joke was actually funny.

An hour later, the guests are still inside the church. The chatter slowly fades away. Only the women still have arguments, while the men are beginning to feel uncomfortable with the silence.

Anna, waiting for someone she knows will never come, looks at Uncle Ernest, sitting next to her father. It is the first time she sees him after Matt's confessions and, if she could, she would kill him with her bare hands. She wants to tell her father everything, but she can't. Matt has made her promise never to tell anyone, after all, it's part of his past and he doesn't want to go back to those terrible times.

Alfons looks around him. On the one hand, the women who, although exhausted, are keeping each other company; on the other, the men, puffing with boredom, going in and out the church, taking the opportunity to smoke a cigar to distract them.

Not exactly what the colonel has imagined for the wedding of his only son. His tolerance is stretched to the limit when a whisper interrupts the uncontrolled murmur:

"Maybe Matt has run off with the first man who passed him on his way here."

A female giggle follows.

Anger begins to cloud Colonel Offman's eyes. Suddenly, he sees it all clearly. The puzzle is complete. His son, his only son, is not cured. He is still ill, and what is even more serious: he has been mocked. He cannot believe that the scoundrel has done it again, first in front of his colleagues and now in front of friends and relatives.

It is too serious an insult, too disrespectful. The joy of his recovery was so great that it blocked his ability to understand it, blinding him completely. Now, however, it all comes back to him, now he sees everything clearly. The colonel takes Anna by the arm and leads her out of the church, away from prying eyes.

"Tell me, Anna, where is your brother?"

Anna looks at him with both amusement and terror, but she hides it.

"Dad, how should I know? I've been here with you the whole time."

Angrily, he begins to shake her from behind.

"You and your brother are very close, you're as thick as thieves. He would never have done anything so irrational without telling you. I want to know where he is. Tell me right now, otherwise I swear that, when I find him, I'll kill him with my own hands... And you know perfectly well that I am capable, don't you?"

Two demonic eyes pierce the little girl. Now she is truly terrified.

"I don't know!" she shouts as she shakes her head from side to side, trying to avoid eye contact, but it is stronger.

"You are an ungrateful daughter. After all your brother has put us through, you protect him now?"

"I'm not surprised at all, from someone like Matt, it's to be expected!"

A male voice reaches Anna's ears. She turns and sees the last person she would have imagined would have the courage to utter those words: Uncle Ernest.

Anna's eyes fill with hatred and anger, and as her father continues to shake her, she bursts into uncontrollable tears, screaming at the top of her lungs:

"How have you the nerve to speak? It's your fault if Matt's sick! It's only your fault."

Anna has just broken her first promise.

With both hands, Alfons grabs her head, forcing her to look him in the eye. He grips her tighter.

"What do you mean, Anna? Look at me, what does it mean?" The tone of his voice is low and very serious.

"What I've said. Your brother abused your son when he was only seven years old. He is the source of all your problems."

Anna has stopped shouting, but the tone of her voice is very stern and her reproachful gaze reveals the indecency of what has happened.

Ernest is stunned for a moment. 'How could Anna have found out about this?'

Those words have a devastating effect on Alfons. Ernest is his older brother; he can't even imagine such a thing.

"How dare you say such things? You're a little liar."

Then a hard slap lands on his daughter's face. But Anna does not give up easily. At that moment, all the guests are outside the church, silent spectators of what is happening.

"Why don't you confess, Uncle? Why don't you tell my father why you didn't want me in the middle when you were taking Matt to the country?"

Looking around, Ernest notices that family and friends are watching him. He must do something to take control of the situation, and the easiest way seems to be denial.

"This girl is crazy! Alfons, you've really done very badly with your children, one sick and the other crazy and a liar."

At that precise moment, without anyone expecting it, Alfons sees his wife approach his brother and slap him.

"Don't you dare insult my children ever again, you disgust me!" She spits in his face and, turning to her husband, continues: "Alfons, what Anna told you is true. When I found out, she begged me not to tell you anything, otherwise you would have killed him with your own hands. As much as I wanted to, I didn't. Together, you and your brother would have killed your mother and the good name of this family. But now I can no longer tolerate it. Your brother is a disgusting being."

Alfons can't believe it: his older brother, his best friend and confidant, is the cause of all his ills. After the death of his sister-in-law, he gave him the strength to overcome the pain, but now he deserves nothing but death.

Ernest starts to run, and the colonel impulsively follows him. He soon catches up with him. Ernest is quite robust and finds it hard to move; Alfons, on the other hand, is fitter thanks to his work.

Once away from the prying eyes of the guests, he approaches his brother and, looking him in the eye, asks him to confess, but Ernest has always been a coward, and Alfons knows that perfectly well.

"Tell me the truth and you'll save your life."

Ernest has never seen his brother so demonic, but he knows how to reassure him.

"Wait, wait! You don't believe what your wife and daughter told you? They're just fucking lies. They tell you these things because they've always been jealous of our relationship."

Alfons gets even more irritated.

"Lies? Then why did you run away like a coward? I thought you were a good person." As he utters those words, he picks up his gun. Ernest is not yet ready to die.

"All right, all right, I confess it. Yes, it was me. Are you happy now? It was me!"

Those words he wanted so much not to hear come mercilessly and like bombshells.

"Why did you do it? Why with my son?"

Alfons' tone of voice is loud, angry and disgusted.

"I was alone, you knew how much I was suffering because of my wife's death, and your son was there...

The fresh air and his innocence helped make it all easier. I'm sorry, brother."

"You disgust me! You're a monster!"

With a tear trembling down his face, Alfons pulls the trigger and shoots straight into his genitals. A non-lethal shot, but one that will undoubtedly render him harmless for the rest of his life.

Alfons has not finished with him, but for the moment he has vented his anger and decides to postpone the settling of scores.

Now it is Matt's turn. Aware that his son was not born sick, he is still very angry with him because of the continuous humiliations he has put him through and, in particular, the teasing of him, so he approaches his daughter again.

"Have you seen what I can do, Anna? I shot my brother, and if you don't tell me where Matt is right away, as soon as I find him, I'll do the same to him."

Anna continues to shake her head without saying a word. She has already broken one promise and she doesn't want to do it again! The guests have left and Alfons, realising that he has been left alone with his daughter, decides to face the situation more calmly. He takes a deep breath and, looking into Anna's eyes, he says:

"I want to make a pact with you. You have done one thing for me today by telling me the truth about my brother, and now I want to do one thing for you. I promise you that, if you tell me where Matt is and who he's with, I won't kill him. You know very well that I will succeed in finding him, and in that case, your brother's murderer will be you, because I have given you the choice."

Anna knows that her father is serious. He is able to find him in a short time thanks to his contacts; and, in view of his latest humiliation, he is actually capable of killing him with his bare hands. But, as much as he is full of evil and can do horrible things, she knows he can trust him. If she's learned anything from her father, it is that his word is sacred, which is perhaps why he is so angry with Matt.

Betraying his brother again is the only way to save him from certain death.

"He's with Peter."

She says it with a firm voice and with all the pain in her soul.

As Tom narrates the story, Anna's face fills with tears and Ben, with a lump in his throat, says nothing, not a comment, not a question.

Tom continues his story, while the cup of hot chocolate waits on the table next to the video camera.

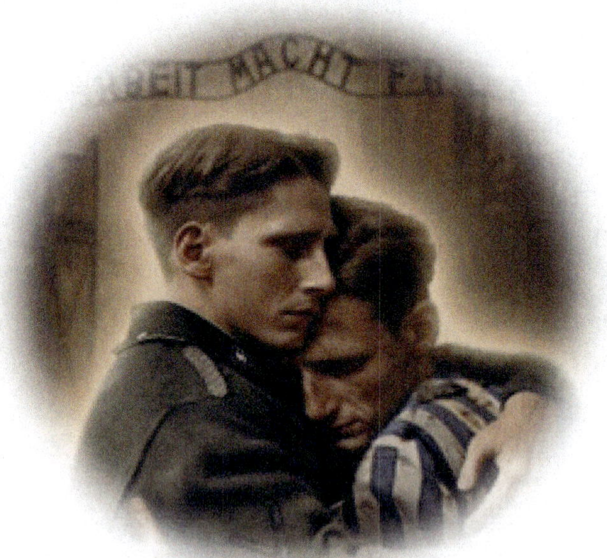
MACHT

27

The humiliation suffered by Colonel Offman is so great that he decides it is time to put an end to it. How much more will a respectable man like him have to endure? He has always been a 'fully grown man', always overcoming all the difficulties of life. From a young age, he always had to fight for what he wanted given his father's extreme discipline, which he always saw as a role model. Given the great results obtained, he set out to follow in the same footsteps.

In fifty years of life, he has encountered quite a few enemies along the way, but thanks to his innate intimidating skills, he has always managed to crush them, and if now his worst enemies are his son and brother..., he feels sorry for them!

Colonel Alfons Offman, a week after the supposed wedding, is sitting at his desk in the barracks office, thinking about how to deal with this situation and what measures to take in order to punish his son fairly.

After all, he has already been warned by the higher-ups that if he does not solve the problem, they will carry it out themselves, threatening the rest of his family as well. He has already resigned his rank of general because of his son. He has not been able to cure him, even though he gave him his word, who knows what awaits him!

Thanks to Anna's ratting him out, he managed to arrest him at the home of another gay man like himself.

Although Matt was ready to escape with his backpack in his hands, Peter's doubts about the repercussions of such a decision caused them to lose time.

Fortunately, the colonel promised Anna not to kill him, because with the rage inside him, he would have shot him in the brain with a single shot.

But things are calmer now. Time has diluted all kinds of emotions. Even the pain has gradually disappeared.

In the office, however, things are very different. The more time goes by, the more people find out what has happened.

Friends, relatives and, in particular, colleagues never miss an opportunity to remind him of how depraved his son or, even worse, his brother is. The colonel has always been a respected man in the barracks, but now things are changing. Suddenly, SS Army General Becker appears before him.

"Colonel Offman!"

Alfons jumps out of his chair with his right arm raised and shouts at the top of his lungs:

"Heil Hitler!" With his head held high and his gaze fixed, he continues: "It's me, sir."

General Becker walks towards an empty room and, with a signal, orders the colonel to follow him. Once inside, still standing, he rests both hands on the desk and looks Alfons straight in the eye.

"Colonel, I heard some rumours this morning, and I'm here to find out if they are true."

"Yes, my General, it's all true."

"I haven't told you yet what I've heard, and already you're telling me the rumours are true. Look, Colonel, this is just what I like to see: my SS officers who are not afraid of anything and face everything with their heads held high. But today you don't need my help. Everyone here is making fun of you. If you want it all to end, you must take serious action. If so far we have not intervened with more... let's call them drastic methods, it is because we have respect for you, for your position and for your professionalism. But you don't deserve to be the laughing stock of the barracks, or am I wrong?"

The colonel immediately realises that this is a suggestion and is impatient to hear it.

"Yes, my General, you're right. What do you propose?"

Becker, now with his arms folded, replies as when a friend needs help.

"Have you heard of Dachau?"

"Yes, I know they do horrible things to prisoners. It's a model for all Nazis. I know that they have recently started to build a large building complex in the area that houses the original camp, using prisoners to finish the work. It is a terrible place."

"Nonsense, it's only a rehabilitation centre, and besides, don't they deserve the most merciless punishments anyway?" He looks at the colonel, still puzzled, and continues: "If it were you yourself who ordered the imprisonment of your son and your brother in that camp, you would soon be respected again and would emerge victorious, like a real man, because that is how a perfect Aryan behaves. Besides, I don't have to be the one to remind you that you could lose your uniform for the embarrassment caused to the Reich..."

Alfons is not at all happy with the suggested proposal, no one knows what really goes on inside the walls of that centre, no one has ever come out alive.

But this is his only option, his only chance to win back his reputation and the esteem of his colleagues, who for some time now have done nothing but mock him. He thinks of Anna and the promise... He would not break any oath, because, whatever happens, he will not be the one to kill him.

"Thank you for such a valuable suggestion. Consider it done, my General, but, if I may, I would like to ask you a favour."

The general, without saying anything, nods and invites him to continue.

"I ask for special attention for my son, Matt Offman, while for my brother Ernest I want no preferential treatment. I want this monster to disappear from my family for good, and the best way to do that is to disown him as a brother. As soon as he enters Dachau, he will be nothing but a stranger to me. That is why I demand that he be treated as one of the worst criminals, because that is what he really is."

General Becker, with a big smile of satisfaction between his lips, congratulates him and escorts him to the door. Once there, he invites him to keep his word.

Offman calls two men, including Aaron, and orders them in a loud voice to listen to him:

"Discharge my son and my brother, both of whom will be transferred as soon as possible to the Dachau concentration camp."

In the office, all standing with their right arms raised because of the presence of the Army General, they listen to him in astonishment. They are shocked and bewildered by the atrocities to which the colonel is about to assign his own son and brother.

"Grandpa, that's terrible, how could he condemn his own son to certain death?"
No answer; eyes lowered and silence.

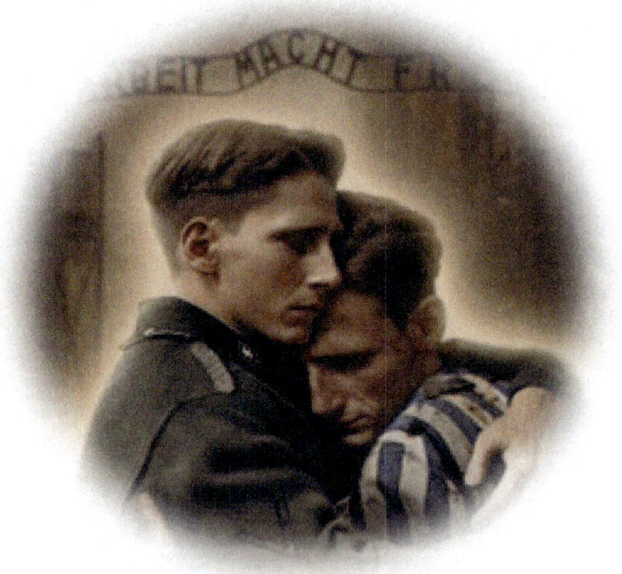
MACHT

28

In any case, the terrifying Nazi madness was going like wildfire, destroying everything in its path and converting other nations. In May 1938, Hungary adopted a Nazi policy, and in the summer of the same year, the manifesto of the racist sciences was published in Italy in the journal La difesa della razza.

In August, in Vienna, the Central Office for Jewish Emigration was created under the leadership of Adolf Eichman, a Nazi Germany institution whose purpose was to manage the departure of Austrian Jews. Similar offices were also opened in Prague and Amsterdam. For the Jews, there seemed to be no escape, the hunt was on: wherever they went they were harassed.

Mussolini himself, on 18 September in Trieste, from the balcony of the town hall in Unity of Italy Square, on the occasion of his visit to the city, had a huge box set up on which the word 'dux' could be read, where he announced the enactment of the famous anti-Semitic racial laws. An indelible stain on the Fascist regime and the Italian monarchy.

At the beginning of October, the passports of German Jews were considered invalid. On the night of 9 and 10 November, Germany, Austria and Czechoslovakia were shaken by a terrible echo. The crystal sky had been shattered by anti-Semitic savagery and terrible violence. The pretext was the murder of a secretary at the German Embassy in Paris by a young Pole of German origin, Herschel Grynszpan, the son of a deportee. All that hatred echoed across the sky, crashing into the heavens, and shards of glass fell amidst the deafening noise of shattering glass. Jewish synagogues, houses and shops were attacked.

   The police were ordered not to intervene and the fire brigade was left only to watch that the fire did not attack more buildings. Seven thousand five hundred Jewish shops destroyed, one hundred and ninety-one synagogues set on fire, and seventy-six destroyed by vandalism. Thousands of Jews murdered and tortured. More than thirty thousand deported to the concentration camps of Dachau, Buchenwald and Sachsenhausen after having been expropriated of all their property.

   Ben narrates it with a firm tone in front of his video camera. A historical truth told with a touch of poetry that serves to dilute that pain, that feeling of anguish and the desire to vomit and cry for all that he has heard from his grandparents' stories.

   "I had warned you, Ben, that it would be difficult to listen to this story. If you wish, and if you deem it appropriate, we can end it here."

   "No, Grandpa, I want to know. I beg you to continue, not only for the sake of my research..."

29

It's lunchtime. I'm not very hungry, how could I be with everything that's going on? There seems to be no escape for my father and me. Semitic extermination seems ever closer and events are happening with breathtaking speed. Many nations have adopted the Nazi policy.

How can I open my bleeding stomach?

Nevertheless, I know I must return home to keep my father company, he looks old and too tired. I lost my appetite long ago, and not just because of those days of atrocious violence, I lost it when my best friend was arrested for the second time.

I eat like an automaton; I am forced to feed myself in order to cope with the severe working day that awaits me every day. This morning, as every morning since Matt can no longer lend me a hand, despite the hour, I find myself still walking through the countryside on my way back from the city, after having scurried in vain through the streets of Berlin and having managed to sell only a few of the loaves of bread that I manage to hide well under my clothes.

The few customers who don't care if the bread comes from Jewish hands start to back away for fear of being discovered. Only a few have the courage to risk their lives for these oddly shaped loaves, the rest prefer to starve. But no one, absolutely no one, is assiduous in ordering their bread.

Forced to hand over my old bicycle to the Nazis, I travel exclusively on foot, with the consequence that the amount of bread is limited, which is why I also lost quite a few customers and, as if that were not enough, I am forced to travel several times a day regardless of the weather and the circumstances.

Today I walked the same route three times until, partly from the heat, partly from fatigue and partly from malnutrition, I fainted. I was rescued by a passer-by who, seeing me unconscious, tried to revive me by offering me some water, without me showing the slightest sign of recovery.

More people approach me, unbutton my shirt and, to their great surprise, see the bread I am hiding.

Someone gives me something to drink with a taste I can't recognise, and I recover quickly. All around me I see a lot of people, all Jews, fortunately, or so it seems. I am barely aware of the situation and reconstruct what happened, button up my shirt, stand up, thank them, and leave as quickly as possible for home, thanking God that no Germans have seen me.

I enter the house in silence and surprise my father sitting in a chair with his head in his hands. Today he seems more discouraged, so when he asks me, reading the fear and worry on my face, if anything has happened, I lie and tell him that everything is fine, everything as usual, and that we'll have something to eat today as well. I open my shirt and take out the bread I haven't managed to sell.

My father rests a hand on my back and sighs.

"Who knows what else will happen?"

"Indeed, Grandpa, recent events do not bode well."

In less than a year, Adolf Hitler had gained command of the German armed forces and, on 12 March, conquered Austria, which had been under the rule of the Kingdom of Prussia, incorporating it into Germany and bringing 125,000 Jews under Nazi regime.

Increasingly blinded by power and in a fit of omnipotence, Hitler announced his desire to incorporate the German-inhabited Czechoslovakian territories, the Sudetenland, into "greater Germany". On 29 September, the Munich Agreement was signed by Hitler, Mussolini and Chamberlain. As proposed by Mussolini, the agreement approved the incorporation of the Sudetenland into Germany, effective as of the following 10 October.

Czechoslovakia lost an area of more than 25,000 square kilometres, a region rich in mineral resources and of vital military importance, since it possessed a natural bulwark in the event of a possible German invasion.

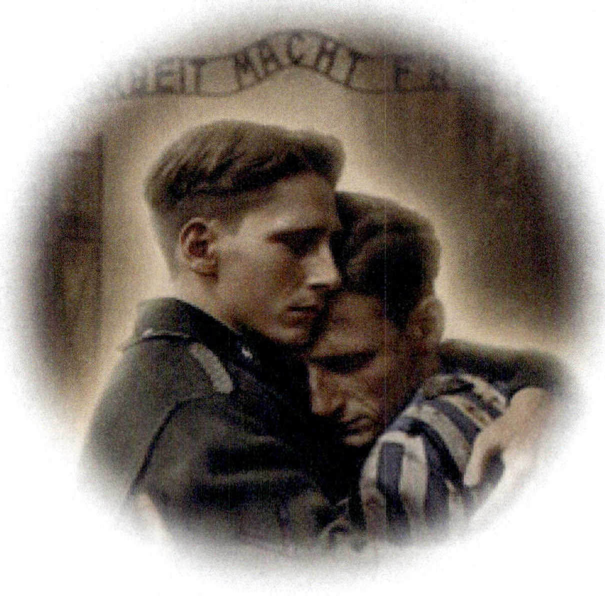
MACHT

30

"And, after having lost first all their rights and then all their property, the Jews also lost their names. From January 1939, by order of the Führer, all Jewish women had to be called 'Sara' and the men 'Israel'; the Germans did not need to differentiate them at all; for them, all Jews are the same, like a flock of sheep. Sounds terrible, they were all considered the same: dirty and no good... Jews! Jews! And that was only the beginning."

"But my destiny was different, I was different, I tried to convince myself that I should breathe and not die prematurely from panic. In fact, I had long had the feeling that someone was following me. I repeated to myself that it was the nightmares that were present, and I continued my pilgrimage, trying to sell a loaf of bread."

"Your nightmares were real, dear Grandpa."

On 1 September 1939, with Nazi Germany's attack on Poland, war breaks out. Hitler's expansionist policy was unstoppable.

Poland was the first stage towards the conquest of the whole of Eastern Europe. Thus, while on the Western Front, the French and Germans were fighting behind opposing fortification lines, Germany, in a blitzkrieg, with 2,700 tanks and paratroopers, defeated and conquered Poland. France and Great Britain immediately responded by declaring war on Germany, but were totally unprepared militarily.

Hitler split the army in two: one part occupied the Channel, the other headed towards France, defended by the English who were forced to retreat as the French arrived in defeat. From then on... Hell!

The world war had begun, an atrocious and endless war that claimed countless victims.

31

That feeling that I am being followed is not just a figment of my imagination and a latent fear that leaves me breathless and without reason. Probably, when I fainted, someone among the people who were present saw the bread and in exchange for some favour may have denounced me to the SS, or perhaps they followed me first to observe me and then denounced me…

In the evening, just before dusk, the Germans accompanied by their faithful German shepherds set off on a journey across the countryside to Colonel Offman's property. My father and I, as usual, are working with the oven at that time. It seems like any other evening, when suddenly my father hears noises coming from outside. My heart starts pounding harder and harder, as if it is about to burst out of my rib cage.

Without showing my uneasiness and anxiety, I put my ear to the old wooden door that separates us from the outside. I quickly grab two large buckets of water and turn off the oven; I do it in complete silence, trying to make as little noise as possible, and drag my father into the hole created under the oven.

My father understands everything, in the situation we find ourselves in, it doesn't take many words to understand each other. In silence, once inside the hole, I place the firewood that should cover the passage and we settle in the secret compartment created exclusively to deal with dangerous situations like this.

A few minutes after the arrival of those cars, two soldiers open the door violently. Right after that, General Becker enters and orders other soldiers to search the outside of the house with the help of the German shepherds specifically trained to do so.

Offman, after receiving the report, analysing all the details and hoping to clear his name and stay out of trouble, sensing the truth, suggested controlling that land and his house, which has been abandoned for a long time.

He stands in front of the door, impressed by the great changes the house has undergone. Silently, the general and the two soldiers begin to search the house, which, though small, is capable of providing good hiding places. After about three minutes of searching, Offman decides to shout:

"Thomas Potter, I know you're here, come out. It's an order!"

Becker stares at Offman, as if asking for an explanation. The colonel, keeping his voice too loud for me to hear, turns to the general and adds:

"Mr. General, Potter is a friend of my son's. He is a Jew whom I have never given the slightest importance because I consider him harmless, but he's the cause of the trouble in my family. I'll bet he has the same disease as Matt, don't you, Potter? Come out now!"

Hearing those words, despite the heat inside the oven, I break out in a cold sweat. I am relieved only because of my father's grip on my hand, which brings me back to reality, helping me to react even for his own good. I know those words are true, but no one else can confirm it except Matt, David and Anna, and none of them would ever betray me.

The situation in the oven is only getting worse. Since the fire has just been extinguished, the space we occupy is still hot and, in addition, the way the oven has been put out has generated so much smoke that it is almost impossible to breathe.

Feeling ignored, Alfons decides to continue his shouting, but the general immediately shuts him up.

"Offman, there's nobody in here, stop shouting!"

But the colonel knows he's not wrong, he knows I'm in there and decides to ignore the general's order. He begins to look cautiously at the oven, noticing that it is still hot and has been turned off in a hurry. He knows I can't have gone far. At that moment, the soldiers enter the house after having searched the area outside.

"General, we've searched the entire perimeter, but we haven't found anyone."

That statement reinforces the colonel's conviction that I am inside the house. He closely inspects the inside and outside of the oven, and orders the soldiers to light it. The guards point out to him that it is too damp and therefore cannot be lit.

But Offman doesn't give up.

"Go at once and get the can of petrol that is in the car. I've said this furnace must be lit, and so it will be."

The SS agents return with the can of petrol and manage to rekindle the embers. In the back, the air is becoming increasingly unbearable. It is not the smoke that bothers us, as it rises upwards and we are hidden at the bottom, it is the heat that is making us suffer.

I realise that my father is starting to breathe heavily, and the heat is practically cooking us alive, so I decide to leave the hiding place through that small opening covered with firewood.

"I knew I was right, but I didn't expect to find your father too."

Alfons Offman is now more than satisfied!

He has managed to arrest two Jews who were illegally trading on one of his properties. And, on top of that, he has managed to regain the confidence of General Becker, who could inform the higher echelons, and win a transfer to the camps.

32

"And at this point, history speeds up its course and, along with your story, Grandpa, the history of Europe is also speeding up."

Time ran fast. The war pressed on and embraced wider and wider areas. Mussolini was determined to help Germany, fighting on three fronts: in the Mediterranean, in North Africa and in East Africa. But he was defeated by English troops, and the Germans were forced to lend him a hand, not only in England, but also in Yugoslavia and Greece, which were fought off only thanks to German intervention.

After these victories, Hitler prepared to confront Russia. The attack began in 1941. The Germans managed to break into the territory, but the Russians, acting with cunning and intelligence, let them advance, waiting for winter to arrive. Hitler's soldiers, taken by surprise by the unimaginable cold, unable to withstand the snow and ice, were forced back by the terrible freezing cold.

Meanwhile, the Japanese, interested in controlling the Pacific area, attacked the American military base at Pearl Harbor and provoked the entry of the United States into the war. Having defeated the Japanese in several areas of the Pacific, in accordance with agreements made with the English, they began to fight the Germans.

On the home front, the war was no less ferocious. From 14 June 1940, the Auschwitz concentration camp was set up, where the number of prisoners was between 15,000 and 20,000.

On 3 September 1941, the deputy commandant, Karl Fritzsch, experimented with an anti-parasitic, Zyklon B gas, to exterminate 850 Jewish prisoners. From 8 October, Birkenau was operational, a vast camp in which more than 1.100.000 people, mostly Jews, Russians, Poles, prisoners of war, homosexuals, political opponents and Gypsies, would lose their lives.

The camp experience became a valuable testimony, because only those who have lived through it themselves and miraculously came out alive can know the whole truth.

"Ben, we and, if I'm not mistaken, not many of the German military, including Matt's father, really knew what was going on in there."

It's been a long time since Dad and I were interned in Berlin prison. Life here is not at all easy, but outside things are even more difficult.

We have no idea what is going on in the rest of the world, but we thank heaven that we have been allowed to live through these terrible days together. Together we survive, giving each other a little strength and courage. We joke, we make fun of how ridiculous and unkempt we look, and we say whole speeches to each other in rhyme; it is very distracting and helps us to build a parallel reality in which to take refuge; my father, in his saddest moments, recites poetry.

Although there is really little to have fun with, we hope that, when all this is over, at least our hearts can remain as they always were, given that our physical appearance has visibly worsened.

We haven't killed anyone. We don't deserve to spend our whole lives in jail. I suppose.

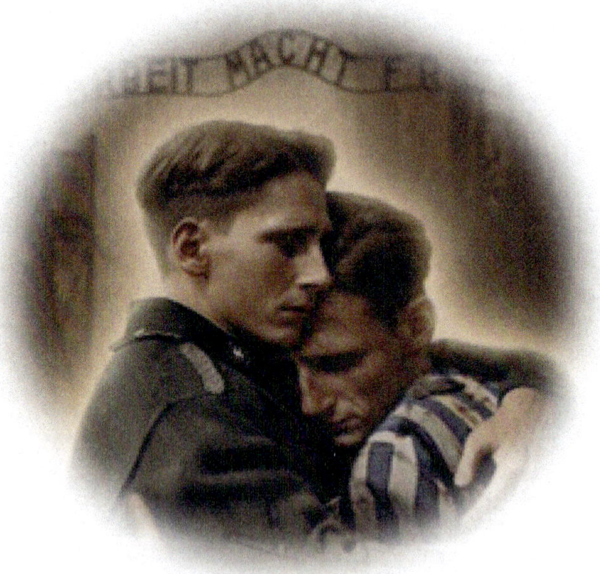
MACHT

33

The roar of bombers piercing the sky is continuous, we wonder if prison is a safe place or if we risk ending up like rats on a sinking ship.

Although the war ravages outside, nothing changes in our dungeon, except today. This morning, we smelled something strange. Outside the cells there is a lot of commotion, more shouting than usual, and planes are constantly flying over the walls.

"Potter, on your feet! Hurry up, we have to go."

An SS guard, in an unfriendly tone, orders us to leave. Convinced that this is about our freedom, I ignore the guard's manner of speaking and, euphoric, rush to wake up my father, who is still asleep.

"Dad, hurry up, wake up, I think we're being released. Come on, we're going home at last."

The agent, who doesn't like my euphoria at all, tries to destroy it with a few words:

"Home? You no longer own a house. Neither you nor any of your people. You're just being relocated. We have created more suitable places for your kind."

I can't even close my mouth in amazement. My father, resigned and still drowsy, decides to follow me without saying a word. When we reach the exit, we are ordered to line up in pairs and follow the guard.

As we walk, other groups of people join the already existing line, including children and women. Along the way, we see familiar places, full of memories, moving away.

In the distance, a park bench catches our attention. We are near the clinic. It is the same bench where my father and I promised to always support each other after my mother's tragic death. And this bench, once again, is a silent witness to the renewal of that promise.

The walk lasts about thirty minutes, until we finally arrive at a station. We are ordered to wait for a train that will arrive in a few minutes, but the minutes multiply until they become hours; hours of waiting in the street, unable to drink, eat or pee, and all in silence, a silence marred by a terrible commotion.

I try to find out something about what has happened while we were locked up, but I only manage to collect unconvincing and disorganised stories because some time ago everyone here was banned from having any kind of electronic device, such as a radio. Each of them tries, in a low voice, to contribute to the conversation, so, little by little, the puzzle is pieced together.

My father seems confused. He keeps trying to find out more and more, but he only gets bad news.

'They are taking us to a labour camp'. 'Now they will make us do forced labour'. 'They will kill all those who can't work'.

These are only suppositions, voices, the echo of terror, but my father knows that, if they were true, he would have nothing to worry about, he is aware that he is sloppy, but he can still work. He has done so all his life, though at the sight of that crowd of children, pregnant women or women his age or, worse, the sick and crippled, he shudders. He wishes it were only hearsay, rumours stemming from fear of the unknown.

No one is sure of what they say, they rely on a "heard say". It cannot and must not all be true. They cannot exterminate an entire race. It is true that Hitler has many followers, but no one in their right mind would back him in this madness.

In the meantime, the train arrives; one only has to look at it to realise that it is too small for all these people.

The prisoners, unaware of the train's final destination, begin to become impatient.

Those who have been famous doctors, bank managers, jewellers, fruit sellers or bakers, and many other things, are now nothing more than a bunch of people who really stink, tremble with fear... and don't know what the future holds for them.

On the journey, you see people whimpering everywhere. I am terrified since I discovered that people are killed in the middle of the street by the SS for no good reason. One man told me what happened when they entered his flat to deport them.

They were ordered to leave the house in one minute, not a second more, not a second less, taking with them only their most precious possessions; anyone found inside the house after the minute had elapsed would be killed.

The man lived with his wife, his two daughters, aged two and five, and his father, a seventy-five-year-old man who had lost a leg during the First World War. Noting his father's difficulty in getting around, he decided to help him take a suitcase with little clothing and an old photograph of his mother taken on their wedding day.

He reassured his father that he would carry the suitcase, but he also had to hold the child, so he asked him to lean on him and move as quickly as possible. The soldier started counting down from ten.

Adam, the man who is telling me about it, breaks out in a cold sweat. Worried about the girl, he asked his father to keep moving on his own, that he would come back for him as soon as he got the girl to safety. He went downstairs, his only thought was to get little Lussy out of the house and back as quickly as possible so he could save his father. He hurried out of the building...

As soon as he stepped through the doorway, a gunshot rang in the family's ears. One of the girls, the oldest, burst into tears. The man who had just emerged from those walls with his little girl still in his arms, turned around wishing he could see her father behind him, but he did not. He confirmed the fact with a simple sentence uttered by an SS officer as he left the dwelling: 'That mutilated man would have been of no use to us'.

As the story ends, Adam's face fills with tears. The man, a father of two girls, weeps silently. How can he care for his family now that he does not have the power to do so? My father, who fully understands how Adam feels at this moment, gives him a big hug with a heavy heart.

"Son, I'm so sorry, there are no words to describe what happened to you, I only ask you to be strong! You must do it for your wife and for your two girls."

Dad tries to be supportive; he knows there is no consolation for such a situation, but showing solidarity, perhaps, can help.

During the journey, each passenger has a terrible story to share, but either way they all consider themselves lucky to be alive. There is talk of abuse, murder and even suicide.

After all, I feel strangely fortunate to have spent the last few days in prison. Not knowing the destination of this journey creates confusion for many passengers and for one in particular, nicknamed 'the Madman'. The fact that he knows nothing disturbs him, for him it is something impossible to bear.

"We'll all die. They'll burn us alive, work us to death. We're all the talking dead," he shouts often, but only when a moment of silence is created.

The fear and desperation are evident in everyone, but that boy seems to have been put there on purpose to make the situation worse, which is bad enough as it is.

The train stops several times to allow even more passengers to board. Although the carriages are packed to capacity, more people are pushed inside, turning what was already a harrowing journey into an impossible one for many.

It is not possible to sit down, we are piled on top of each other, the heat is suffocating. The only water that arrives is that which the SS agents spray from outside the train through the tiny windows of the carriages. People crowd together to try to get at least a small drop.

The stench of sweat, urine and vomit prevails.

After almost twenty hours, the train with an unknown destination stops.

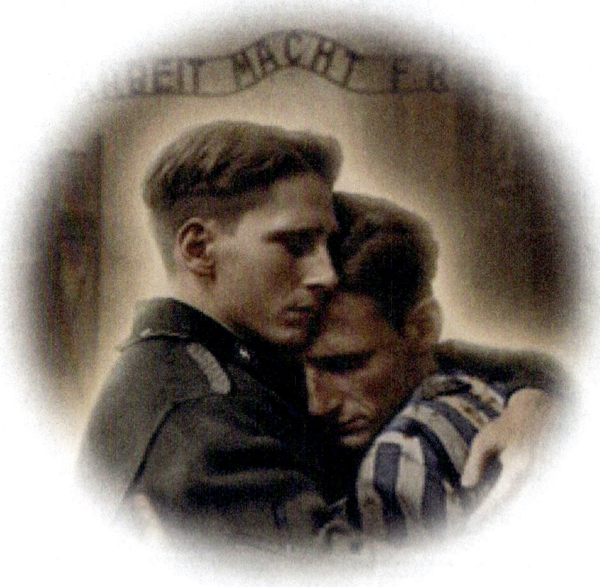
EIT MACHT F

34

A whistle orders all the passengers to get off. Unaware of what awaits them, people rush in desperately, creating great confusion.

My attention is immediately drawn to some chimneys emanating a strange sweet smell that I can't identify, despite being an expert on ovens. When I see them, I smile, a smile that is immediately erased by the circumstances. If I had thought my oven was big, I now know that there are much, much bigger ovens. Who knows how much bread they can bake in there!

I take Dad by the arm, to make sure I don't lose sight of him, but something disturbs me: the Madman. He's about to get off the train when someone behind pushes him, makes him stumble to the ground and they stomp on him several times. I didn't see him get up, and, without thinking too much about it, I continue on my way with my dad.

As soon as we get off the train, the men are separated from the women and children. An officer, perhaps a doctor, walks past us, scanning us one by one in detail. When he touches or points at someone, other officers move them and line them up in another row in front of us.

Among the SS there are men in striped pyjamas who, strangely enough, are not treated as prisoners. It is obvious that the commandant is the doctor who, in his white coat and rather friendly demeanour, gives the impression of being a very kind man. He speaks softly, caresses the children's faces and accompanies the women when he decides to move them to the front row.

None of us here can imagine that this man is actually deciding our fate, confirming our immediate death sentence. I am almost at the end of this long row, continuing to hold my father's hand tightly, praying to God not to let them separate us in the same way they have done to a lot of families present, separating husbands, wives or children without any apparent explanation.

The doctor is about to arrive in front of my father when he is suddenly distracted by the barking of a dog, which is dragging an SS officer forcefully towards the rails. Wary, he calls in more agents to get a better grip on him. They stand in a semicircle around the place indicated by the dog, and one of them shouts in an authoritative tone:

"We know you're under there. You've got five seconds to get out, otherwise you'll come out dead. One... two..."

The officer doesn't get to three when the Madman comes out of the rails under the astonished gaze of everyone. If up to that moment I thought he wasn't so crazy, now I'm absolutely sure he's a madman.

The doctor, who was inspecting those who had just arrived, approaches the man to get a better look at him, orders him to stand up, and finds that he does so with great difficulty. The SS officer, the next highest-ranking after the doctor, sighs nervously at the scene: he would have liked to teach him a good lesson right there in front of everyone, but he knows he can't do it.

Before it all goes to hell, the doctor decides to take matters into his own hands, gives the madman a hand and accompanies him to the front row of women with small children, the elderly and the sick. But the officer is not satisfied, he wants to make him pay and has other plans. So, rudely, he orders him to stand in the row of those who seem to be in good health. The doctor, at that moment, understands everything and, with a wry smile, continues to select the rest of the men.

My heart, inexplicably, begins to race as the doctor, passing in front of my father, after looking him straight in the eye, continues his walk and moves on to the next man: me.

The moment I come face to face with the doctor I realise that it is really me who is in danger. Until that moment, I had seen my father as an old and needy man, but now, for the first time, I see in him a strong man, tall and sturdy, unlike me, skinny and weak.

Suddenly, my old father is no longer old, but rather a man who has fought in the war, who has overcome the terrible loss of his beloved wife and who has always worked to ensure a decent life for me.

I would like to beat myself up for thinking, even for a moment, that my father could not have survived without me, but in reality it is the opposite. Between the two of us, I am the one in danger.

Despite all my doubts, and my thoughts, the doctor, after having touched my arm muscles, moves on to the next man who, unfortunately, is not as lucky as I am.

Once the selection is over, the group of old people, invalids, women with disabilities or very young children, are asked to leave their belongings on the train benches and are told that, after a shower and a hot soup, they will be able to retrieve them again. In a line of five, they are made to the 'showers'.

When they arrive in the changing room, they are asked to take off all their clothes and place them on hangers whose number they must remember to avoid confusion when they return from the shower. To further reassure them, pieces of soap and towels are distributed. Once inside, the doors are closed for a few minutes. When they open them again, no one comes out alive.

"They were gas chambers, Grandpa!"
"That's right, Ben. Let me go on."

The second group, to which we belong, are forced into trucks. While Dad is standing in line, he asks me if I can imagine where we are. I shrug my shoulders, but the answer comes clearly from one of the SS agents in the back:

"We are in Poland, in Birkenau."

Everyone looks at each other, indifferent, because none of them knows that they are actually in an extermination camp. The smell emanating from the chimneys reveals the truth, but only to the most attentive. The trucks leave loaded with people, unaware of their next destination. This time, the load brought by the train has been halved. Barely three kilometres in, when the caravan stops for the umpteenth time: no one knows it will be the last.

I thank God that I am still with my father. I don't know what the future holds, but with him I know I can face it all. No one here can know what is really going on, but once we arrive at the new building, many breathe a sigh of relief.

A sign welcomes us to the new camp: *Arbeit macht frei*[4]. It is confirmation that we are here to work.

I tell myself that, if I manage to work hard enough and well enough, even if I know I won't be released, at least I won't be killed.

---

4 Work frees.

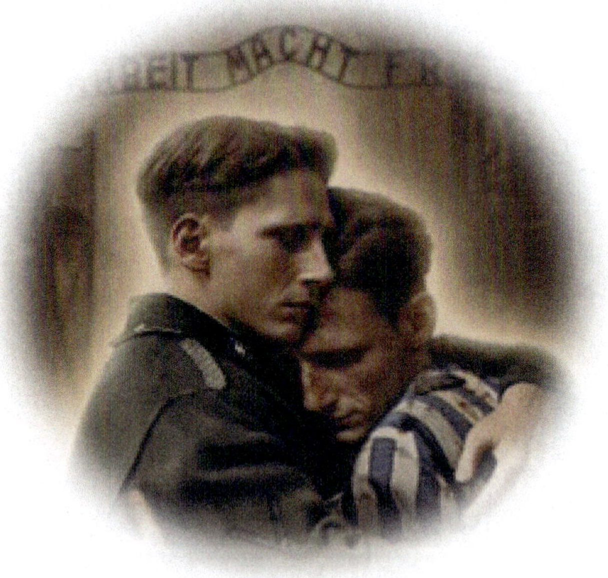
BEIT MACHT F

35

Once past the threshold of the camp, the women are tearfully separated from the men. They were asked to hand over everything they had: documents, suitcases and all their accessories, except for their trouser belts and a cloth handkerchief.

We are forced to undress completely and a barber waits for us with a razor to shave all parts of our bodies, including our private parts. Immediately afterwards, we are taken to the showers, where we are washed in the worst possible way: ice-cold water alternating with boiling water. We all panic.

Many of those present have already heard of the gas chambers, and this moment foreshadows what for many is to come.

Cries everywhere, everyone is terrified: my father and I start to get nervous too. In prison we have lost all contact with reality and with what is really happening in Germany and in the whole world, with the Jews and the other minorities; that is precisely why we are the most sensible among those present, but to see all these men crying out of fear or despair at having lost their family, perhaps forever, is heartbreaking. I wonder why bother shaving and washing us if we are going to be killed afterwards.

On top of that, there is the Madman who shouts nervously:

"You see I was right? We're all going to be murdered. And I was the crazy one, wasn't I?"

Although it's terrible, the showers are carried out without any victims and quickly. The shaved body parts are disinfected with damp cloth and a disinfectant liquid. Then we are handed dirty striped pyjamas that do not fit us. Finally, a pair of heavy wooden clogs. But the torture does not end there. Each of us had a number tattooed on our left forearm, which from then on would be our name.

We are ordered to learn it by heart, and all foreigners are forced to learn to pronounce it in German so that they can recognise each other when they are called. Apart from the tattoo, the same number is sewn on the jackets and trousers of each prisoner, accompanied by a symbol that has a specific colour, depending on the category of the detainee. We, being Jewish, have a yellow triangle, but I still don't know if, being a homosexual, I should have had a pink one as well. Finally, we are asked to fill in a form with our personal details.

After registration, all the men are taken to old barracks called Block where there are many three-bed bunks. Block 21, where my father and I are taken, is quite large, but not large enough to guarantee a bed for each individual. The number of men sleeping there is beastly, some beds are shared between three, and others are strangely empty.

New arrivals are ordered to share a bed with at least two or three other people and to make themselves comfortable at each other's feet. My father takes my arm and positions me on an already occupied bed. He seems to be a decent, if dirty, malnourished man, like all the rest, but he is young and, seeing him alone,

Carl's paternal instinct is released. Strictly in German, they explain to us some rules that we must respect if we don't want to be punished.

The prisoners, once the commotion is over, are allowed to go to the toilet.

Once inside the latrines, I am literally shocked: a very long concrete platform, about ten centimetres high, wide enough to contain two rows of holes, with nothing, and dirt underneath. There is no water and a disturbing writing informs: *Eine Laus ist dein Tod*[5].

5 *A louse is your death*

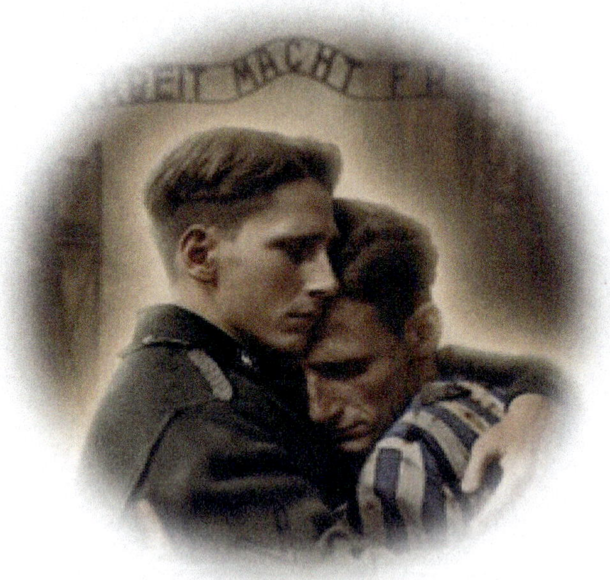
MACHT

36

It is nine o'clock in the evening when the SS, before leaving, announce that the Block is now closed. Dad, finally breathing again, decides to introduce himself to his bedside neighbour, trying to understand more about the atmosphere around him.

"I'm Carl and this is my son Tom. What's your name?"

"I'm number 12590; you are no longer Carl, just as he is no longer Tom."

I look down, as if I've been scolded.

The boy is right, from now on we can't make a mistake. I am no longer Tom or Israel, now my father and I are a number and, if we forget it, the punishment is death.

Very early in the morning, after we have tidied up that mass of straw called bed, we are sent to the labour camps. Dad and I are sent to the coal mines.

After the lousy night I spent because of the bed, the terror of what we are about to experience, the stench in this room and also the fact that I slept with the unclean feet of a perfect stranger practically in my face, I don't feel ready for this kind of work, I find it exhausting.

I haven't slept a wink all night, even though I'm used to getting little sleep; after all, I'm a baker and an early riser. Besides, in view of the number of SS men ready to stimulate the detainees with extreme violence, I decide I'd better hurry up and do things properly.

While I work listlessly, dad does it with great commitment and dedication, he seems to have been born to do this job.

I look at him with great admiration. After my mother's death, I have always seen him as weak and in need of help, but these last few days I have realised how wrong I was: my father is actually a lion.

After ten long hours of gruelling work and a tiny plate of onion soup with a piece of stale bread, we are allowed to return to the barracks to rest. The straw bed could not be more comfortable.

37

Before entering the block, we are introduced to a man we must obey. He is an individual in a prisoner's uniform, not very tall and rather robust, who immediately arouses my curiosity: how is it that a man in our uniform can be so robust? And, above all, why does this man have so much power, if he is also a prisoner like us?

The answers are not long in coming.

My bedmate, hearing us whispering, decides to intervene, revealing everything he knows.

"That's our Kapo. He's a murderer, and that's why he was brought to the concentration camps, but, being German, he enjoys certain privileges. His duty is to keep us in order, and in return he is offered enough food and a few other favours..."

I can't believe my ears, a privileged murderer? A murderer who enjoys favours just because he is a German!

"You see, Grandpa, I was just telling you... Then I don't understand why Matt had to go through all that he went through... By the way, did you hear any more news from him?"

"Be patient, Ben, and let me continue..."

This murderer is tasked with ensuring discipline and, if necessary, killing Jews just because they don't do what he orders. What I hear is really terrible, but I have the feeling that it doesn't end there.

"What kind of favours are you talking about?"

The words come out of my mouth with great indignation. 125901 seems concerned, but deep down we are all in the same boat and it is better to be informed about what might happen.

"You have to know that every Kapo chooses his man, a man with whom he can have sexual fun whenever he wants…"

At that moment, Dad, who is God-fearing and has a great sense of decency, dignity and a deep respect for people, incredulous, opens his eyes wide.

"Excuse me? A man with another man? Why not choose a woman?"

A small chuckle escapes me, my father is so straight that just the idea of being with another man, even in this period of extreme deprivation, is incomprehensible to him. Who knows how he would react if he found out that I was gay and that my great love was a man called David.

"Yes, Grandpa, but about this David, after you told me about your first meeting, you haven't told me anything more."

"Ben, either be patient or we'll leave it here."

Ben gets angry, and Anna decides to intervene.

"You can't even imagine how bad your grandfather and I feel when we remember those days. Our dignity doesn't allow us to express all our pain and despair. Don't be angry if your grandfather has raised his voice, believe me that this story he is giving you, emotionally speaking, has a very high price."

"Forgive me, Grandpa, I won't interrupt you anymore. Go on!"

After that fleeting thought, I listen again to my fellow captive. There is one thing that doesn't sit right with me in the speech, and I ask:

"How can a man be allowed to choose if homosexuality is condemned?"

"They simply believe that gay relationships are dirty and sick, while those between straight people are considered innocent because they serve to compensate for an absence."

My father and I exchanged disturbed glances.

125901 bursts out laughing at the sight of us with completely different expressions. Carl, shocked and outraged by those words; me, disgusted, wondering why the difference. The boy has been in the camp for so long that it's hard for him to remember when it all seemed strange to him too, but eventually it all becomes normal; it's as if one gets used to these strange and terrible things.

"Listen, I apologise if I've disturbed you with what I've said, but I swear that being Kapo's favourite is not a bad thing, quite the contrary..."

"Boy, how can you talk like that? Of course, it's a bad thing! It's an abuse in every way!"

Dad still can't accept those words and tries to bring the boy, who apparently is not averse to the situation, to his senses.

"It's obvious that you've only been here for a short time! In a place like this, where surviving even one more day is an achievement, if someone offers you an escape route like a little extra food or, who knows, a bit of soap, giving him sex in return is not such a bad thing."

I am increasingly curious:

"You talk as if you want to be the chosen one."

"Indeed I am."

Carl can't believe it, 125901 has surrendered to war. This boy of tender age, who made a number his name, has submitted himself to another man just to survive and, what's worse, seems to have no dreams or desires. His gaze is empty, his words are apathetic and, above all, he is indifferent to his surroundings.

Dad decides he should not judge him, but prays that God will come to his aid. Never have his prayers that God will come to his aid. Never have is prayers been so intense.

38

After a month in captivity, I begin to bond with little 125901, who for everyone is the Chosen One. At that time, I also appreciate my Kapo. He looks like a real bastard when he is in the company of the SS: he offends, spits, hits everyone, even 'his Chosen One', but deep down he is not so bad. He allows his ward to bring more food into the blocks to share with the other prisoners and, when someone gets sick, he lets him bring medicine. I was convinced of his good heart once, when he called the Chosen One in the middle of the night, as is often the case, to satisfy his wishes.

It seems like any other night, nothing indicates that, in reality, tonight it will not be the Kapo who will satisfy his desires, but that it will be the Chosen One who will satisfy one of his own.

It's nine o'clock, I'm in bed when, together with Dad and our barrack mate, we realise that something is going to change.

125901, next to me on the edge of the bed, looks impatient and strangely happy. I don't immediately notice this enthusiasm because I'm distracted listening to the strange noises that seem to be coming from outside the camp, like screams. It is an undefined sound, difficult to reproduce. Intrigued, I ask the Chosen One who, with a strange smile, answers me that it is the 'Singing Forest', insinuating that it is something good, but he does not have time to explain because his Kapo orders him to leave immediately.

My father and I can't understand him. After a few hours, during which I slept, three SS men burst into the cellblock.

"Everybody out! You have ten seconds!"

Drowsily, we get up of what everyone now calls 'bed' and rush out of the barracks in the shortest possible time.

In front of us, there are some German officers and two soldiers trying to pull the almost dying Kapo to his feet.

"Something unacceptable has happened tonight. One of those things that we hope, for your sake, will never happen again."

From his tone of voice, the SS officer seems to be furious, but no one present understands what could have happened.

"A detainee escaped," continues the SS officer.

All the detainees begin to look at each other, hiding their satisfaction as best they can. The SS officer continues abruptly:

"Don't rejoice too much because he won't get very far. The SS agents will have already arrested him and, obviously, killed him."

We all look around to find out who is missing, and it is clear that the little Chosen One is not there: his place is empty, he is the fugitive.

"I'm sure by now you've figured out who it is. We think that your Kapo has let his Chosen One escape. Now I imagine that many of you will want to see this man dead, so, why don't you tell us that number 125901 was his Chosen One? Come on!"

I look at everyone else, they are petrified, no one

has the guts to open their mouths. It is obvious that the Kapo is a bastard, but we are not so bad off with him either. He has given us food and medicine, and only beats us when ordered to do so by an SS agent. He is not the worst evil in here.

All the detainees in Block 21 have the chance to take out a nasty German son of a bitch, but none of them think he is the right person.

So, very scared, but sure that no one will tell on me, I step forward, keeping my head down.

"I'm sorry, I'm his Chosen One. Tonight, Kapo was with me."

The man, bruised and bloody, opens his eyes in surprise. He finds it hard to believe. Without further questioning, all the detainees start nodding, confirming my words, except my father. He cannot believe his ears. His heart races for fear of the consequences. Then, suddenly, it all becomes clear to him. I am a good boy, and if I have told these lies, I have done it to save this man's life - even if he is German!

Right now, Carl is proud of me.

At this point, the SS officers throw the bleeding Kapo to the ground; the officer crouches down close to his ear.

"We give you one last chance just because you're the son of one of our own! Next mistake, consider yourself dead."

The man, lying on the ground, nods his head, leaving us speechless. Then the SS officer, addressing the prisoners, orders him to be taken inside.

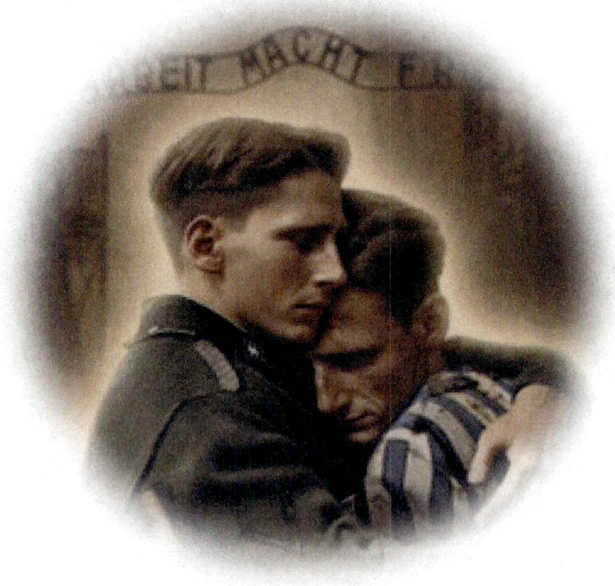
MACHT

39

"Grandpa, did you see the Madman again? Do you know what happened to him? Sorry if I've interrupted you!"

"Yes, Ben. About a week after his admission to the Auschwitz concentration camp, Putti Gad, christened from the outset the Madman, despite having behaved like a perfect, hard-working, untroubled inmate, was transferred from Block 24 to Block 17, also called the 'Death Block.'"

The Madman was not really a real madman, but for some reason he knew and announced to the other prisoners what was going to happen. That was why, in order not to go crazy because of that anticipated reality, I preferred to believe that he was actually mad, rather than believe what he was saying.

After what he had done on the rails in Birkenau, Putti knew he would not get away with it, but he did not understand why they waited so long to kill him, until one morning, when he woke up, he found the same SS officer standing in front of him who had pardoned him that day in Birkenau.

As soon as he opened his eyes, he knew that his end would not be quick and painless like that of the prisoners exterminated in the gas chambers, but much more cruel and painful.

Like every day, he was sent to forced labour, but at night, instead of his well-deserved rest, a very special treatment awaited him: hanging on a crossbeam.

They grabbed him by force. He twitched nervously as he tried futilely to save his life, or else to bring about his death more quickly. They dragged him out of the camp and reached a forest next to the camp, to be exact: on the other side of the barbed wire fence through which electric current was passing. It seemed that in that dark and terrifying place, even the wind was screaming in pain.

Among the trees a small grotto was formed where two large poles had been planted, and, in these, men were tied up, though they were no longer men, but human larvae awaiting sentence.

While the Madman was still writhing, they tied him to some poles; he was suspended in the air so that his feet did not touch the ground. They reserved for him one of the most atrocious procedures: spinning him around.

Inhuman screams and moans spread rapidly through the branches of the forest, over the barbed wire and into the camp. The inhuman chanting pierced the gates of the Block, penetrating the souls of the prisoners, causing them an anguish that was more suffocating than death itself.

When the soldiers had exhausted themselves spinning him around, suspended between the poles, they went away, leaving him there with the tips of his feet unable to touch the ground... until dawn.

The condemned were alone, like Christ and the thieves: the Madman and two other men, one on his right and one on his left.

During the night, he began to falter and the screams were uncontainable. The desire to abandon himself, to let himself die was strong for Gad, but the spirit of survival was even stronger.

He was about to leave when Walter, the SS man who wished him dead, realised that he was still alive... Agonising. Three men had been hanged, but he was the only one who had held out.

"I think you're the only man so far to survive the 'Singing Forest'! Congratulations!"

Walter, one of the youngest SS officers, recruited only a year earlier, loved to play with the detainees. That was what he loved about his job, that was the beauty of war.

He was especially excited that day, he was approaching his eighteenth birthday, and just at that moment he had the perfect opportunity to celebrate it properly.

It was about half an hour before the rest of the detainees left the camp for work, so he decided to release the Madman, under the watchful eye of a fellow sentinel. Walter approached the dying prisoner and whispered to him:

"Escape as fast as you can. Get up and run, go! Take the forest path, there you'll find salvation. I'm sorry for what I have put you through. Believe me, I'm sorry and I want to make it right."

Putti could not believe it, assumed he had auditory hallucinations and did not dare to take a single step, but the SS agent continued to pressure him. The Madman, thinking that the soldier had truly repented for what he had done and wished to free himself from his guilt, summoned all his strength, aided by the adrenalin triggered by the desire for freedom, and, limping from the excruciating pain in his legs, began to run along the path that his executioner had indicated to him.

A hundred or perhaps a hundred and fifty metres was the distance he managed to cover when a shot to the head stopped him. After the sentinel declared that he had seen the prisoner escape and that the SS officer, by shooting, had merely prevented his escape, young Walter was not only rewarded with a day off on his birthday, but was also applauded for his responsible and immaculate behaviour.

40

It has been several months since we entered the labour camp. By the way, they couldn't have come up with a more appropriate name, given that there is nothing to do in here but sweat and starve. Also, 'concentration camp' is a perfectly appropriate name. Thanks to my instinctive act of daring and altruism, we have survived Camp 11.

Sunday is the only day off for those who work in the mines and, therefore, it is the only day I live inside the camp, witnessing all the atrocities taking place.

At this point in the story, Anna can't hold back the tears and Ben, out of respect, turns off the camcorder, taking advantage of the pause to change the memory card, which is almost full. Anna walks away, perhaps to wash her face or get a glass of water.

With his voice cracking, pretending that everything is fine.

Ben breaks the silence:

"Grandpa, I'm ready. If you want, we can start again."

"Of course..."

It is Sunday and I am woken up by the chaos outside my barracks. The SS officers order us to get up and rush out into the courtyard, which is only a few metres away.

There is a large number of detainees lined up in a

semicircle. In front of them, three dogs on leashes and five SS men holding a detainee.

It is not unusual for someone to be shot just to set an example and deter the other prisoners; every time we are called outside, we all look at each other to find out whether it was one of us or a prisoner from another block.

But now it is different: in the centre of the courtyard is a naked man sitting tied to a chair. The SS agents immediately make it clear what is about to happen.

"Detainees, you are here to witness something very important. Now you will see what happens to fags, to serve as a lesson to all of you.

This man, apart from being a fucking fag, has infected a full-blooded German, which is why he deserves to die in the worst possible way. This disease must be nipped in the bud."

This time, I feel very affected, although nobody here knows it, not even my father. Every time I hear about torture inflicted on homosexuals, I am ashamed to the core and feel like a coward because, in order to protect myself, I am denying who I really am.

As I'm not very tall, it's hard for me to see what's going on, but suddenly a gap opens up in the crowd and I freeze completely. It's Matt!

The man standing with his hands tied, forcibly held by an SS officer, looks like Matt.

Willing to make sure that who I have seen is really my best friend, long gone, I move closer and closer, trying to make my way through the mute and unwavering crowd.

I walk through the crowd, hoping with all my heart that it's not really him. I hope I've imagined it, deep down I miss him so much that a hallucination would be acceptable and predictable. Maybe it's all in my imagination, I think to myself when I hear a strange noise. Three dogs, purebred German shepherds, big and strong, start barking at the poor naked boy tied to the chair.

The Germans spill raw meat from a can over his body; the dogs, smelling and seeing the blood, pull desperately to pounce on the food.

The soldiers place a metal bucket on the prisoner's head and, immediately afterwards, release the beasts, who throw themselves into the pile of dead and living flesh, immediately biting the man in front of everyone, just because he is gay.

Desperate cries of pain tear through the air and reach our consciousness like piercing blades.

That man is almost certainly Peter, the doctor. Although I can't get a good look at Matt, I have no doubts now.

A dog bites Peter's private parts, right in front of his beloved's eyes, at the same time as another one goes for his arm, and the other one, for his hip, tearing him to death; a slow and painful death, too painful even for us, who receive each new violence as a personal death and nothing serves to anaesthetise the soul.

Matt's screams, wanting to die too, and those of Peter, no longer able to bear the pain, pierce my heart and ears like sharp nails that come in like violent projectiles.

I burst into tears; my eyes completely blurred as I lose sight of my beloved Matt. They take him away, unconscious, who knows where, while the dogs continue to eat that body, like lions do with gazelles.

"But... but Peter is... is... dead," stammers Ben, who, though he has never met him, has learned to love him from Grandpa's stories. Although the narration has been clear, he asks because he can't believe what he has just heard.

"Yes, Ben, Peter died a slow and excruciating death, torn to pieces by the dogs who bit and tore his flesh to shreds, and ate all his pieces."

Ben gags at the story.

"Are you all right, Ben?"

"Yes, Grandpa, I'm sorry, it's all very strong." He takes a deep breath. "Go on."

Anna returns to the living room with two steaming cups of tea for her and me. Ben still hasn't finished his hot chocolate.

> About a week has passed, I have searched for Matt everywhere, even at the risk of getting into trouble, but he is nowhere to be found. For all those I asked, Matt is just a fag who was not murdered because he is German; indeed, between the two of them, the only one who was slaughtered in front of everyone was the gay Jew.
>
> I know they're probably right, but they can't even imagine that Matt would have preferred a thousand times to die rather than see Peter die, and probably, if he hasn't been killed already, he'll be dead in life, a corpse crawling around waiting for death to take him into the arms of his beloved.
>
> It is a cold December morning in Poland, the weather is freezing. Besides being malnourished, I am desperate and psychologically devastated. Today, like every day, I am working in the mine. They are prepa-

ring a big load of coal for me to carry out, but I don't feel strong enough to carry it all at once, so I decide to divide the weight. But I didn't know that an SS guard was watching me. A kick in the hip knocks me to the ground and leaves me breathless.

"Hey, are you trying to be clever, you fucking Jew?"

Those screams reach the ears of all the detainees, but none of them have the guts to look up to find out what is going on, it would be too risky.

I barely manage to raise my head while thinking what to say, how to justify myself, when another kick hits me in exactly the same place.

The pain is terrible.

Carl and the other SS officers come over immediately. Dad can tell that I'm in serious condition, from the shortness of breath, from the colour of my pain-stricken face; he's sure that I've broken a bone. He also realises that the situation is getting out of control and that, if I remain lying on the ground, I could be kicked to death or shot in the head with a shotgun. Dad would die for me.

He bursts in front of the soldier who is slaughtering me and shouts at him:

"Stop it, stop it! I beg you, he's just tired."

None of those present among the SS and the prisoners would ever bet that I would recover; I'm already dead to them all. Many much more robust men did not make it through the three months, why should a man like me, so thin and emaciated, make it through?

I faint amidst Carl's pleas.

One of the SS officers, who has just arrived, watches me lying on the floor, passed out, as if I were dead: he can't believe his eyes. Without giving many explanations, hiding his own emotions well, he orders the other guards to leave, he will take care of the corpse. He congratulates my executioner, who must have been his subordinate:

"Well done, now restore calm, I'll take care of this human larva that is more dead than alive."

He thus avoids giving further explanations and decreeing my death or my salvation. In this way, he would have to take me to be cured and return me to the Block without arousing suspicion or, in the best-case scenario, let me escape. Poor deluded man!

The SS agents walk away, ignoring Carl's desperate cries.

"Tom, Tom, can you hear me?"

Carl can't believe it, the soldier not only pronounces his son's real name, but what's even stranger... he knows him.

The soldier, very kindly, asks him to move away so as not to arouse suspicion because, from that moment on, he will do everything he can to save my life. My father doesn't know who he is or how he knows me, but his sixth sense tells him that he must trust and, after giving me a kiss, dirty with blood and coal, he walks away without saying anything

41

Without allowing much time to elapse, just long enough to get to the camp, trying to remain unnoticed, David runs to the doctor to see me.

The doctor is an old man, with un-German features, not at all gentle. After examining me in front of David, who tries to hide his worried look, he walks away and diagnoses me.

"This man has a broken rib, but that's not the problem. He's on his last legs, he's too tired and malnourished to survive in here; in short, he's doomed to die, so it's best to finish him off right away."

After a moment, just long enough to come to terms with the bad news, David tries to find out more, keeping his tone cold and distant, though his eyes betray him.

"Doctor, but is there really nothing to do?"

The doctor becomes suspicious and nervous - why would a German want to know more about the state of health of a fucking Jew?

"I've just said he is exhausted and malnourished, like all the prisoners in the camp. What do you intend to do? Let him rest for a month and feed him? He's a sick man, therefore useless. We have no use for guys like him. Killing him is the only solution. Take him immediately to the gas chamber."

David realises he can't keep his cool any longer, so he decides to play along - the doctor has inadvertently given him all the instructions to save my life anyway.

"When you leave here, you must call the Sonderkommando and send him to his destination."

"The Sonderkommando, Grandpa?"
"Yes, I thought you had studied it: prisoners ordered to rehabilitate those destined for the gas chambers, then burned. It had to be done secretly, without giving the victim any hint of what was in store. If anything escaped from their mouths, they were killed."

If David wants to save me, he must find a quick solution.

"Perfect, doctor, I will take the prisoner and drag him out without giving him to understand what will happen, and then hand him over to the Sonderkommando."

The doctor has no reason to distrust a German and nods without even raising his head, waiting for them to leave the room at once and let the next prisoner in.

Turning to me, David says gruffly.

"Come on, fleabag, get up, we're going back to the Block. And don't complain about the pain, you're lucky to be alive."

Then he pulls me towards him, even though I struggle to stand up. Once outside, he doesn't call out to anyone, he grabs me under his arm so he can pick up the pace. He remembers an old, half-destroyed barracks, and that's where he takes me.

When prisoners walk with a German soldier, no one usually asks questions because the answers can be uncomfortable. Many soldiers take prisoners away to torture them, whip them and have fun with them.

If anyone sees us, they will probably think that David will do the same.

We reach the barracks, though with every step I take, my broken rib is riddling my flesh. That journey seems endless to me.

From the looks of the building, it must have been an old infirmary, but it's almost empty. Half the roof is missing and it stinks. The dampness is such that fungus is growing on the wooden walls. Once there, now that he has finally found me, he is willing to do anything for me, even risk his life.

After having slept for a whole day, I finally wake up. I'm alone... and I don't understand where I am.

I try to remember what happened, but it's all very confusing. I try to stand up, but a pain in my side prevents me from doing so, so I start to remember some things: the coal, the kicks, my father and also him, the man I have loved most in my whole life. It's probably a dream, it can't have really happened. That can't be the man I'm madly in love with, no.

It can't be my beloved David. How did I get to this place?

I even have blankets. Someone tried to make a bed, with a straw mattress and a blanket, and I even have more blankets to cover myself. One, two, three, four, and one more folded to look like a pillow – that's five blankets! As I look around, I see water, bread and soup just to my left. It looks like a mirage.

I try to chew the bread, it's very hard, but it's edible if I soak it in the potato soup. The sound of footsteps startles me. At last, I can find out who has done all this for me. For an instant, the thought of seeing my beloved David in uniform terrifies me. My man, whom

I have wanted and loved so much, cannot be one of these monsters. But suddenly I recoil: David materialises in front of me.

"What am I going to do with you? You can't stay out of trouble!"

He tells me in a tone that is both sweet and sad, trying uselessly to get a smile out of me.

After that sentence, a flashback comes to my mind. The day when three young Germans got out of the dark car to beat me almost to death; that day, the voice I heard before I lost consciousness was his voice, David's voice.

I wasn't imagining it, it was real!

And now I also understand why Peter didn't want to tell me any more about the young German who took me to the clinic after he saved my life. He had to arrive in uniform.

From our first meeting, it was all obvious, when he said he couldn't afford to be himself, to kiss me, to let himself be carried away by our magnificent story. How could it have occurred to me that he was a journalist?

I am disappointed. My David is part of those damned German bastards who are doing all this damage, and he, like everyone else, is responsible. Resentful, frustrated, but even in love, I decide not to forgive him, at least not right away.

"Why did you bring me here? Why didn't you kill me? It was you who saved my life the day I was attacked and then disappeared, wasn't it?"

"I never forgot you, Tom. From the first day I saw you in that place, I couldn't keep you out of my heart. I know, it seems absurd, perhaps, in another life we loved each other and were happy, and today our souls have recognised each other. Unfortunately, reincarnated in two bodies too different, too distant. But I love you all the same, Tom. I love you as I have never loved anyone.

That's right, the day of the attack, I saved your life and then I disappeared. I was afraid you wouldn't have accepted my role, and I couldn't have tolerated your rejection, so I preferred not to see you anymore and let the sweetness of our first meeting live on."

I don't even look at him, but I remember perfectly the moments we lived together.

"I was ashamed, Tom. I didn't know how to tell you the truth. I thought about it a thousand times, but I couldn't do it. And when I saw you in that mine, it was terrible for me. You don't know it, but I watched you. I wanted to protect you from everything and everyone, but it's not easy for anyone here."

Seeing that I still don't deign to look at him, after filling his lungs with air, he continues with his monologue, in a sad attempt to be forgiven.

"Unfortunately, for a German like me, there are not many alternatives. I had to enlist. My father had enlisted and died while fighting in the Great War. I was just a boy then, but I have always grown up with the conviction that I would follow in his footsteps. I'm very sorry, Tom, I never killed anyone. You'd be surprised how many good people there are in the SS. We're not all sons of bitches."

David looks for understanding and comfort in my eyes, but finds none. Then I start to speak. A deep, stern look pierces David.

"I don't care. The mere fact that you support Hitler disgusts me."

David's gaze is lost in the void, in an infinity that only he is capable of perceiving; and then, in a low voice, he confesses, more to himself than to me, that he hates Hitler, his beliefs and all the rest of it.

"But I can't back out, Tom. Do you understand how hard it is for me? I've been unable to do anything but watch over you from afar, ready to step in if necessary." As soon as he finishes the sentence, he kisses me, and we spend the whole night talking about everything that's happened while we've been apart. And then memories, hopes, dreams and desires are the only protagonists of our talks.

Despite the fact that we are in a makeshift bed, in a barrack that stinks of damp and, even though I feel quite ill, we spend, after a period that has seemed eternal, a magical night, cuddling together while we tell each other beautiful things but, above all, the misery of the last few years.

42

Through my eyes, David begins to see all the atrocities his people are causing. He knows perfectly well that this is all wrong, he's always known it, but being there to minimise the damage is enough to give him a reason to fight.

David was drafted before the war began, just as his father and grandfather had been. At first, everything seemed normal and right for the homeland, but his father would certainly never have accepted all this. He was good, just like his mother, but the Great War took him away and now it is his turn, he has to show the world who he really is.

Unfortunately, he is fighting on the wrong side. David hates Hitler, has hated him from the first moment, from the first time he heard him speak in public. He continues to wonder how someone like him can talk about a perfect race, just him, who has nothing perfect about him. But not all Germans are such bastards.

I listen to him with great interest, I want to know everything about him, and I'm glad to know that not all members of the SS are fucking insane, in fact, some of them, even a small part of them, enlisted in order not to let the situation get worse or because they were forced to do so.

Having ascertained that my father is in good health, I have another favour to ask of David: to find my dear friend Matt. Now that I know he is alive and, more importantly, that he is in this very camp, I have to talk to him and be there for him. With all that he has been forced to endure, Matt must be a broken man inside.

After two days of searching, David, as usual, comes to visit me in the barracks. But this time his countenance is much more serious than usual. After all the hardships I have been forced to go through, I immediately think of the worst. My heart begins to race and my eyes fill with tears when I see someone peeking through the door.

"I just hope I don't have to be jealous of your complicity." David winks at me.

I raise my head and, with great happiness, shed a lot of tears for seeing my best friend again after so long.

"I can't believe it! You're here. It's great to see you again."

Matt gives a small smile.

"I'm happy to see you too, but it honestly breaks my heart to know that you're here too."

I hug him tightly and realise that he has changed a lot. The fabulous hair that used to cover his head has disappeared. His eyes, capable of lighting up an entire room, are now dull and his gaze is absent.

His physique, which has always made me envious, is now exactly like mine, weak, frail and malnourished. And besides, the old Matt would have taken it all lightly, as if it were a game; now the young man I hold in my arms is a devastated, war-torn man. Not to mention that damn pink star stitched on his jacket. The more I look at him, the more I think about what it might tell of Matt's true nature.

I've been good at hiding, but just the fact that I

don't have the pink scarf sewn on gives me the feeling that I repudiate who I am and who I have been.

"I'm sorry about Peter, I really am, I'm very sorry, but how are you? Tell me everything. I want to know what you've been doing all these years."

We sit on the floor; David leaves the room to let us talk like two old friends.

"The last time I was arrested, they didn't seem to care that I was the son of a member of the SS, as has happened in the past. First, I was taken to Dachau with my uncle Ernest, and then I was brought here to Auschwitz, where I found my Peter. At first, despite the harsh living conditions inside the camp, I was happy, because I was not alone. I really loved that man and, when I could, I tried to be with him, but we were discovered."

"What? How? Why? Unfortunately, I know the end of the story, but I can't understand how it could have happened."

"Peter worked in the Sonderkommando. You know what they are, don't you?"

"Yes, at least I think I know. They are Jews in charge of smiling, keeping calm and not revealing anything about what is about to happen to the people they accompanied inside the gas chambers."

"If you only knew how many children he has seen die. Women in perfect health who were about to give birth, old people, invalids. It was terrible for him. All the people he used to cure he had to accompany them to death, without being able to do anything to prevent it.

Every day, feelings of guilt killed a part of him, his best part. I tried to support him as much as I could.

That damn day, I went looking for him, you don't know how sorry I am that I did it: it's as if I had killed him myself. I regret it and I'm sorry, but it's not going to bring him back..."

Matt cries desperately and beats his legs.

I'm at a loss for words, I don't know how to comfort him and I honestly don't think there are adequate words, so I have nothing left to do but hug him.

Matt, sobbing, wipes the tears from his face and continues:

"That night, I went to look for him, we went to a secluded place, it was dark, I can't tell you where, but it was a place Peter knew well and I trusted him unconditionally. He was the one who guided me. Without thinking, he started kissing me, I couldn't imagine, it was dangerous. It was so passionate, so irresistible…, as if he knew it was our last time. And suddenly, as in our first sober meeting, a light blinded our eyes and two SS agents began to insult and beat us. It was terrible!"

Matt starts crying again, but this time I have something to tell him:

"Listen, Matt, not to make you feel better, but I'm sure it wasn't your fault what happened to Peter..." I pause to take his face and get him to look me in the eye. "I think that if the work he was doing in the camp was as terrible as you say it was, maybe Peter had, in a way, planned for it. Maybe his heart wanted to put an end to that pain and not have to continue to witness that atrocity day after day, so that he would no longer be part of this crazy and cruel project."

"Do you think I haven't thought about it? But it's difficult. Besides, did you see how they killed him?

They're merciless fucking monsters."

"Yes, I don't think your doctor would ever have imagined that he would be killed in such an atrocious way, but we are in Auschwitz. I'm so sorry, my friend! I too felt heart-rending grief at Peter's death, and for you, after the execution, I didn't know what had become of you or whether you had been harmed. But now tell me about yourself. What are you working on in here?"

I try to change my speech to distract him from such terrible thoughts.

"Work? I wish! I'm locked up in a laboratory all day. The Nazi doctors have used me for scientific experiments, trying to discover the genes for homosexuality so that they can cure future Aryan children unfortunate enough to be born homosexual. Dr. Vaernet is the most wicked and wretched of all SS doctors. He is conducting a study of a hormone-based mixture that he has prepared himself.

He is experimenting on us homosexual prisoners in the Buchenwald camp. The cure is based on huge doses of testosterone, 80% of the prisoners who have undergone the treatment have not survived. I, too, have been forced to undergo the treatment and, since Peter's death, I have been subjected to experiments on my eyes. I don't even know what they are for, but they don't work at all, in fact, I can hardly see anymore."

Story after story, several hours have passed and David returns to the shed to clear up our doubts.

"They are experiments to understand what Aryans born with brown eyes lack in order to become perfect. They study blue eyes to try to change the colour of those who were not lucky enough to be born with sky-coloured eyes."

We give him a look of contempt because of the uniform he wears. I love that man, but I have a lot to say about his race.

"I can't believe it. You Germans are sick."

David, looking at me, replies with a hint of sarcasm:

"Very much so, unfortunately." Then, turning to Matt, he continues: "I wanted to tell you that I'm sorry for what happened to your beloved, but you should know that he was a Sonderkommando."

I don't understand the nexus of the speech, what exactly David means by that sentence.

"So what?" The question comes out of Matt's mouth and mine at the same time.

"I shouldn't say it, but anyone who is selected for that job can't live more than six months."

A lowered gaze and a mournful tone of voice accompany these words.

"Obviously, because they're the only ones who know what really goes on in those showers."

This time, Matt seems enraged, outraged and dismayed. I, on the other hand, am puzzled.

"So why the fuck don't you guys do that nasty job? After all, everyone knows what goes on in there."

At this point, David decides to sit next to us.

"It's not easy to say, but the only reason why it's not us accompanying you, but one of you, is so as not to give anything away. The victims must not know that they are walking towards certain death, and if one of them accompanies them, nicely and gently, any suspicion disappears. I'm sorry, but it's the terrible truth!"

After a few minutes of silence, where any words seem superfluous, David leaves, saying goodbye first to Matt with a pat on the back and then to me with a light kiss on the lips.

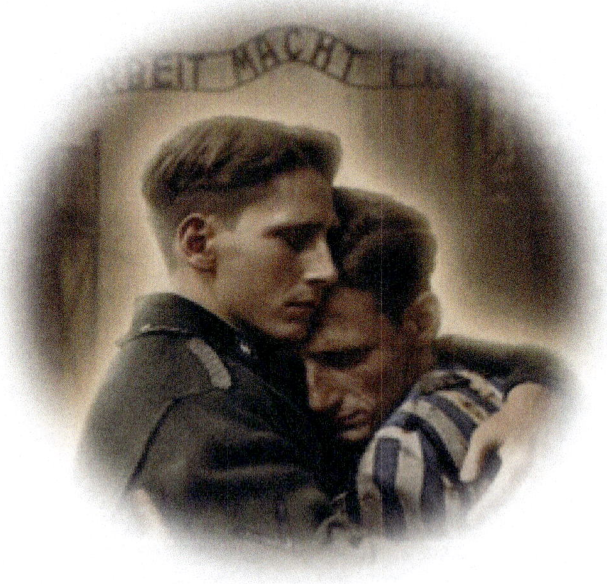
MACHT

43

After a few days, David learns that the number of war casualties has increased and that, as a result, measures are being taken to expand the camp and create more barracks.

The first area to be restructured is precisely the one I am in, the old infirmary without a roof, which, secretly, for two weeks, made us home. Although I am starting to recover, I am not really out of danger yet. David must immediately find a solution and find some way to get me back to the Block.

He has proposed to himself to give everything for me, to save my life, to protect me. Unfortunately, he can't do anything for others, but for me he would risk everything.

Since I have managed to win the trust of my Kapo with that heroic gesture of mine, it occurs to David to use this situation to our advantage by asking him to get me into my block somehow. It is fortunate to have someone on our side; apart from my father, he is the only one who knows the truth, which is why he has never denounced my death.

The Kapo does not hesitate for a moment to offer his help and immediately puts himself at our disposal; after all, he owes me his life. There are so many prisoners that no one will notice if there is one more. Among the men who die, the men who are moved to other areas and those who are assigned to other destinations, there is chaos. A field of creeping ghosts, who no longer have the strength to think whether they will ever see another dawn.

On the other hand, the roommates, the few who still remember my bones, have no idea that I have been destined to die, and the SS will never think that there is another prisoner, if anything they will check if anyone has escaped... It is relatively unlikely that prisoners will appear out of nowhere. Apart from the fact that the only one in charge of such checks is the Kapo.

Of course, if I had caused any trouble at work or felt bad, it would have been a real disaster.

So, back at the Block, the Kapo makes me push my way back in and shouts:

"Next time... There won't be a next time, and may the punishment you have been given serve as an example to all."

I'm back sharing my old bed with a new stranger and with my father, who is such a smart man and has immediately understood that this was not the time to talk or show any emotion on his face. David has made sure that he has always heard from me, but he has not seen him since the day I fainted in the mine. The other prisoners realise that something doesn't add up, but they don't dare ask questions because they have understood that on my side, as well as that of the Kapo, there is also a German soldier.

It is Sunday. No prisoners, except for some who clean the factories, are working.

I am sitting next to my father and at last we can talk. It is one of the few pleasures and distractions we have left. In our bed there is a newcomer, a young man of twenty-four with a double stitching on his uniform: a yellow star and a pink triangle.

I realise that he is bleeding from his rectum. I try to wake him up, but he already knows: he's been tortured in the worst way because he's gay.

My heartbeat gets faster and faster.

What else has this man had to endure just because of his sexual orientation?

For them, we are just fags, torturing or hurting us is normal.

As the boy continues with his story, I unintentionally start to tear up. My heart keeps pounding, as if it wants to break free from the chest wall and finally be free.

Why does being gay have to be a problem for others? Why is it wrong when for me and for many others like me it is natural? Why can't I shout to the whole world that I have found the love of my life and that he is a man like me?

The more I reflect on that pink triangle sewn on the young's jacket, the more guilty I feel for hiding my true identity and not wearing that pink triangle with dignity on my striped uniform.

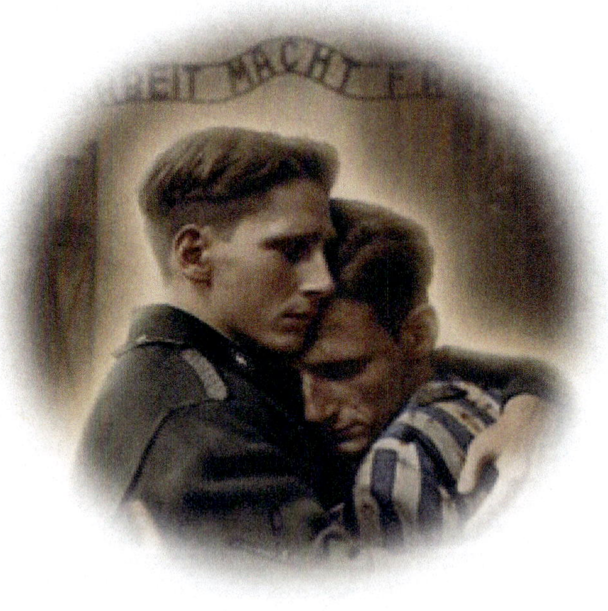
MACHT

44

The sun has not yet risen, all the detainees are still in their beds, sleeping. With the arrival of the young prisoner, we are all forced to sleep with our arms outside the blankets, so that the arms could can be seen. Now there is a homosexual among us and the disease can spread.

I sleep soundly. Suddenly, the doors of the Block burst open. Three SS agents, still standing in the doorway, shine a powerful torch into the room. One of the three shouts my full name out loud:

"Thomas Potter!"

It is impossible not to hear him, but no one answers, and it is strange that a prisoner is called by name and not by number.

"I've said Thomas Potter. Where is he?"

The SS enters the Block and illuminates the detainees one by one with the strong, violent light of the torch. All the detainees quickly stand up and line up.

Carl, frightened by the shouting and, above all, by the fact that I have been called and summoned using my real name and not the number, squeezes my hand tightly. He thinks I'm doomed, and I think so too.

Did someone rat out David? Did someone mention that I've come back out of nowhere? But who... who?

Nobody but Matt knows about us, and Matt would never do that. Maybe I've left a clue in the old infirmary where I've been, but what? Nothing personal, nothing that could give me away.

But it is an order, and here we must obey orders without complaint, since we have no other choice, so, on shaky legs, I step forward and answer:

"I am number 829014. Thomas Potter is my old name, Sir."

Two of the SS approach, and another continues to inspect.

"You have to come with us. Hurry up, come on!"

Not knowing if this is a goodbye, I turn to my father and hug him intensely.

Who knows where they will take me, who knows where and how they will kill me!

But I am sure, seeing all that has happened, that they will do it in the worst way, or even worse: first they will humiliate me in some horrible way and then they will kill me.

I feel I am in the olive forest, I tremble, I sweat, I am afraid. And I can't imagine how my father will feel when he discovers my homosexuality: shame and disappointment will kill him.

Dad, too, hugs me intensely and bursts into tears when he hears his bed mate say:

"Maybe they just want to have some fun. A father can't accept something like that."

Carl would never have agreed to me experiencing all the inhumane atrocities that most prisoners have had to endure. He knows that, unfortunately, he has no choice but to watch helplessly, but it is worth a try.

"Take me, I beg you!" He rushes towards the SS officer and kneels down in front of him. "Leave my son alone, I beg you, take me! Do with me what you will."

But the SS man in front of him is not interested in

the old man.

"We don't want you; we want the boy."

Carl bursts into tears of despair, grabs the German's leg from his uniform and pleads again in tears:

"No, no, take me!"

The SS officer kicks him hard to get him off.

"Go back to your place immediately if you don't want to end badly. It's him we want. Go away, you old fart."

So as not to make things even worse, I decide to follow the SS wherever they lead me. But first, I give my father one last greeting, a kiss on the forehead, intense, deep and sincere, whispering in his ear:

"I've always loved you, Dad. Don't ever give up... Do it for me."

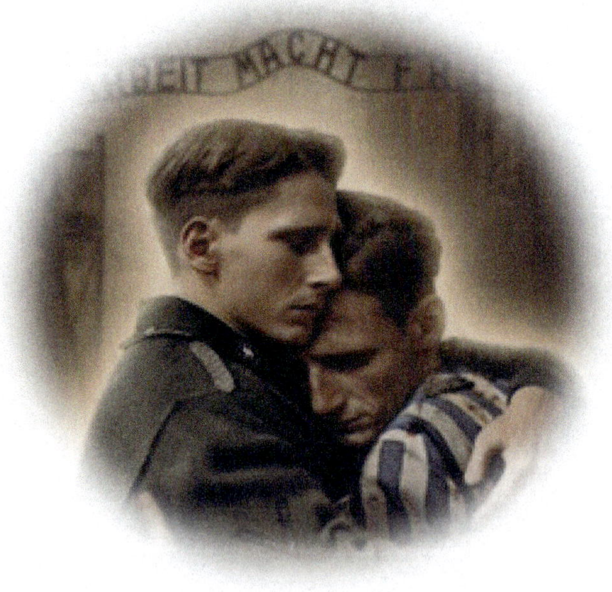
MACHT

45

It is almost dawn, maybe five or six in the morning. It is very cold. I follow the three agents, wondering what they have in mind.

Will they kill me or will the dogs kill me, like poor Peter? If they have discovered me, then David is in danger too.

I am terrified and worried. The more I think, the more obsessive my thoughts become, they become unbearable.

The SS officers talk to each other without saying a word to me; after almost ten minutes of walking, we reach the end of the road… At the door of a small building. Once inside, they order me to undress. From that moment on, everything becomes clearer to me. It's the gas chambers and I'm about to enter.

It is certainly not the end I expected, but it is the most dignified and least painful death I could wish for. Who knows if the same fate has been reserved for David.

Completely naked, I take small steps to get into the shower, but the SS agents are too late and speed up, kicking me into the shower.

"Hurry up! Quickly!"

"Can you move?"

I am surrounded by these four walls in front of three members of the SS. As one of them passes me the soap, I look up at the shower, if that's what you can call it, thinking that soon all this will come to an end.

"Grandpa, you weren't betrayed, were you? David had sent for you, didn't he? Tell me I'm not mistaken."

Matt, David, my father and even little Anna invade my thoughts. I'm so immersed in them that I don't realise that what's coming out of the shower is water and that it's getting me all wet. Cold water, but anyway... it's water. I've been brought here just to wash myself. It's just a stupid, bland, normal shower.
When they turn off the water, one of the SS gives me a brand-new uniform.
"You're lucky, Jew, there are few who wash themselves with soap and who have a new uniform... One that hasn't belonged to anyone before."
During the whole time I don't have the courage to say anything. After the shower, I am taken to a new place, Block 10. Looking at the uniforms, I quickly realise that they are all Germans, no one in there is wearing the Star of David on their jacket, only me, but instead they are all wearing a pink or green triangle.
I am among Germans! But why? Nothing makes sense any more. A few minutes after I enter Block 10, I notice that Matt is two beds away. I go over to talk to him, but just then I see my beloved David come in. I am happy and content, but increasingly confused.
I would like to ask him to explain, but this is not the time to do it in front of everyone else. All the prisoners line up next to each other when, in a serious and distant tone after roll call, David names my number, asking me to follow him.
When we get to the kitchen, we are alone: just Da-

vid and me.

"Can you tell me what's going on?" I ask him a thousand questions in order to understand as quickly as possible what is about to happen, because I still have nothing clear.

"But have you seen where we are? This will be your new job. Aren't you happy?"

David, after giving me a quick kiss, tries to explain that he thought it would be a pleasant surprise. He tells me that one day, while he was at the table with all the other soldiers, a soldier remarked that what he most needed was bread, not bread that was soft or salty or overcooked, but bread that was meant to be. At that moment, David had an enlightenment. Since he had sent me back to my Block, he was not at peace; he felt that I was no longer safe in that place, if I ever was. So it was that, after the meal, he hurried to the kitchens of the German mess halls.

A short, thick-set man, kneeling on the floor with a rag in his hand, was about to start cleaning up. David, before making himself noticed, paused, took a deep breath, cleared his voice and attacked:

"Gustav, why are you on the floor cleaning up? Is it with those dirty hands that you prepare our food?" From the tone of his voice, he sounded like one of those SS Germans, an authoritarian bastard.

"I'm sorry, sir, but I'm on my own."

The cook, Gustav, is a good man, but no one can really tell, as his days are always spent within those four walls; when he doesn't have to cook, he has to clean. David was overcome with a great euphoria that he could hardly hide when he heard those words.

The satisfaction of having got it right gave him the

adrenaline to go on and finish in style:

"Well, then from tomorrow you'll have a helper. It really disgusts me to know that with those hands you clean the floor and then prepare food for us. It's really disgusting."

"Thank you, thank you very much. I have asked for help many times, but nobody seems to care. My last assistant was killed three months ago, and since then..."

"Excuse me? Why?"

For a moment, David blanched, he thought the kitchen was the safest place in the camp.

"He was a German prisoner. He came to help me with the cleaning, until one day he tried to poison the food. I noticed it myself and reported him."

"Then let's try it with a Jew, because even the Germans can't be trusted."

46

I don't understand anything, I'm a bundle of nerves, I start talking quickly:

"Happy? You could at least have warned me, don't you think? This morning, I had to say goodbye to my father, the poor man almost got himself killed for me. And then I thought they were going to kill me in the gas chambers, and..."

David, without letting me finish, hugs me to shut me up, but above all to calm me down. At any moment someone could walk into the kitchen, so David sums it all up for me:

"Forgive me, Tom, but I wanted to surprise you. From now on you'll be working here. You'll be in charge of the cleaning. You'll have access to all the food you want and, if you're very careful, you'll be able to give some to your father too. Besides, aren't you glad I put you in the same Block as Matt?"

I look down.

"Yes, I'm sorry, it's just that I got really scared. I would never have guessed that you were behind all this. But now I'm very grateful!"

An hour later, in the German kitchens, cleaning the floor, oven, cooker and all washable surfaces, I feel happy.

Gustav proves to be a good man. From the very first day we talk to each other calmly, as if we knew each other all our lives.

He is a man in his mid-fifties, the father of a son who was

also in the SS and was transferred to Falstad in Norway. Like Carl, Gustav lost his wife to an incurable disease. For this man, talking to me is a blessing, as he has been alone for a very long time.

47

"David was trying to save your life in every way, and the truth is that getting a few days back in that period could make all the difference, as events, once again, suddenly came rushing in."

1942 was the year of the counteroffensive. The Allies rallied for 'the unconditional surrender of the Germans', and Russia forced Italy and Germany to withdraw from Stalingrad. The Rome-Berlin-Tokyo axis was irreparably weakened.

For the Jews, the year started in the worst way. On 20 January, the 'Final Solution' began. The plan was the annihilation of the entire Jewish population, which included the systematic extermination of all prisoners, after they had been exploited to the maximum.

Genocide and mass destruction represented the culmination of a decade characterised by increasingly harsh discriminatory measures, some of which, on the one hand or the other, marked the lives of the protagonists of our DocuFilm. Tom, my grandfather; Anna, my grandmother; Matt, who I discovered was my uncle; Peter; Carl, my great-grandfather, and also David.

'During that time, other concentration camps were opened: Belzec, Sobibor, Treblinka, and in June, Himmler ordered Birkenau to be expanded from 125,000 to 200,000 places, and the Buna-Monovitz camp, called Auschwitz, was created.'

"But, Grandpa, you go on and tell us how things turned out for you and your loved ones."

"I was very happy in the kitchen. Gustav liked me so much that he even let me send food to my father, thanks to the help of the Kapo, who, after saving his life, remained loyal."

"Grandpa, do you see how doing good is always rewarded?"

"I'm sorry, Ben, but isn't that what I've been trying to teach you all your life?"

We smile, and then I go on with the story.

I continue to sleep in the dormitories of the German prisoners, it is not easy for me, but there is my dear Matt. Unfortunately, because of the numerous experiments, he has become completely blind. It is difficult, but with me he copes with everything, even though the situation can never get better.

As he is the son of one of them, instead of killing him, they decide to exploit him even more. Given his blindness, they have taken what they consider to be the most appropriate decision: to subject him as a guinea pig to different kinds of scientific experiments. This time, it is not about studying the perfection of the Aryan race, but the imperfection of homosexuals.

Since the hormone treatments have not worked on what they consider to be a 'disease', they decide to try other cures.

Matt is forced to undergo multiple sexual relations with lesbians forced into prostitution because, although lesbians are women and are useful for procreation, unlike men, they consider women to be curable and, above all, useful. Subjected to repeated unprotected sex, Matt, in little more than a month, contracts numerous venereal diseases.

"Poor Matt!" Ben can't keep quiet.

Poor Matt. His health condition is serious and worsening day by day due to fatigue and malnutrition. For him, the end is near. One more day in this place could cost him his life.

Having punished him enough, considering that he is a German and that his father plays a very important role, Colonel Offman is asked if he would like to take his son home to say goodbye and, who knows if with the right cures, save his life... Life, or what's left of it.

But Alfons, very resentful of his son's behaviour, of his brother's situation and of the great shame that a son suffering from homosexuality has caused him, declines the offer and abandons poor Matt once again.

"What a son of a b…!"
"Ben!" Anna catches his eye.

The boy, realising what he has said, changes the subject.

"But... What happened to the guy? Was he punished as he should have been for not respecting life, childhood, kinship?"

A year has passed since the colonel was informed of the terrible death of his brother, killed while trying to flee. Alfons still remembers that day with great satisfaction.

It was five o'clock in the afternoon when he received a call from a colleague in Dachau to find out whether the relationship that the prisoner Ernest Offman claimed to have with him was true.

Alfons immediately asked the reason for these questions, and the SS officer on the phone was quick to answer.

"We discovered him while he was trying to escape with other prisoners. He managed to get under the barbed-wire fence through a hole that no guard knew about. The other two were killed in cold blood, as ordered by our general, but the other man kept saying, 'Don't you know who I am? I am Colonel Offman's brother. I beg you, in a way, I am one of you.'"

Alfons laughs.

"It's an amazing and funny story. Since he wants to escape so badly, instead of making him climb under the electric fence, let him climb over it... It will be amusing to see him climb over it, knowing that he will be instantly struck down. That man, to me, is nobody, so carry out the general's orders and finish him off," he orders angrily, satisfied with revenge. Putting the matter to rest, without waiting for an answer, Alfons, his hands trembling with rage, ends the conversation.

The day after, the same SS agent contacts him again.

"Colonel, I wanted to inform you that the man who kept claiming to be your brother has received an appropriate punishment."

"Has he climbed the electric fence?"

"He would never have done it, so we decided to make him eaten by the dogs, and so, in order to escape from those fangs, without a second thought, he himself, out of desperation, climbed it. He died in a mangled state. You were right, it was really funny."

"Poor Grandma. But did anyone, her father, brother, you, Grandpa, stop to think about how Anna was?"

"Thank you, Ben, you're thinking about it, and this comforts me, makes me feel loved and makes me feel good." Then, looking in the past, she takes the floor: "I knew about the dynamics of escape and my uncle's death, and everything Matt was going through: the violence, the tortures he suffered day after day. I felt totally guilty... I remember those days well...

One thought kept drilling into my brain and soul: it was my fault, just my fault if Matt was forced to endure all that. It was because of me that Peter had been torn to pieces by the dogs, and because of me and my stupid idea that Tom and his father had got into trouble. I'm a mess, my conscience will be stained forever."

"Stop it, Grandma. You're not to blame for anything. Why do you have to torture yourself like this?"

Anna keeps trembling, as if she is really reliving those moments.

> The bakery idea seemed like a good one, but it has been my doom. I keep thinking about these things over and over again when I decide to make a gallows out of a sheet and hang it in the rafters of Matt's room.
>
> Suicide is the only possible option, I can't bear the weight of these blood-tinged thoughts any longer, I seem to hear the screams of each one of them and a voice inside me repeating: 'It's your fault, Anna, it's all your fault! How can you, how can you live with the weight of this boulder?'
>
> Suicide is the only salvation for many Jews who take their own lives out of fear of what awaits them.

It is also for many Germans, too good to endure the atrocities of war.

But now it is my turn: death will be my peace, my escape from this hostile and cruel world. It will be the atonement for my faults. A last act of courage.

It is not easy to find the strength to hate a father, the man who brought me into the world. But the truth is that I can't help hating him and, with my death, I want to sink him too, once and for all; to lose two sons for the party, for a bullshit ideology that really has nothing to do with him or with us.

"My God, Grandma, did you really want to do it?"
"I wanted it with all my heart, I was fully aware that I wanted to end it all."
"And what made you change your mind?"
Tom answered, taking the burden off Anna's shoulders.
"Your grandma didn't change her mind."

Anna enters her brother's room to end her life. In spite of everything, since Matt is no longer at home, their father is unable to sleep, probably because of the weight of his conscience. So, the colonel, in the middle of the night, hears some noises coming from the room of the son he cannot forgive, although deep in his heart, perhaps, he has already done so, but out of pride he cannot admit it.

Alfons hears something fall to the floor, as if it were a chair. Sweating and struggling to breathe, he decides to get up and check that everything is in order.

When he reaches Matt's room, he sees something white hanging. He immediately realises that it is his daughter in her nightdress. He quickly tries to free her and lays her down on the floor. Teary-eyed, he takes her narrow face in his arms, praying to his God to save her.

That same night, Alfons tries to bring light back into his life, but the darkness, in which he chose to live, is not easy to illuminate.

He immediately grabs the phone:

"This is Colonel Offman, bring my son home immediately!"

He is answered sympathetically:

"I am sorry, Colonel, I told you that he was ill, but you did not want to hear of it. I called you personally to tell you that you could take your son home if you wished, given his serious state of health, but you replied that you were not interested and ordered us not to tell you anything in case anything happened to him. I am sorry, but…"

"Wh… what? What do you want to tell me?"

Although it is clear, the colonel refuses to believe those words, he knows perfectly well what he said, but that was before, before Anna's extreme decision, before he came to his senses.

"I am sorry, but your son died two days ago."

Alfons hangs up the phone without further explanation and bursts into tears, realising that he has been a merciless man and that he has received his just punishment: eternal suffering.

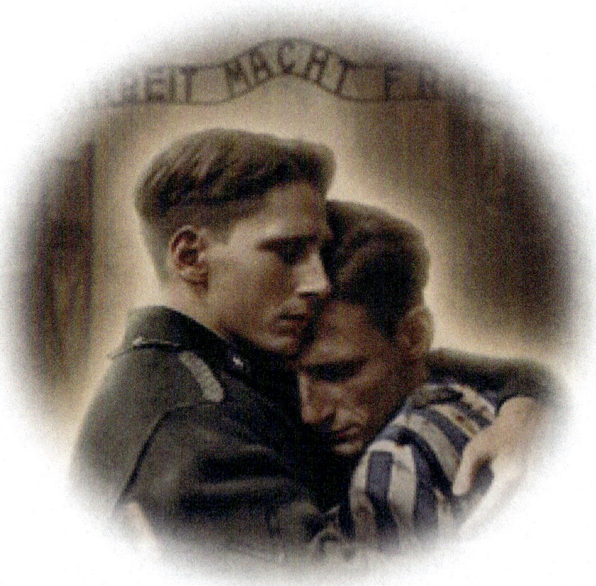
MACHT

48

"And so poor Matt didn't make it." Ben picks up the transmission.

And Italy, which surrenders to the Allies, cannot make it either. We are in 1943. The Fascist Grand Council issued a vote of no confidence in Mussolini and, meanwhile, in Italy, civil war raged between Mussolini's followers and the Partisans. On 10 September, the Germans occupied Rome and much of Italy, liberating the Duce who proclaimed the Italian Social Republic.

On 14 November, during the first congress of the National Fascist Republican Party, which arose from the ashes of the National Fascist Party, the Verona Manifesto was drawn up, which represented the birth certificate of the Italian Social Republic and defined the political programme. Among other things, it declared that Jews were foreigners and belonged to enemy nationalities.

On 13 October, Italy declared war on Germany, but once again, in the maelstrom of war, it was the Jews who bore the brunt.

On 16 October, the Jewish quarter of Rome was sacked and the deportation of Italian Jews to Auschwitz began. New trains, new departures and new arrivals. Lines of people, like cattle, divided in two: the most fortunate, destined for forced labour, and the rest... for the showers.

Ben's sensitively stripped-down narration, mitigates the fire that is spreading because of the memories.

49

"I remember well those terrible moments, which will haunt me for the rest of my life. They are remembered by Carl, the Madman, the Kapo's chosen one and all the others."

It's been several months since Matt has been gone, and yet I remember that moment vividly.

In Auschwitz, some prisoners, perhaps Jewish or possibly German, manage to steal a lot of provisions that the SS has available in the mess hall storeroom. Gustav is forced to denounce when it happens one day, since there is absolutely nothing to cook and, as expected, all suspicion falls on me.

In the morning, the SS agents show up in Block 10, where I am still asleep.

I wake up with a start.

"829014, tell us immediately where you have hidden the food from the storeroom."

Without being fully awake, I know that these accusations do not help me at all.

"I've hidden what? Why me?"

"We know it was you. You are the only Jew who has the keys to that storeroom."

"Was it me because I'm a Jew? I slept until now, I don't know where the food is."

"I don't think you've understood: we want to know where the food you stole is!"

The soldier points a rifle straight at my head, I don't know what else to do to convince them that it wasn't me. At that moment, two other SS soldiers rush into the Block to announce that the food has been found.

While I still have the rifle to my temple, I see David enter the Block, his eyes wide with panic, his concern evident.

"You will pay for this offence. The responsibility for the storeroom is yours."

The soldier looks furious. He never wants to admit he was wrong and must take his anger out on someone. David closes his eyes, he doesn't want to see me murdered, I am the man he loves more than anyone else.

Matt gets out of bed. He is blind, but not deaf.

"No! Stop! He has nothing to do with all this, the responsibility is mine."

The soldier laughs his head off.

"You're blind, you fucking fag! How could you have done it?"

I look at him terrified.

Don't do it, Matt! I beg you, don't do it, I scream inside me.

Matt smiles cheekily, as if wanting to provoke him further, and responds:

"How did I do it? I fucked the guard. Just like that!"

The SS officer withdraws the rifle that was pointed directly at my head and approaches Matt.

"I was about to shoot a Jew, accusing him of something you actually did. Why did you save him? Why didn't you let me take him out?"

At that moment, I see the same old reckless, shameless boy in Matt. After all this time, I am reunited with my old Matt.

"I stole the food just to starve you to death, just like you do to all of us. You bastards! I don't care about saving the Jew's life, what's more, when you're done with me, you can kill him too. He'll be just one less fucking Jew!"

Matt's tone is strangely calm and relaxed. He does not see the rifle resting on his forehead, but he feels the coldness of the steel, which makes him imagine the circumstances perfectly.

David is not troubled by Matt's words, indeed, he knows full well that, by saying those things, he is pressuring his colleague to keep that dirty Jew alive, just out of spite. His reverse psychology reverberates around the block like a new light.

"Get out of here, at once!" The soldier orders everyone out to attend the execution.

As I look at Matt, I let a tear fall, lean closer to him and whisper:

"Why, Matt? Why did you do it?"

"I'm already dead, Tom. At least I'm out of pain and hopefully I'll find my beloved Peter. I want you to know that you've been much more than a friend to me, you're my soul mate... You've always been a brother, or rather, a sister!"

A small smile accompanies those words out of Matt's mouth.

Among tears, a faint smile comes to my face, accompanied by a thousand memories of when everything was still beautiful: our first day at school, when we discovered our homosexuality; the barbarities we endured, all the confessions and the presence of both of us in the most important moments of our lives.

We have always been together throughout our brief existence, and I am not yet ready to say goodbye forever. The pain and fear of losing him is so strong that I am paralysed without realising that I am the only one left inside the Block.

A shot rings in my ears. I rush out, I feel like throwing up.

The last image I have of Matt is of a man with fantastic blond hair and a hole right in the middle of his eyes, which have long since lost their fantastic sky-blue colour.

See you soon! I love you very much, my friend!

50

"Poor Matt, but he would not have survived anyway, because while Germany was in global decline, the SS were rushing to get rid of the prisoners. The Soviet counteroffensive against the Germans continued."

On 22 January 1944, the Anglo-Americans landed at Anzio and Neptune, and on 4 June they liberated Rome. On 6 June, the Allies reached Normandy, giving the green light for the liberation of German-occupied territories. It was not an easy moment even for Hitler, who on 20 July, inside his headquarters in Rastenburg, East Prussia, suffered an attack by some German politicians and military officers who, by means of a coup d'état, sought to establish a new government capable of negotiating peace with the other Allies to prevent a military disbandment and the invasion of Germany.

After the coup failed, some 5,000 people were arrested, most of whom were later executed or interned in camps. Paris was also liberated on 25 August, and in December Germany tried to recapture Belgium and divide the Allied forces along the German border in a final attack.

I continue to work in the kitchen, every day: I clean the floors, the cookers and whatever else is needed. My relationship with Gustav is getting better and better: he sees me and treats me like a son. He allows me to visit my father often and bring him food. Despite that, Dad is getting more and more tired and fatigued, and he is also very weak.

Gustav doesn't know him, but I tell him a lot about him; if there's one thing they have in common, it's a big heart.

Gustav understands everything and, without saying anything to Tom, decides to go and meet him.

Dad has always been a kind, good-natured man, but also a great fighter. The fact that he was left alone with me after mum's death gave him another reason to fight.

If I think about the past, he has nothing to regret, there is absolutely nothing he would change.

Life has not always been kind to him, but he has always lived it intensely. There are so many moments that he remembers with great happiness and so many sorrows that he remembers with pain, but it is thanks to the latter that he always faces life with enthusiasm, because it is suffering that gives you the strength to start again.

After all, how can you know what happiness is if you don't know what pain is?

Inside the camp, it is not easy for him. There are many who suffer from the fact that they are Jews.

Inside the kitchen, thanks to the art of hiding bread, acquired over time, I always manage to bring him extra food, just enough to keep him on his feet and give him the strength he needs. But, knowing my father well, I can imagine what he does with the food.

Dad has already received a lot from life and now it is the turn of those who have yet to start living. He knows full well that the war won't last forever, so he decides to give the younger ones all the provisions I bring him. I'm sure Dad is not looking for death, but helping the weakest is a way to make him feel at peace with himself. Besides, he says, if he helps someone, maybe someone will help me.

Day after day, he distributes every piece of bread I bring him to the younger ones. Other times, he donates them to the sick: people who, according to Dad, are most in need.

I am on the fringes of all that, but with the help of my accomplice, Gustav, I manage to bring a little more each time.

David joins me in the kitchen, rushes to me, hugs me tightly and, as he holds me close, reveals that Dad has taken his last breath.

I burst into tears, I can't believe it, but strangely, deep in my heart, I was expecting this news.

David squeezes me tightly, and I half-faint in his arms. Gustav, who is there, tries to hold me up, douses my face with some water and lays me down on the floor.

I recover, but I'm even more upset and more discouraged. My world has collapsed!

From Gustav's words, I realise that all my suspicions were right, but the anger I feel is growing.

"Dad, why think about others when in this world there is still me? What do others have that I don't have? Maybe I wasn't up to your standards? I'm sure I'm not perfect, but does everyone really deserve more than me? Dad, why did you do this to me? Why to me? Why? First Mum, then Matt, and now you. Now I'm alone!"

Gustav, crouched on the floor, hugs me tightly, whispering in my ear:

"You're not alone, I'm here for you."

David, his eyes full of tears, crouches down.

"I'm here too!" Lifting my head with both hands, he adds: "I'm so sorry, Tom, there are no words that can comfort you or help you get better, but I want you to know that I'll always be with you, because you're the best thing that ever happened to me in this world." Wiping away my tears, he hands me a sheet of paper folded in four. "This one is for you, the Kapo gave it to me."

Gustav looks at David and then at me, nodding his head.

David thinks it's time to give me some privacy to read the letter and, with the cook's approval, accompanies me to the storeroom, where I can be alone. But it's not solitude I'm looking for, so I ask David if he can stay by my side.

We sit next to each other. David puts his arm behind my back to make me feel that he is with me at that delicate moment.

I open the paper. What I thought would be a letter written by the Kapo, to give me some explanation or comfort, is actually a letter from my father.

I would recognise his handwriting even from a distance, because I learned to read and write with that handwriting.

That paper, yellowed and crumpled, reads:

Beloved son:
I asked that this letter be given to you only after my death, because I'm afraid that you'll make me regret

what I do. I don't want to leave you, I don't want you to cry for me, especially after all you have been through. Anyway, I won't live much longer, I won't make it out of this place alive.

I want you to know that I loved you very much and that you have always been in my thoughts. I thought I had lost you on more than one occasion in this horrendous place, the bearer of terror and suffering, but you, as always, made it through.

You have a good and gentle character, for this reason you'll never be alone, and I'll leave with fewer remorse and regrets.

This world, which makes humans hostile to each other, is really a cause of shame for all of us, so I want to settle the score by showing our God that we are not all the same.

It is shameful how human beings use one of the Lord's most precious gifts.

Free will is undoubtedly the most beautiful gift after love. Today, the Germans have decided to offend God the Father Almighty by ignoring this gift, following the ruthless orders of a single being: Hitler.

It's terrible! That's why I ask your forgiveness today if I leave like this.

I wish you to know that it is not an act of cowardice, I don't want to leave this stupid world for fear of facing it, on the contrary, I am leaving fighting. I confess that I have given the food supplies you gave me to those who needed them.

I'm sorry I did this to you, but now I want you, like me, to fight for this world, facing danger and surviving it.

You've been lucky enough to meet many good people along the way and, thanks to your character, you have put them on your side.

Who would have thought that a Jew's best friends would be Germans?

First Matt, then Gustav, David, even our Kapo, and don't forget sweet Anna.

Fight with them and for them!

For my part, you've already fulfilled the first miracle, and now you only have to live to continue your fight.

I, on the other side, with my sacrifice and with your involuntary help, have given many young people another chance to fight, because that is all I want.

I want every individual to have the chance to leave their own grain of sand in this world, because with every drop a sea can be formed. My son, I'm proud of you and the great man you have become.

I love you and will always love you very much!
Forever yours,
Dad

51

David too, having lost his father, knows how I can feel but, in reality, he is also aware of the special relationship between Carl and me.

I have reread his letter at least ten times, being more and more moved by the words: 'My son, I am proud of you'.

Why should I fight for the Germans who are exterminating my race, to save them from sin? Anyway, these are words of hope for a better world, and I also want to contribute. Of course it is not easy, and I keep repeating to myself: 'Where do I start?'

Everyone here needs something and everyone deserves it, so there is a lot to do.

David also wants to do something and, as a first and perhaps last mission, considering the danger of the plan, he wants to get me out of this damned place. He knows I have suffered enough in here, and I certainly can't take much more.

It is 30 April 1945, in the camp there is a confusion never seen before. The soldiers don't stand still, they come in and out: they look like ants going crazy.

Actually, for some months now, at the end of 1944 to be more precise, they have been eliminating every day a group of fifty or sixty people to empty the camp before the arrival of the Red Army.

Today it has been decided to eliminate all prisoners. The executions are carried out in the 'firing corridor', a narrow alley between two high walls between the Bunker and the crematorium. Prisoners are shot in the back of the head in the presence of the camp doctor who finishes them off with lethal injections. The bodies are then burned.

The Soviets advance faster than they could have imagined, and the bosses continue to give orders, hysterical, shouting to hurry up, to finish everything and try not to leave any clues.

It's chaos. The alarm is sounded, we are all alerted. Everyone has a precise role to play. All the evidence of the extermination must be hidden, the documents destroyed, the crematoria burnt, the camp emptied, the prisoners who are still alive killed, and we must flee quickly.

In a very short period of time, hundreds of prisoners are escorted to the firing squad. The chaos works in David's favour and he manages, by pretending to push me towards the death corridor, to make me escape.

This is how my journey to freedom begins.

In that hellish chaos, where it is practically impossible to understand who is running away from whom, and who wants to kill whom, I pray to God to help me.

While the Germans try to kill the last prisoners, the Russian tanks advance, killing and capturing the Germans.

As I flee disoriented, not knowing which way to go, I see the Russian tanks approaching. It is they who save me. At this moment, it is David who is in danger.

Suddenly, everything takes an unexpected turn: the roles are reversed. I am safe, but nothingness awaits me: I have no one, no home and no job.

But I have my life and a young girl I want to embrace again to share with her Matt's death, which has not been mourned enough.

The day I return to Anna, there is a person standing next to her. After a few minutes in shock, I find myself completely paralysed and dumbfounded, confronted by the one man I had hoped never to see again in my life: Colonel Offman!

Anna, seeing me, throws herself into my arms. I smile at her, discovering with joy how much she has grown. She is a wonderful woman, becoming more and more beautiful and more and more... like her brother.

The colonel has wanted to accompany her; by welcoming me, it is as if he were forgiving Matt, Peter, my father and all the people who have suffered to death because of him.

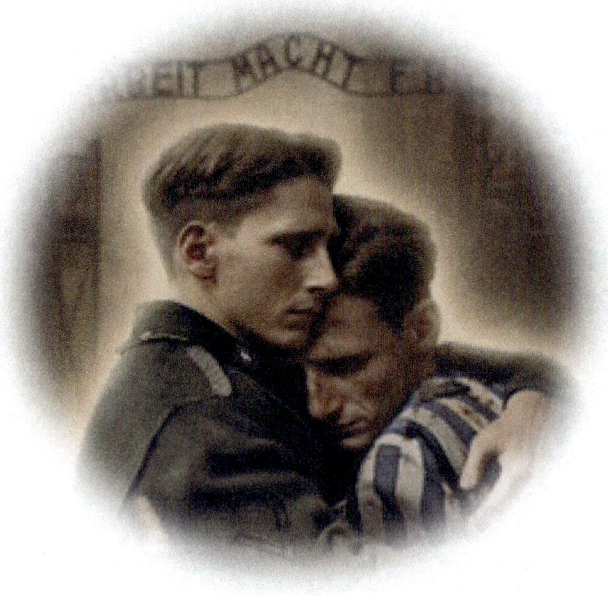
MACHT

52

On 27 January 1945, the Auschwitz concentration camp was liberated by Soviet troops during their swift winter journey from the Vistula to the Oder. The first group to enter the camp was part of General Kurochkin's LX Army from Marshal Ivan Konev's First Ukrainian Front.

They found about 7,000 prisoners still alive; the others, those whom the Germans failed to kill before they fled, were forced to leave the camp, heading for certain death.

The Russian army was horrified by what they found in the camp: thousands of abandoned items of clothing, various objects that had belonged to the prisoners, and eight tons of human hair, packed and ready to be transported.

The Nazis were forced to withdraw, but this was not the first extermination camp discovered by the Russians: previously, they had liberated the Chelmno and Belzec camps, veritable death factories where deportees were immediately gassed, sparing only a few special units.

On 24 February the last group of Jews left for Bergen Belsen, and, in April, the Americans arrived in Nuremberg.

On 15 April the Bergen Belsen camp was liberated, and the next day the Russians reached Berlin.

The situation had already been precipitated.

In Italy, Mussolini was executed by partisans, while Adolf Hitler, on 30 April, committed suicide in his Führerbunker in Berlin, shot in the head with a revolver after ingesting a cyanide pill; his wife, Eva, met the same fate: she committed suicide by ingesting poison. Their bodies, according to the Führer's instructions, were carried down the stairs to the emergency exit of the bunker, doused with gasoline and burned in the garden of the Reich Chancellery.

53

To atone for his sins against his son, Alfons Offman takes me into his home to help me put my life back in order.

When I tell Anna about Matt, the colonel turns away; every time he hears his name, deep feelings of guilt are triggered and eat him up inside.

But, after a while, it is he himself who asks me about Matt, as if trying to find someone to blame for everything that has happened. For my part, I haven't forgiven him for remaining indifferent and, above all, for refusing to take his son in his last moments.

I want to leave, the very sight of him makes me nauseous, but I know Matt would want someone to take care of Anna, and that someone can't be her father.

I am sitting on the stairs in front of the Offman's house, the same stairs where I have spent hours and hours with my best friend talking about this and that.

Thousands of memories invade my memory enough to make me smile. My thoughts are interrupted by a voice I can never forget.

"Hello, Tom!"

I raise my head, and, straight ahead, I see my beloved, just as I have known him, unarmed, out of uniform, and without that horrible hat.

My David is here, right in front of me!

His hair seems longer, he looks more and more beautiful, and seeing him alive makes me cry uncontrollably.

"Come on, Tom, don't be like that... As you can see, I'm alive. I told you I'd keep my promise. After I helped you escape, I tried to save more lives, and then miraculously managed to escape and save myself."

David, still in front of the stairs, tries to keep control, but seeing me so moved, he gives in too.

A strong and intense embrace unites us. We keep silent, it is the beating of our hearts that speaks for us.

The silence in the street ceases when a little old man, standing upright with the help of a cane, passes by and spits on the ground right at our feet.

"But didn't they have to kill you all in those camps? How disgusting!"

David turns suddenly, as if he wants to kill him, but I stop him by taking him by the arm.

"I beg you, don't do it, it's not worth it!"

David knows I'm right, that old German man, after all, can know nothing of the love that unites us: a strong, intense, passionate, but above all... true love.

Even though the war is over, prejudices are still alive. Jews are still looked down upon by most Germans and homosexuals still have to hide from the world.

David knows that it will not be easy for us to face a serene and peaceful life, but we must try. He loves me more than anyone else in the world and he doesn't want to give up this love.

The days after returning home are wonderful. Alfons Offman gave me that famous country house in Ahrensfelde, partly in order not to leave it abandoned, and partly to apologise once again.

The knowledge that he condemned to death all the people he arrested causes him deep remorse, which his subconscious makes him pay for at night, giving him horrendous nightmares.

But deep down he is not really sorry: he thinks he did what had to be done. But his conscience cries out for revenge and he wants to do something for the one who was persecuted. It is a good way to win back the trust of his only daughter and not be tormented by the demon of his dead son.

But I know perfectly well that I must not trust him completely.

There is not a single day that goes by that I do not remember my father, my best friend and all those I have seen die in front of my eyes.

It is terrible how poor Peter was taken from this world.

On the bright side, I now have my David.

Of course, I suffer the absence of all my loved ones, but sweet, scary David helps me to carry on. Facing life, with him by my side, is so much easier.

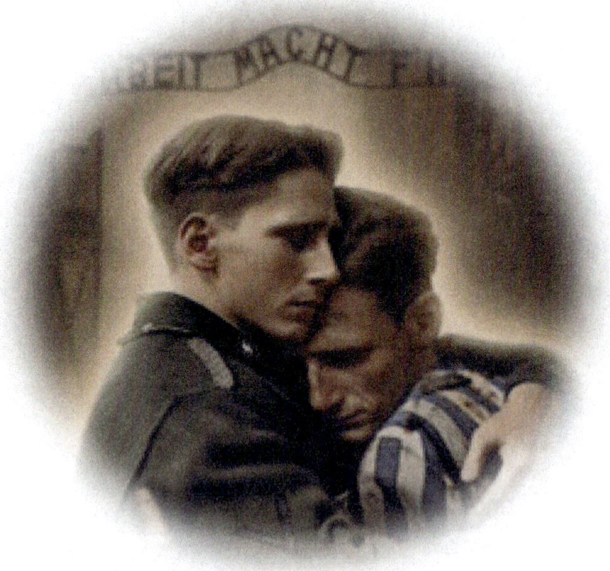
MACHT

54

20 November. In Nuremberg, the international war crimes court opens and, after his reinstatement, David is summoned to stand trial.

I don't take the news well at all, I swear to myself that I will do anything to save my love from jail, after all, he has never done anything wrong.

On the contrary, David expects to be punished.

For him, it is only fair to serve his sentence, after all, he is one of them. Although he has not killed anyone, he is still a German executioner like the others.

The first phase of the trial, to everyone's delight, ends very badly for the defendants.

A few days before, I begged David to run away with me: to go far away, where no one could find us. We have just started living our new life, it can't end here. We have our whole lives ahead of us.

On the day of the trial, David, surprised, finds me in the witness box. After having sworn to tell the truth and nothing but the truth, I made my statement:

"If I am here today, sitting in front of you, it is only thanks to this man. Many detainees today could say the same about him. In there, he was a freak. I almost died because of the hard work in the mine. That man, instead of taking me to the gas chambers as the doctor ordered, assisted me until I was almost fully recovered.

He found me a job in the kitchens, giving me the

possibility to bring food to the other prisoners. The food rations inside the camp were so meagre and insufficient that a man could die in less than three months. Thanks to this soldier, my father and I managed to survive for a long time in that hell. He brought bread, water, soap and even shoes for the prisoners. Yes, it's true, he was one of them, but he could be trusted."

In order not to compromise the final decision, I do not mention our relationship, but I try to explain comprehensively how indispensable David was inside the camp for many Jews.

Torturing my hands and mouth during the statement, I haven't managed to say everything. The emotion and the fear of losing him have literally taken the words out of my mouth. Waiting for the verdict, I feel strangely calm. I know my David doesn't deserve prison or the death penalty, he doesn't, and besides, the other SS soldiers tried before him, who were certainly no freaks, got off scot-free.

Colonel Offman himself, whom I consider one of the worst murderers, regardless of his desperate desire for redemption, has been acquitted as he was never inside the camps, so his actions were limited to carrying out orders.

Each individual adopts different defence mechanisms to survive the hostilities of life. I, up to that moment, as a defence mechanism, have adopted the suppression of memories.

It hurts me too much to remember, to relive those moments of my life, the worst ones, to see again what my eyes have been forced to look at, my ears to listen to and my heart to suffer.

There is a person in the room who, when I see him,

worries me, a Jew who has always played dirty, selling out his people, if only for a piece of soap.

He is called to testify right after me.

"But why him? What does he have to say about David?"

"I am a Jew, straight and not a criminal. Being a Jew, I know very well what was going on in that camp, and I have no reason to hide it. Everything that the previous witness said is false. The truth is that the two of them are lovers."

In the room, everyone is murmuring.

I don't understand why this man could harbour such hatred towards us. He may have been paid by someone who wants to remain anonymous, or he may be driven by envy, or possibly he is a homosexual who has not been able to accept himself, and is now pouring out his hatred and frustration on us.

I try to understand why this kind of man is saying these things. Deep down, he has nothing to gain and nothing to lose, and David, many times, has also helped him.

But evil and envy know no ethnicity or religion, they don't need specific motives to explode, and Nazism is the proof.

I will never know the truth about this guy and his ruthlessness, but I will certainly never forget the effects of this hatred on our lives.

The man, with a smirk between his lips, continues his speech:

"The SS agent Koch is exactly like the others, he beat me, raped me and more than once threatened to kill me."

I look at David, deeply angry, but at the same time

resigned to the fate that awaits him.

When asked to say something in his favour, David decides to remain silent. Nothing of what the man has said is true, but it is easy for the judges to believe him - after all, he has described perfectly what most of the SS were like.

At the end of the trial, David is sentenced to ten years in prison. The accusations against him are terrible, although in his defence he could have said that he was carrying out the orders.

I burst into tears and desperately look for the sold-out Jew in the crowd to ask him for explanations. But it is he who finds me and, with the same arrogance he had during the trial, he explains everything to me.

"At last things are going as they should! Tom, I wanted to make you suffer and I've finally achieved my goal. The truth is that I couldn't stand everything you've had. I didn't deserve to stay in there, whereas you deserved it because you are a disgusting homosexual. You deserved to be in that camp more than anyone else, and yet no one has discovered your homosexuality, and you have managed to befriend an SS man in order to achieve your goal: escape.

Your father took his own life for a good cause, while you're cunning and manipulative. With that good and gentle character you seem to have, you have won everyone's heart, even Gustav's, who, after you escaped, instead of hating you, was happy for you. Yuck...! You disgust me!

The best way to make you pay for it is to take away what is most important to you: love, that love I've never known. You have no right to be happy..."

A blow to the jaw interrupts his fervently delivered

speech. I am furious.

"Why? Have I taken away your freedom? I never stopped you from escaping!" I shout, and shake him violently by the shoulders.

He puts his hand over his mouth to massage it. I'm thin and small, but I certainly don't lack strength.

"I had to be in your place in that kitchen. It was me he had to help first. I had asked him to do it!"

I let him go, I don't want to touch that despicable being any more, and with an indignant expression I leave without so much as a glance or another word.

On 30 September, the Nuremberg trial court condemned the SS, declaring it a criminal organisation. The judges underscored that judgment by holding that the SS used it for purposes which were criminal and which included the persecution and extermination of Jews, the savagery and executions in the concentration camps, excesses in the administration of the occupied territories, the administration of the slave labour programme, and the mistreatment and murder of prisoners of war.

The judgement went on to state that the suspicion of war crimes would have involved all persons who had been officially accepted as members of the SS who became or remained members of the organisation knowing that it would be used to commit acts declared criminal under Article 6 of the London War Crimes Statute.

On 16 October, all the defendants sentenced to death in the Nuremberg trial were hanged.

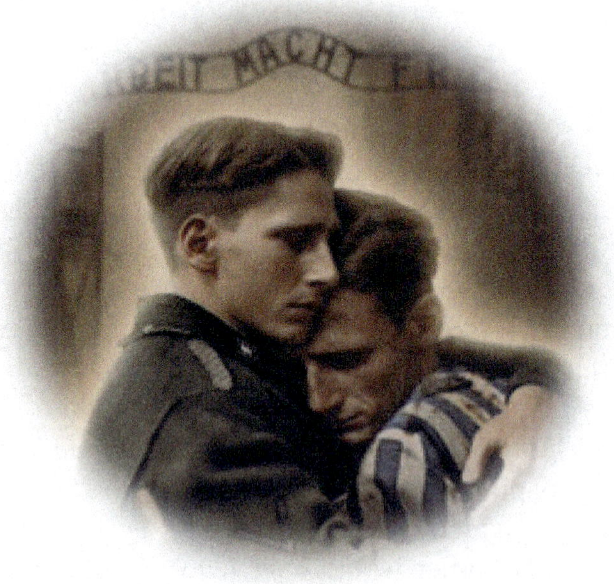
MACHT

EPILOGUE

Given David's great love for me, he decides to leave me in order to push me towards a life with sweet Anna.

Prejudices towards homosexuals are not, and perhaps never will be, completely overcome, so David decides to sacrifice his happiness to give me a decent life, at least for me.

Anna can give me a social life, children, and also love, given her beautiful sweetness. On the contrary, David thinks he can only give me a life where hiding from the world is inevitable.

He really loves me too much to drag me into an existence plagued by secrecy and shame. I "don't deserve it".

Although with great regret, oblivious to the real reasons, I have learned to live with the idea that David will never be the man of my life.

My heart and mind will jealously guard his memory forever, but my eyes will no longer see him, my hands will no longer touch him; I will no longer enjoy his wonderful scent and my lips will no longer kiss him.

This makes me suffer a lot, but now there is someone who considers me really important, someone who has waited for me for a long time, someone who has been infatuated with me since I was very young.

Anna is now a woman.

Having known true love, I know that the affection

and respect I feel for Anna is not at all the same, but I married her, and with her I had two sons, Carl and Matt.

She has always been my partner, my accomplice, my friend, and the pain of what we have been through has made us unbreakable.

"Do you understand now, Ben? Do you understand how much pain?"

I clasp Anna's hand in mine and squeeze it tightly; our eyes are both lost in a parallel dimension.

Ben immediately takes that image, focuses the lens on the hands. The grandparents, without realising it, are giving him the most beautiful and meaningful image to write about.

To my friend Adolf.
Thank you.

Printed in Great Britain
by Amazon